THE HOUSE ON ESPLANADE

THE HOUSE ON ESPLANADE

William Biery

Mason & Lipscomb PUBLISHERS   NEW YORK

Grateful acknowledgment is made for authorization to quote
from the following songs:

"You Are My Sunshine," by Charles Mitchell and Jimmie
Davis (p. 6). Copyright 1940 by Peer International Corporation. Copyright renewed Peer International Corporation. Used
by permission.

"Shrimp Boats (A Comin'—There's Dancin' Tonight),"
words and music by Paul Mason Howard and Paul Weston
(p. 17). © 1951 by Walt Disney Music Company. Used by
permission.

"True Love," (p. 29), copyright 1955 and 1956 by Chap-
pell & Co., Inc. Used by permission.

For Robert Kruger Biery

THE HOUSE ON ESPLANADE

Mark Dennick's last hitch on the long journey from San Francisco took him through the canefields of Louisiana. The country was desolate in late winter, lost in a gray February mist. As was the custom, the fields had been harvested and left to lie fallow, the stubble of hacked-down cane sloping to the red trenches bordering the highway. Along the road, gas pumps marked the presence of villages where homemade signs nailed to trees sold crawfish, fresh eggs, and alligator pears. On the bayous that crossed the road under narrow bridges, fishermen sat in pirogues, becalmed as floating logs on the water.

Mark spoke as the truck entered the oil-rich air of the Norco Refinery, twenty miles west of New Orleans. "You going downtown?"

"I get the ferry at the foot of Canal," the driver said.

The route would save Mark a bus ride through the city. His father's house was on Esplanade Avenue, a short walk from Canal Street. "I'll hop out at Rampart."

The driver adjusted a bunch of bananas he had stacked against the windshield, his *lagniappe* for the haul to Beaumont. "You on the bum?"

"I was. I'm home now."

"Funny how young people like to do that. I did it. At first it seems exciting to take off on your own. Sometimes they have a little fun. When they get their fill of misery, they come home. You have any fun?"

"Not a hell of a lot."

The driver shrugged and insisted that Mark take a banana. Mark took one out of gratitude for the ride, strapped it in his bag, and jumped and waved as the diesel groaned on toward the river.

He was home. This time he had been away only two months. The time before, a year. The total seemed a long time lost. Days lost by the absence of familiar things to grow warm in his hands, nights he had stood on dark roads without the solace of a car's headbeams. The aloneness had made him weep inside while his face was as pale and blank as clay. He remembered the times of wearing dirt like a crust, the weariness that built inside him, eternal extremes of cold and heat. He had had a little fun. The driver was right about the misery.

On all those dark streets of his past, Mark had asked himself *why*. Was the truck driver right? A Huckleberry Finn search for adventure? But Huck had a reason. He wanted to be a pirate on the Spanish Main. Reasons can be written down and understood. Mark had written a list and discarded it because no one cared to understand. Still it loomed in his mind but vaguely, and he was a very poor rebel without a complete definition of his cause. In time it became everything at once, and his resolution grew so old that its benign purpose seemed forgotten.

But as he walked along Rampart Street, he knew his disenchantment had to do with the city and its people. A town has a personality, a temperament. New Orleans of 1956 was a victim of its own neglect. Its mood was as mean as its climate. Whole neighborhoods were crumbling. The areas of Central City, Treme, Desire, the Irish Channel were nearly unfit for human habitation. Raw sewage was being pumped without conscience into Lakes Borgne, Pontchartrain, and Maurepas. No one cared a damn. The decay was ignored as if it might just go away by itself. The city ate its great food, slept, and ignored its troubles.

Worse than its physical condition, the city seemed to be on the verge of a mental and moral breakdown. Led by its colorful governor, Earl Long, self-styled, "the last of the red hot Mamas," and heir to the throne of the Long dynasty, the state seemed to be going mad. Maybe that happens. When the head of a family inspires insanity, the children follow his example. Surely a good leader can inspire goodness. The Governor reflected his people, the people, him. Earl was a sick man when he entered office on a whirlwind. He was now making international headlines by heaping verbal abuse on practically everyone in the state. Even his close friends thought he was heading for an insane asylum. But everyone had a good time laughing. Earl laughed with them or at them and ran the state as if it were his personal possession, outdoing even the Kingfish himself in flamboyant style. When he came to New Orleans it was to argue with the local politicians and to visit a personal friend, a stripper on Bourbon Street. Banana Republic politics at its best.

The city followed the example. It was a relic anyway in thought and spirit. Bigotry is a kind of insanity. Ignorance was the common disease. Pageantry stood in the place of humanity. Rex and Comus and Proteus were the gods of the Pickwick and the Boston Clubs. Like a light-headed, self-serving child, the city reveled in the gaiety of Mardi Grass and side-show politics while it turned away from responsibility. Although the Negro had been granted first-class citizenship by the United States Supreme Court, every white New Orleanean still considered him half animal and about fit to empty the cesspools of Metairie.

A favorite joke circulated after every hurricane: How many niggers did you save during the storm? Answer: None.

Split your sides.

Political corruption was rife. It was the New Orleans of a hundred years ago. The Old Regular political machine did favors for you if you voted for the demagogue of your choice. You might have a traffic ticket fixed or the tax books altered.

The headlines were always good for a laugh: EARL SAYS, "IF I'M CRAZY NOW, I'VE BEEN CRAZY ALL MY LIFE."

Huey P. Long, the second to last of the red hot Mamas, was a martyr. The Earl of Louisiana was fast becoming one. Racists like Leander Perez, the boss of Plaquemines Parish, and Lincoln Rockwell, the Nazi, were modern heroes. The city was sick. The symptoms were abundantly clear to Mark. He was revolted because he feared he would become like these people, hateful, distrustful, self-serving. He had to get out.

3

In 1956, the year he was graduated from Loyola University, Mark made his decision to leave New Orleans. He was twenty-one years old. Papa Dennick was shocked; he had envisioned a railroad career for his son. The boy would not have to start at the bottom splitting rails as his father had. Still the old man offered no opposition. The career could wait until Mark got the wanderlust out of his system. Never did Papa approach a true understanding of Mark's real reasons for leaving, nor could Mark successfully explain them to his father. The most he could manage was a lame explanation. "The city is living in the past, Papa. Nobody cares about anything here. The outside world is changing." Papa listened attentively, believing his son was seeking adventure as young men do, and he tried not to make an issue of his disappointment. Mark would come home in time.

What did in fact begin as an exciting adventure turned into a dark year in Mark's life. He was young. He decided to hitchhike to Los Angeles. But along the arid roads of Texas he had many misgivings and had to struggle to keep himself from buying a bus ticket home. Sour memories of the city kept him on his way. He made it to Los Angeles, weary, alone, and much confused about his new freedom. The problem was what to do with it. He did nothing. He got a part-time job in a bar on Santa Monica Boulevard called the Pink Pussy Cat. The changing world he had sought became one of waiting on tables, of girls dressed like pussycats and swinging from the ceiling. His new world was one of dark places that smelled of beer and urine, of drifting shadows, a bed in a room of impersonal furniture, and a running war with the classified section of the *Los Angeles Times*. He read the help-wanted ads every day. Jobs were plentiful for college graduates who wanted to work. Mark turned down a thousand. He didn't want a job because he didn't know where he wanted to be. Never New Orleans, but what would he put in its place?

Gradually in his loneliness he began to wonder if the malaise he had diagnosed in his home town was really in himself, the confused drop-out with a vague definition of his cause. The sweet times of the past began to haunt him. Whenever he was out on the bright beaches of California, he thought of the dark forest of his father's twenty acres of land in Saint Tammany Parish.

There were memories of his brother Matt, and how it had been for them as boys. The old Negro hand, Phoebus, had taught them to swim, to track animals, to find their way through the woods without getting lost.

The icy current of the Bogue Falia River had been no small challenge to a ten-year-old boy. Phoebus was ever cautious. "Keep yo feet kickin' when yo is in the high water," he would say and call out the warning, "Kick, Mark—kick!" Mark remembered the commands and how it felt to have the big black hands snatch him out at the last moment. He had promised to kick harder next time. He was never afraid when Phoebus was around.

Phoebus taught them to distinguish rabbit droppings from the dung of the larger animals and how the rabbit's legs went deep into the mud when he was being chased by a cat. When Phoebus killed a rabbit, he showed them how to skin and quarter it for the skillet, which parts you had to throw away, and which parts you fed to the stray cats to keep them from hunting your rabbits. He taught them about hunter's traps and snares and how to tree a possum. They learned how to dig for turtle eggs, catch flying squirrels and lightning bugs, hook catfish without a pole. In those days, Phoebus knew everything about the woods.

On a hunting trip he would point to a crooked tree. "See that bent tree? They ain't no other like it in this wood. I knows 'cause I knows every stick o' this wood. When y'all sees this tree yo Papa's house is jis up the river bank. Y'all cain't get lost if yo knows this tree." The boys learned the lesson well, but even with the bent tree and landmarks of rocks and dead tree trunks, they still got lost. It could be that they only pretended because their forest seemed so much larger that way.

Conjuring memories of times Mark could never resurrect was painful enough; his loneliness was finally made intolerable by a beautifully sad letter from Matt's wife, Marylene. She had a grasp for every detail of the Dennick household. She knew the whereabouts of every flower and stone of the house on Esplanade. She understood the quirks of Papa, of Matt, and most disturbingly, Mark's own. Her newborn child, which Mark had never seen, looked like a Dennick, she admitted, but most of all like Mark. Moreover, throughout the four perfectly written pages, there was an implication of great sadness soon to befall the Dennick family. There was an underlying foreboding in her tone, an indirect wish that he were there. A ruse to get him home? He thought not. The tone was too genuine, the prose too sincere. An hour after he read the letter, Mark was on a bus bound for New Orleans.

Three restless days later he was home. There was a grand reception. Papa was thrilled to see him and held a backyard party in his honor. He boasted that his boy was older and wiser now. He had gone out and learned about the world. The family came to verify it, aunts and uncles and their children, Matt and his new family, even neighbors. They all exclaimed on his good looks, shook his hand, patted his back. He had purged the roaming from his system. Now that he was home, the railroad job was waiting. He could gather up the threads of his life.

But Mark was never more confused. He saw no evidence of an impending sadness. He saw only a family that had voluntarily adapted to the meanness of its town. The poison had sunk deeper in its system. Niggers were still blamed for all crime and taxes and the deterioration of everything on earth from the levees of Louisiana to the Capitol in Washington. There were new headlines on the Earl and new versions of the hurricane jokes. While the Governor was still clowning, a similar buffoon was standing in the wings. The folks of Louisiana were singing his tune:

> You are my sunshine, my only sunshine,
> You make me happy when skies are gray . . .

As Mark's first day home wore on, he eyed Marylene warily for making him the dupe. He would have left immediately for another bar in another town had something not happened that he would later consider the most important event in his life. He saw Michelle DeJoie again.

He remembered her as an undergraduate. She had seemed aloof, untouchable. Now she was a graduate of Loyola and a librarian at the University Library. She was Garden District middle-class perfection, much too responsible to understand Mark's fuzzy disenchantments, but she fell immediately in love with him. It was a wonderment to him that he had managed to

6

blunder into her life. Her beauty was softly understated by an absence of paint and powder like the neatness of her mind. She was a girl of delicate contrasts, black hair over fair skin, features open and bright, command without the post of sophistication. She was petite and strong-boned, as well-fitted for her life as the words she chose to press out through her perfect lips.

As Mark remembered their first meeting at the library, he had to struggle with an unhappy memory of their first sex together. He had begged her and she masturbated him in his father's car, in the romantic shadows of Lakeshore Drive, turning her head as if her hand belonged to some ghost. He helped her hand to the rhythm, and quickly came. Surprised by the discharge, she jerked her hand away, spreading the seminal fluid like drops of candle-wax on his pants. He would always regret debasing her in that way. He charged it to an account, one he swore to repay. There would be a reckoning in a more mature time of their lives, a long way out from the thrills of childhood. Mark knew he would never love anything quite so perfect and so vulnerable.

Michelle never mentioned the incident, and in the two months they spent together, she did a lot to change Mark's estimate of himself, one he had learned and settled for in the twenty-two years of his life. He was brown, dark to his hair and eyes and in to his spleen. Ruddy for official things like driver's license and draft card, but coarse, Sicilian. The name had been shortened from Dennicola by Papa's immigrant father. Before the turn of the century it was popular to assimilate, become an American. Mark was like the Dennicks, heir to sloped shoulders, powerful arms and hands, veined with popping circulation. His arms were his strongest point. He often wished it were his head. Like his father, he was thin-featured. No rugged jaw. No swarthy beard. No sleek mouth of choppers. But those strong arms, a sun-toasted Latin with a corrected name. Michelle, sweetly, had called him handsome. She came close to teaching him tenderness and that he had a strength that was not in his arms.

In the weeks of the past autumn they had gone everywhere together, weekends on the Mississippi Gulf Coast at Pass Christian, nights alone in the park or on the steps of the seawall of Lake Pontchartrain. Mark was happy for a while. Being with

Michelle was a joy for him. But the oppressive days at home seemed endless. Papa pressed him constantly on the railroad job, pointing to Matt as an example of a young man who was making a life for himself. Matt was raising a family, building a house, while Mark was dawdling away his time.

In the afternoons when they sat on the gallery to talk, the conversation invariably came around to the railroad job. Papa's ambition for Mark was to see him start as an operations trainee and work up to an executive position with the Southern Pacific. The business was entering a new era. The old L & N Station at the foot of Canal Street was closed. Another on Basin Street had been demolished. The scattered depots were being merged into the new Union Station. There was a grand future ahead. Mark could be a part of it if he wished.

Papa had seen the bright young college graduates coming in. They were the future executives, the moving force behind a modern railroad. They were the heirs to the new technology, computers, electronics. They would be working with equipment never dreamed of forty years ago, refined methods of laying ballast, putting down rail, braking, switching. Operations executive was a job Papa would have enjoyed had he lived in another time and had a better education. There were other trainee positions in sales, finance, purchasing, but operations was where a man could dig his hands in.

To Mark it seemed his life was being prescribed for him. Each time they discussed the railroad, he would carefully try to explain. "Papa, try to understand. To work for the railroad I would have to be here. I don't know that I want to settle in New Orleans." Papa would listen and shake his head scornfully. At that point the conversation was generally lost with nothing understood or resolved. Mark's inability to communicate with his father was a tragic disappointment to him.

At last he secretly decided on San Francisco. This time it would be no life in a bar and a boarding house, for his plan was to take Michelle with him. One evening they were parked at the Audubon Park Aviaries. He asked her to go with him.

"San Francisco?" she said. "Mark, what's wrong with here?"

"You know how I feel about this town. I can't stand the ignorance and bigotry. People here don't know what's happening in the world. No one even cares. They sit around laughing at their politicians and waiting for Mardi Gras to happen. I'm sick of it. Why put up with it if we can go someplace else?"

"Because it's our home. You're not ignorant and bigoted. Everybody doesn't think that way."

"You should hear my Uncle William. He would send all the niggers back to Africa where they belong. He never says where *he* belongs. Michelle, it's a sickness. How many times have you heard it? This town will never change."

She had heard it many times, but never in her own home. She was sorry that Mark had to be the unlucky one. "I've heard it, but I'm not sure the answer is running away. I can't do that to my family. It would hurt them terribly."

"Yes, I know it will hurt Papa when I do. But if I let him stop me now I'll never get out. If you don't speak out against stupidity, you become stupid yourself."

"Fine, then speak out. Maybe you can do some good. The way to make change is to do it."

"I'd wind up beating my head against the wall. Everybody in New Orleans is a hundred years old."

Michelle had long ago sensed Mark's rift with his father. She discerned the bitterness in his tone whenever he discussed his family. Now that it had come into the open, she instinctively took sides against him. She knew the town and believed that someday the old attitudes would change. "There's bigotry everywhere, Mark. You can never escape that entirely."

"I can try."

"What will you do in San Francisco?"

"Get a job. Start a new life."

It sounded so simple and foolish to Michelle. She looked at him, pleading. "We could start a new life here."

"Michelle, I have to go. Please come with me."

"I can't do it, Mark. I could never do it."

As she spoke the final truth, Mark felt more alone than he ever had in his life. Failing to gain her support, he felt he had lost all. Of course, she was correct. He had no right to disrupt her life and substitute an uncertain one thousands of miles from her home. It was too much to ask of her. Mark's disenchantment, real or imagined, was his own affair. Because he accepted her refusal as rejection, he became embittered. Bitterness soured his thinking and inured him to his own feelings.

He packed a bag and left that night, saying goodbye to no one. As he waited for a ride on the highway, his thoughts were all of Michelle and the happiness of their weeks together, memories that would be with him for all of his time away from her.

The city was excessively warm for the season. As Mark approached his father's house on Esplanade, his shirt was dripping. His throat was dry with a burning thirst. He went into the yard and drank from the garden hose. The water was tepid. He let it run for a long time and wet his hair.

The garden was snarled with debris, evidence that Papa had been in Saint Tammany Parish for some time. The house, empty, flaked with rot, had lost some weather strips below the eaves. Inside it smelled of moth and rust. The floor was gritty beneath his feet. On the dining room table, there was the same checkered oilcloth, threadbare at its creases and corners. The Dennick home, now sadly run down, had been part of Papa's promise to them of a better life than the one they had been born into in the poverty of the Irish Channel.

Papa's Italian immigrant parents had come to New Orleans to find their place with a lot of other Italians and Irishmen, jammed against the *batture* of the Mississippi River in an uptown area of the city bounded by Tchoupitoulas and Magazine Streets. Called the Irish Channel, it was an odd place for an Italian family to live. To escape the stigma, Grandpapa had shortened the name and had given non-Italian names to his children, Emma, Stephen, Delia. He flew a small American flag every day from his gallery.

Because Papa grew up in the Irish Channel, he swore he would get them out of it. He would do it with hard work and an indomitable spirit Mark would later view with awe. How proud Papa had been that he started with the old Southern Pacific Railroad as a teenager, splitting ties and laying rail. Like Abraham Lincoln! There was a lot of hard work still to be done then. In later years he worked in the yards as fireman and engineer. He loved those years most of all. Recently he had been brought into the office as dispatcher. It was his reward for a life of service. His job was to know the whereabouts of every train from Louisiana to the Texas panhandle. He prepared schedules and reports on equipment and right-of-way. A map in his office pinpointed the positions of boxcars and engines. The logistics of the railroad could turn into chaos without his constant attention. Still Papa disliked the job. He had never been a man for paper work, no matter how important. Papa yearned to be out in the yards running the trains himself.

Yet the twilight of his career was dear to him. The railroad had been the stabilizing influence of his life. It taught him to work and gave him the strength to seek a better life. Papa lived for years in the tiny house in the Irish Channel, sitting on his gallery in his tank undershirt like the rest of the bewildered poor, making promises that would have frightened lesser men. He had to get his family out because he knew the result of a life of bitter hardship. He had buried both of his parents while they were still in their fifties.

Just as his family knew he would, he found the way. He went into business for himself making hogshead cheese in his yard, a food popular among the poor because it was cheap. Mark remembered the trips to the slaughterhouse to buy the heads, the great kettles of boiling meat, the discarded skulls turning white in the sun. As if challenged to do so, Papa did it all by himself, working at night after he came home from the yards of the Southern Pacific. He would chop the onions and garlic, add the spices according to a secret recipe, stir the big pots and pour the final liquid into the molds to form the loaves. He did it all with great joy, tasting the pots and offering portions to the children of the neighborhood.

On Saturdays Papa loaded his old car with cheese and made the deliveries. Mark or his brother could come along to help if they wanted, but he never forced a boy to give up a Saturday against his wishes. In an eighteen-hour day, he covered every grocery store in the uptown area. He always came home with an empty car and his reward, the money that would free them of the Irish Channel. On Sundays, Papa was always a very tired, happy man.

Papa's ambition was to own a house on Esplanade Avenue.

12

He pointed to the one he wanted one day as he was driving along, admiring the grand houses and great oak trees. The presence of it, the fact that he would someday own it, made him work harder. As the business grew, he had to hire men to help him run the cheese factory. That was when Phoebus came into their lives. He was hired with two other Negroes, Cher Alvarado, and a man known as Lemon. Mark could remember his father screaming in the yard, "Never have I seen such shiftless niggers!" But under his supervision, they turned out a remarkable amount of cheese. Soon there was a truck for deliveries, a dozen pots, and a brand name, "Dennick's Cheese." "Nigger, somebody named you right. You are a Lemon!" Papa shouted and they worked. If he caught them "Standing around with their hands in their pockets up to their elbows," he might poke them with a fork. But he paid them well. If they got sick he had Trudy, the housemaid, care for them. When they got drunk and ran away he always took them back. They were "his" niggers and he was responsible for them.

The Dennick family moved into the house on Esplanade when Mark was only eight years old. He had never seen a house so splendid on a street so clean. How proud they had been of their Papa! Why they were rich compared to the kids back in the Irish Channel. This was happiness, but the best was yet to come. In another few years, Papa was able to buy twenty acres of piney woods in Saint Tammany Parish, across Lake Pontchartrain from New Orleans. He named it "Our Wilderness." He built a house of creosote rail ties "borrowed" from the railroad. Then he burned the title on a shingle with a poker and hung it over the front gallery. It was a wilderness of high land and trees by a river that ran with hungry fish.

Mark found the telephone and blew away its coating of dust. As he dialed Michelle's number at the library, he again had the struggle with his memory of their first sex together. A woman remembers the loss of her virginity, a man his first cooperative masturbation.

"Where are you?" Michelle said as if she had expected the call.

13

"At the house on Esplanade. I just got here."

"Are you going to say a lot of dumb things and pretend you've never been away?"

"Only that I missed you."

"A postcard could have said that. I'd have written you to stay where you were."

"I didn't have an address."

"And now? Are you just passing through?"

"I'm home for good. Will you go to Pass Christian with me tonight?"

"The beach this time of the year? *Ne quittez pas.*" He heard a distant voice, a question, Michelle answering it, explaining the whereabouts of a book. "You didn't give me time to forget you."

"Can I pick you up around seven?"

Now the sound of breathing, thinking, concluding. "I'll go, but only to talk, and only if we come back tonight. I want to get some things straight with you. I don't know what I'll say to my mother."

"Your mother is very considerate."

"I've given her a bad time with you. I'm waiting for a rainbow, she said."

"I deserve that. But why do you think I'm back? Back to stay."

"I'll change the subject. Clarey Boriakoff is home. He called me twice asking for you."

Mark had heard his good friend Clarey had been wounded in Korea, spent a year in a hospital in California, and then wandered about the country for two more years, refusing to come home. "How does he look?"

"Not very good. One arm is twisted and he looks in pain when he walks. I saw him with that girl friend of his, Gloria."

"I'll look him up when we get back."

Mark hung up. The car keys were in their place, a red dish on the hallway table. Papa generally drove to Saint Tammany in Uncle William's worn-out Studebaker. William's mainstays in life were cars and food and property. He consumed one as the other. He had married Papa's younger sister Delia and sentenced her to life over the kitchen stove, and he already owned much of the property near Papa's in Saint Tammany Parish. He wanted more.

14

On the table beside the keys, Mark saw the picture of his mother. It was old, hand-tinted in an oval frame, the only icon left of her. He wished he had remembered to avoid it. The features, small nose, deep-set eyes, brought back a painful memory. Her smile seemed forced and apologetic, as if she were sure the photograph would give her away for the remainder of her existence. It had, for when it was taken she was a dying woman. She staggered about the house like a drunkard, colliding with objects that seemed forever in her way. Mark remembered the baths of salts to soothe the aching legs and the continual bumping. At last her eyesight failed completely, and she carried a cane to support a useless foot. One day she took to her bed and Trudy, the Negro maid, was hired to care for her. Mother died, they told little Mark, of a tumor in the brain, an illness no one knew very much about. Trudy wept, "Cause the Missus was only a girl," she said, as Mark followed her about the house clinging to a long brown finger. The young Cajun country girl Papa had married was twenty-four at her death. Papa was almost twice her age. He seemed grieved that he had been permitted to live.

Trudy dressed Mark for the funeral in his suit and shiny new shoes, and she stood close to him all day long. He knew it was because she knew he needed someone to be near to. As if it were a week ago, he clearly remembered the funeral, his mother looking out from a dress she had never worn while she was alive, the bologna sandwiches everyone ate in another room, and the shiny new shoes he was permitted to wear on such a solemn occasion.

The phone rang. It was Papa, his voice weakly cheerful, trailing with great effort. Mark would not have to steal the car. He could ask Papa's permission. "How did you know I was home?"

"I never knew your Aunt Emma to miss anything that went on in our house," Papa said.

Mark had forgotten Aunt Emma. Papa's older sister and her husband, Dominick, lived across Esplanade. Gossipy, prattling Emma would have called Papa the moment Mark appeared on the street.

Papa went on, "Venetian blinds must have been invented by a woman. Look out the window. I bet she's bending the slats this minute. Calling up relatives with the other hand."

"Papa, can I borrow the car?"

"You only just got home."

"I have a date with Michelle. We're going to Pass Christian."

"Sure, son. I have to stay here until Sunday morning anyway. William has some niggers cleaning up the place."

"Thank you, Papa."

"Mark, I'm truly glad you're home. I'll be planning a big Sunday. Think you can make it back from the coast by then?"

One of Papa's typical bargains. Earth, life, all of creation was a compromise. In return for the car, Papa expected Mark to be available for a family Sunday, a backyard afternoon under the chokedamp stench of grassfires while the family drowsed to the chew of rockers on bare flagstone. "I promise I'll be back by then," Mark said.

"I'll want to hear where you've been. What you've been doing," Papa said and hung up.

Mark had part of the weekend to make up something. Papa would listen and not hear.

Papa, I had this job in a carwash pulling the cars through. Tough work, but boy was I clean.

Papa, I got this fantastic job in a supermarket weighing tomatoes, garnishing the meat counter with branches of parsley. Meaningful. Creative. I won a prize for the prettiest meat counter in Blue City, Iowa. Meat counter flunkies all over the world sent me congratulations. I'm famous, Papa.

Could Mark make him hear?

Papa, this trip all I did was rob banks. Mostly small, out-of-the-way banks that didn't matter. When I collected a whole suitcase of money, I went to Monaco, gambled it all away. Came back a poorer but richer man. Imagine a whole suitcase of money, and I had to kill only once, an eighty-year-old woman who wouldn't give me all the money in her drawer. I made it painless. Shot her right between the eyes. Pow! Like a Hitchcock movie!

Mark would perhaps tell his father the truth or at least some of it. He would tell of the homosexual, Mandy, who had tried to teach Mark to sell dental drills, his own invention. Mandy (he had changed it from Andy and Mark thought it would soon evolve to Candy) had had all his facial hair removed. Mark had thought only a woman able to endure electrolysis. Mandy

16

swore he was a woman living in the body of a man. His plan was to save enough money for a special operation. He had read about it in a magazine. There was a hospital somewhere in the East where they remove everything and replace it with the same equipment a woman has down there. He knew every detail. They used the skin—epithelium, he called it—of the penis to form a lining for the brand new vagina. They even created breasts—large ones!—with doses of hormones, although he was not very clear on that. With the dedication of a missionary, he dreamed of the future. "When she comes home from the hospital it will all be worth it." What distressed Mark was that Mandy was pretty ugly as a man. He would make a very ugly woman.

Mark tried to learn to sell the drills, but when Mandy became a permanent attachment, it was embarrassing. He looked like Plastic Man without any hair on his face, and his tennis shoes squeaked, calling attention to his swish. Mark had to tell him he would not sleep with him even if he had a dozen operations. He sat down in the street and cried and would not stop until Mark agreed to have a drink with him. They went into a bar and after several drinks Mandy had built up to a very messy farewell. He dragged Mark into a pawn shop and bought him a going-away present, a three dollar camera and went away, his large plastic face hanging down.

Mark was hungry. In the refrigerator he found two tiers of Jax beer, one of the condiments. Trudy would have had it packed with fresh fruits and meats. He opened a beer and dug the banana out of his bag.

Why did he think it unfair to call her Nanny? Housemaid "Aunt" Trudy, with skin like chocolate icing and a voice, deep and pure, the strings of a fine cello. *Shrimp boats is a-comin, they's dancin' tonight* . . . She sang it better than any popular singer ever did. Mark knew why. It was because she knew what the boats really meant to the men, chugging back to their homes heavy with the catch. She had eaten those shrimps, and she had danced that night through. There was a sad song too, and Mark knew every word of it, the texture of every note:

> They's a steamboat comin' on a river
> Gonna sweep me out-a ma swamp,

They's a big boat steamin' on a riv-er,
Gonna fetch me out-a ma mis-ry,
They's a fine boat churnin' on a riv-er,
Gonna lif' me on to ma hea-ven,
        On to ma hea-ven. . .

Trudy had a favorite book, *The Oregon Trail,* by Francis
Parkman. Not that she had ever read it. It was her secret place
for messages, notes to everyone but Papa. If it were left upside
down on the shelf, there might be news of a pie cooling on the
back gallery or a dish of pennies for the movies. For the Negro
hand, Phoebus, who could not read, she left drawings. Mark
remembered a drawing of two animals peeking over the rails of a
ship. "My favorite Bible story," she said, "so he'd know I was
to church and I'd whack him if he didn't get everything done
time I got back." Phoebus always slammed the book closed, replaced it tidily on the shelf, and went away, anger sounding in
his workboots.

In the library, *The Oregon Trail* was coated with dust but the
gulls on its spine flew upside down. Inside there was a note
from his brother.

If no one home, Papa is in Saint Tammany. He spends
most of his time there but talks of selling. Guess William is
wearing him down. Everyday he looks for you to come home.
Please call me soonest. Important news.

—Matt

To sell their wilderness amounted to a capital crime in Mark's
mind. William had been after Papa's property for years. He
wanted it because it was next to his, and high, with the best of
the river and the woods, all the things a boy needed in a wilderness. They had slept on wooden floors to be awakened by the
dawn and dogs and geese barking. They had rushed to eat
Trudy's hot biscuits and honey, fought chinaberry wars, learned
from Phoebus to hunt turtles in the shallows of the Bogue Falia
River.

"Real snappers?" little Mark said.
"Sure," Matt said. "You yank 'em out by their tails. Watch

they don't bite. Once they get a finger in their mouth they never let go."

"Will you teach me?"

"Not now. It's getting dark and we got to get that rabbit." They had seen it scamper into a hollow stump. Matt stepped back a few paces, remembered his father's instructions. Breathe out slowly, left elbow tucked under, squeeze. . . .

The shot, a quick stab at the ears, carried through the forest. It was a sound they had never grown accustomed to.

Mark turned his face away. "Did you hit him?"

"I don't know."

"How will you get him out of the stump?"

Matt looked into the stump like a boy does to avoid getting spat on by a polecat. "Phoebus will get him out in the morning. We better get home before dark. Papa'll skin us."

Mark, grateful for the older boy's decision, followed close behind him. The rim of the forest sloped to the river where cedars, choked with moss, hung over their reflections. The boys found the crooked tree and followed the river. Thorned bush grabbed at their legs. Mark wanted to speak, to hear his voice break the hum of the wind in the trees. He did not, for he knew his brother would think him afraid. The night had grown cold. Mark thought of Trudy's warm, food-scented kitchen, the wood stove rich with tentacles of pine fire when she lifted a kettle or stoked it with a rod.

Mark heard a clap, sharp and anonymous in the blackness before him, the sound of a dry limb snapped from a tree. But in the sound there was a foreboding of violence as he saw his brother cry out and slump to the ground. When Mark reached him, Matt's face was a mask of bewilderment and pain. A muskrat trap, jaws like the blade of a mill saw, had crushed his leg above the ankle. Mark screamed with all the strength in him. He hammered and tore at the trap until his hands bled. He called out for his father, Trudy, Phoebus, and helpless, the forest began to swim about him as a great wooded swamp, and he could only watch his brother's boot fill with blood. Then all was quiet and cool. His head was down in the crackling pine needles and he was very tired.

He dreamed of a rag doll, his own when he was a baby. It had button eyes and a smile of bright stitches. If he cuddled it, it said nice things. Left alone on a chair, it was unhappy and its arms hung down. Once it was losing red sawdust through a break in the foot. He gathered the wound but could not stop the trickle. The head caved in. The arms became rubbery. Mark's tears in the sawdust looked like blood. To save the life of his doll he knew he must repair it with a needle and thread. In his dream he begged Trudy to fix it for him.

"We be home soon," Phoebus said. "Trudy fix anything you wants." The Negro had been carrying them, one boy over each shoulder, his toeless boots bursting in great strides through the forest.

Papa inspected the leg, slammed his lantern into the dust. It exploded and enveloped itself in flame. "Damn trappers! They know there's no muskrat left out there!"

Phoebus cowered in the shimmer of the flame, his black face aglow with fear.

From the house came the *slop slop* of Trudy's slippers. Her hands were dripping wash water. She looked at the wound. "This boy's hurt mighty bad," she said.

"Papa, we didn't see the trap," Mark said. "It was dark."

It took a moment for the white man to assign guilt, another for the face of the black man to deny it. Papa reached for a cedar log from the gallery, a doorstop the boys had carved from a driftwood root. He slapped it in one of his great hands to gauge its usefulness as a club. "Is that right, Phoebus? Has somebody been trapping in my woods?"

On a night too cool to sweat, Phoebus glistened. "Nevah ain't been no traps in dis wood befo." Nigger talk, the black man's prayer, might save him a beating.

Papa knew the prize was not muskrat, but nutria, the fur of the coypu, an animal mysteriously new to the area. The pelts were regarded with suspicion, the meat considered inedible. "Damn niggers will trap anything. Even a boy!"

"Hungry folks got to eat, Mistah Steve!"

"Even if they ruin a boy!"

Phoebus had only to look at the white man's face to know

judgment had been passed. He saw the great hands grip the club, the quivering rage of the whitened knuckles. He scrambled to escape but tripped into the burning dust of the lantern. Papa threw the log with all his strength. It missed, and before the black man could regain his feet, Papa had dragged him up by the throat, ignoring his pleas for mercy. A crushing blow cut Phoebus to the ground again. Another made him scream with pain. Papa saw the blood rushing from his mouth and nose and dropped him into the dust. Phoebus crawled away crying, staggered to his feet, and ran into the woods.

Papa watched him go, and then tremors of fear or pity or regret gripped him. He dropped to his knees and spoke some words they could not hear. He went into the house, came out with a bottle of whiskey, and drank deeply. Matt's leg hung down as his father carried him to the car.

Trudy went to her room and kneeled at her bed. She folded her hands in prayer and began her song in the beautiful deep voice.

> They's a big boat steamin' on a riv-er,
> Gonna fetch me out-a ma mis-ry . . .

Mark wanted to cry, but he forced himself to kneel beside her, aping the words as she sang.

Following the surprise call from Mark, Michelle asked her friend Donny to take her place at the information counter. Donny batted his eyes and sighed, an acknowledgment that he understood Mark had turned up. It was a breath of relief, for Donny was the only person except her mother that Michelle had confided in. In his girlish way, Donny had condemned her, chastised her, and forgiven her. His reaction was based on a realistic, if liberal, interpretation of the day they lived in. Today it was simply not necessary to get your man in that way. Not only was it unfashionable, but a bit corny if you asked him.

Donny declined to use the word "old-fashioned," which he said was a description of itself, no longer used in the decade of awakening. People no longer had children just because they slept together. In the modern day, sex is apart from reproduction as much as drinking is from eating. While the two are not mutually exclusive, it is possible to do the former without paying for it with the latter. There are methods to reverse the horrifying biological result. Because mistakes of that kind are no longer made, it therefore had not been a mistake.

His conclusion: Michelle had acted like a predatory Sicilian maiden caught in the hay by the desired suitor. His joke had not lightened it for her. Yet she had not thought him cruel. It was his way of slugging her with the truth, that in the time of change you took a precaution against mistakes and nobody ever thought a thing of it, except maybe the Pope and your mother and father. Trial marriage is common in the time of awakening. You don't take a bed-partner for life without trying him first. To Michelle it was a very scary thing, this time of change, and she was not sure she cared for it at all. When all the rules were thrown out, only confusion was left. Careful. Talk like that in front of Donny would brand her the old-fashioned girl. She knew she was.

The restroom was crowded and filled with echoing and

cascading sounds. Public toilets are not made to be comforting places where a person can loiter, she thought, but she waited for an empty stall where she could be alone. She dug in her purse for a cigarette and wondered how Mark would look and act. It was curious that she somehow expected a change. Expected or hoped for? A new wrinkle in his brow or beginning baldness? Some hint of sobriety, maturity. Of course she knew she would take him without it. She focused on her reason for hiding in the toilet. It was to be alone and reenforce her earlier decision. The modern girl was not going to weep and become the distressed female with that age-old problem. She would tell him or not tell him, have him or lose him, but never sink to the depths of tragic despair.

Foolish girl, she thought, to allow . . . but why allow? Caught. With her pants down. Not funny. They had been down only for Mark. The acceptable, quasi-morality of the new time. Was Donny's theory correct? A subliminal ambition buried in the secrets of her subconscious. Freudian wish-fulfillment of woman's destiny, motherhood? Motherhood planned by the omission of one detail, the precaution. Why that neglect? A person plans most events of a lifetime. Death even. The drunkard has his plan of destruction. The smoker feels decay in his lungs.

If it was planned, then it was botched. Timing is a talent in tennis, comedy, motherhood. She had picked him out long ago for every girl's ambition. It went like this: Girl meets boy, marries him, has children, happiness-ever-after. Along the way the priorities got mixed up. Not an uncommon occurrence according to Donny, but in the new time everything was planned. Michelle had had no plan except the archaic one. The predator maiden went on corny dates, necked, drank, smoked, cornered him. How cleverly she avoided going all the way. A difficult thing to maintain—a passionate arms-length. Instinct or a higher intuition told her the real thing would endanger the affair. She was thinking like her grandparents. Promise. Then tease. But the showdown had to come, and she planned even that because she sensed his frustration and felt him drifting away. She coolly decided to come across, to "put out" as the saying goes among the boys.

She planned the place, a garish motel on Jefferson Highway with neon and crisp sheets, a quarter for ten minutes of music. You get what you pay for. The first time had to be like that, had to be bold. She feigned nervous fright, the proper naïveté about such things. It was all in the script. She was giving up a lot. She trembled and was ashamed and cried softly when it was over. Predictably, out of a love manual, she turned her head so she could not see him naked, erected. At the time she thought it was to save something, at least that, wear a garter or a bra, withhold a kiss or a helpful movement of the hips for that moment when they were legally committed. Oh—blessed matrimony! Later she would understand it was part of the act. Mark never suspected she was not completely there. He did it tenderly, lovingly considerate of her embarrassment, afraid like her. She had thought him awkward, her excited lover who had no thought that night of saving anything for the real connubial bed.

She returned to the information desk and said to Donny, "I'm going to Pass Christian with him tonight."

Donny approved. "You going to tell him?"

"Maybe I will and maybe I won't. But I won't hold him to anything." Michelle knew she had that strength. She could go through it alone if it had to be that way. She knew Mark's quirks. She would not hold him to a bad bargain. She loved him much too much to do a thing like that to him.

Mark had been sitting with *The Oregon Trail* open in his lap. He re-read Matt's note, stopping on *important news*. The sale of the Saint Tammany property could be written about. Something more important could not. A long time ago Mark could have guessed what it was. As boys their relationship had been almost telepathic. It was strange and rather wonderful how they were able to anticipate each other's thoughts and actions, a sibling radar. It was how close they were. Mark had accepted the older boy as the leader, gladly following him, imitating his wiser speech.

The accident in the woods had changed them. For two years in a dozen casts, Matt was forced to hobble behind his younger brother, sadly puffing to keep up. In the end he came out of it with a deformed leg, a cripple for life. But much worse than that, Matt seemed so alone, as if some link between them had been broken as well. Mark sensed it was the memory of Phoebus, the blame for the beating. Papa had never openly regretted it. He never spoke of it. Phoebus could not be laid to rest until he could be talked about. Avoiding him became a habit that led to the absence of any talk of importance, and the telepathic relationship evolved into one of evasion and distrust.

Still, there were fond moments to be remembered and, Mark hoped, someday to be returned to. He wanted to talk to his brother, but to shed those deceptions, not to ring up for a lecture. Matt had given in to Papa's temperament in some ways. Mark was in no mood for it. To prevent it he would be sure to speak to his brother in person. With Marylene present Matt would not be so disapproving, so tolerant of the old man's views. Mark checked his watch. It was after four. Matt would be home by five.

Mark was greeted by a bit of friendly sarcasm from his brother. "It's the world traveler," Matt said to his wife and laughed. Then

25

he turned serious and Mark knew a grave discussion was to take place.

The talk was to be the lecture Mark wanted to avoid. Marylene stayed with them only long enough to tour the new room addition to the house, yet unfinished, a sweating slab of concrete already sinking in the porous Louisiana earth. They tossed sticks for the bloodhounds, animals with sharp bones. They looked over the new colt, inspected his teeth. Marylene brought them beers and left them alone in the fetid dung smell of the stable. "Papa's finally decided to sell the Tammany Parish property," Matt said.

"I knew William would get to him eventually."

"He's going to make William come across with a railroad job for you in the bargain."

"William would almost murder for it."

"For all I care he can have it."

Mark knew his brother had come to blame Saint Tammany for his lameness. The accident had delivered to Mark the railroad job Matt would have cherished. "If only William hadn't got it."

"As you say. No one wanted it quite as much. Besides, Papa considers William his good friend."

Good friends do not compete in petty dishonesties like working a job into a property bargain, Mark wanted to say. Instead, he could only think of their wilderness. "Saint Tammany was the greatest thing we ever had when we were kids."

"We're not kids anymore, Mark."

"Yes."

"And if you don't mind my saying so, I think you're acting like one when you run around the country. Every day Papa calls up to ask if I've heard from you. It hurts him so."

"I don't want to hurt him, Matt."

"Then stay home. Settle down."

"I plan to. I really do this time. I'm going to ask Michelle to marry me."

Matt was pleased. He considered his next remark very carefully, looking directly at his brother over the nervous sway of the colt. "You can hurt him now more than ever. He's going to die."

26

Mark thought of the note left in *The Oregon Trail*. So this was the important news that could not be written down. Something had prepared Mark—Papa's tired voice, Matt's grave manner, or Marylene's sad letter of months ago. She had sensed it long before the truth was evident. Women run on intuition. Mark felt a great sadness in the inevitable end of all life. "You know it for sure?"

"I drove him to the railroad hospital in Marshall. They didn't swear him off anything because it wouldn't do any good. It's cancer of the prostate. They give him an indefinite few months. William forced him to take sick leave. I think he's guessed the truth."

Mark could only stroke the colt, avoiding his brother's eyes. "I'm really very sorry."

"Mark, you've got to talk to him. He broods, drinks all day. Always he thinks of you running around the country, wasting your life. All he wants is for you to stay home and take the railroad job."

"I don't know if I can do that."

"You don't know if you can stay home for a dying old man who wants to make sure you'll have a job after he's gone?"

"Why do I have to work for the railroad?"

"Why the hell not!"

The colt shied at the outburst, reared, and backed into its stall. Mark waited until it calmed. "All right, Matt. I'll take the job. For Papa."

"I know how you feel to have your life prescribed for you. You could take the job for a while, let the old man see you at it. Who knows, you may even like it. I think it'd be better than sitting in an office juggling figures all day." The accountant removed his glasses to clean them, annoyed by his momentary loss of self-control. "The old man did right by us, Mark. My kids won't have to begin life in the Irish Channel. Neither will yours. Papa saw to that."

They left the stable and walked across a field that led up to the levee of the Mississippi River. They climbed to the top, Matt laboriously behind his brother. The bank of the river was clear of junk. A string of barges was being pushed up river by

27

a tugboat. The air was fresh and clean. It was a good setting for kids to grow in, a long way up from the dark back streets of the Irish Channel where two generations of Dennicks had been born. Mark knew that there was no small truth in his brother's statement that their Papa had done right by them. Only he thought it a great pity that they now had to sell "Our Wilderness."

The brothers said no more to each other. It seemed that all had been said. Papa was dying. The Tammany Parish property was going to William. Mark was going to work for the railroad. And why not? Why had he opposed it so fervently? He could remember his father coming home gritty and black with the other men, carrying their lunchboxes. He had been proud. He had run to greet his father like every other little boy. Then why? Had the railroad somehow come to represent the snail's pace of the past, the resistance against all change? Had it come to mean the city and the temperament of its people? If so, Mark felt he had been very unfair to his father's beloved railroad.

Marylene called to them from the house. As they walked to her the dogs ran in howling circles around her. She was pregnant again. She seemed very large in the dimming light, flushed and smiling, walking flat-footed to support her burden. Mark thought her very beautiful, and for the first time in his life he was jealous of his brother.

To kill the remaining hour before his date with Michelle, Mark drove the twisting roads of Audubon Park. He was grateful for the extra time to think of her, to decide what he might tell her. Like Papa, she would expect some kind of explanation about why he had left so suddenly, what he had done while he was gone. As he drove he remembered his war with the want-ad section of the newspaper. Engineers, Accountants, Programmers. It was all very confusing to Mark, this drive of the fifties for deliverance.

He would perhaps tell her the truth about a try and a failure. About Mandy, a satchel, a tube, a drill. Mandy had drilled him on the drill and enjoyed the pun. It was only forty-five words. In the dentist's office, Mark forgot them. He fumbled and stuttered. He ran. Surely Michelle could understand that. He made up a title to tell her: Purveyor of Scientific Surgical Equipment. Mandy would like that. He was hooked on common "Salesman." Nothing in the world could ever again be that simple.

Mark stopped the car near a place they had used earlier that summer. The park, as quiet by day as by night, with its great oaks and cool lawns, had been among their secret places. They had stretched on the grass and listened to the scratchy portable sounds of Bing Crosby: *True love . . . true love.* It was true to them. He remembered. Under a leafy pattern of sunshine like the shadows of diamonds, he had first been allowed to touch the moist secrets of her body, though not to penetrate, not one phalange, into the narrow sheath.

"The grass is softer than a blanket."
"A blanket with bugs."
"You're a Chekhovian hero."
"Meaning?"
"Weak."
"Cut the intellectual stuff."

29

Beneath the sweater, she was small and round. He could imagine the nipples, rosy asterisks. "You're very beautiful."

"Why do big ones make men act silly?"

He touched her below.

The silken layer peeled aside, she shuddered. "Please don't."

He rolled away, ate some grass. On his finger, the faint marine scent.

"Why do boys like to do that?"

"We're crazy. Faulknerian heroes with fathers who pinch their daughters."

"It just . . . doesn't seem right."

"What's right? This is 1957."

"Meaning?" Free love, she thought.

"Meaning you're free to do what you want without fear of reprisal."

"And free not to do it if you don't want to."

He laughed. "One day I'm going to win an argument with you." He lifted her dress and tasted her navel. It was sweet and moist, a halved, pitted plum. "I'm sorry. There's an ogre in me trying to get out."

"Would you marry me afterwards? That sounds awfully square."

"I'd marry you anytime."

She stood and brushed the grass from her dress. "I don't know if I like 1957. I'm afraid of all the freeness."

He extended a hand that she might help him up, but he pulled her down and pinned her arms. "Look into my eyes. You are trapped, under my power. And now, little girl, I'm going to eat you."

She laughed and stopped when he kissed her. "I know what's inside you, Mark. I know it has to come out, but please . . . let me pick the time?"

"A lady has that right," Mark said aloud to himself as he left the park and turned into Saint Charles Avenue. As he approached her home, he searched in his memory for that moment of change, that point when they could no longer lie together in the grass but suddenly required a bed.

30

Mark drove to Mississippi through a torrent of rain, much too recklessly on the narrow road that crossed the state line into Bay Saint Louis. From the start, he sensed Michelle's cautious mood. She sat coolly beside him, and he felt like a boy on his first date, unable to begin a conversation. He reasoned that her distrust was correct. He had run out on her. Now she was annoyed with him for cropping up like an old problem, angry with herself for having agreed to the drive. Mark would have to earn her forgiveness with more than a trip to their favorite place.

Their earlier relationship had been so much less complicated. In the beginning, there had been no need to face the prospects of the future. They had been a boy and a girl in love, on a whirlwind, living the ecstatic days one at a time. At first they could make promises to each other. They could envision the future as if it were a dream, enjoy it because it would be so sweet. Now there were realities to be faced. The girl beside him had grown into a woman. She wanted to know if the boy was going to grow into a man.

Michelle began the conversation. As if to get newsy details out of the way and clear the path for more important issues, she brought up Clarey Boriakoff. "I saw him at the Napoleon House. He'd been drinking heavily. Gloria practically had to carry him."

"Is he very badly crippled?"

"He walks with a limp. No, a list. He's very thin." She stopped on a thought that troubles every woman with a man of draft age. "Mark, will you have to go? I mean, the draft?"

The Army conjured Uncle William in his VFW cap, flags whipping on the wind, the tattoo of drums, William ready with a salute and not knowing how to make it snap. "I don't think so. Korea is over."

"I've been thinking of it ever since I saw Clarey."

"You should have known him before. He couldn't wait for the draft. He needed a fight."

Michelle had once seen two boys fight on the beach at Pass Christian. They were boys yearning to be men, crouching, circling on their toes. She remembered the sound of the blows and the crowd. She had felt a strange excitement. "Why, Mark? Why does he need to fight?"

"I guess it keeps him from running away. Michelle, I'm sorry about the way I left. I know that sounds hollow, but I was mixed up. Papa was getting me down. When you refused to come with me . . . I usually face things by turning away."

It sounded very close to a resolution to stay home. She felt a spark of joy. She wanted so much to forgive him. She took his hand and held it to her cheek. "Don't worry, you're home now."

They stopped near Pass Christian, straddled the rails of a foot pier, and watched fishing boats dig troughs in the sea. The storm ended. They ran in the sand and lost and found each other in a low-hanging fog. When they found shelter in a motel-tavern called the Shamrock, Mark began obliquely a tedious debt of explanation. "This weather reminds me I'm home. San Francisco is quite a bit different."

"Did you like it?"

"It didn't make me think any better of this place, but you were always there."

"No, Mark. I was here in my real world."

"You know me too well. I fantasize. An amiable dreamer."

"You could stop it by trying to decide what kind of world you really want."

"I'm working on it. At the moment all I know is that I don't want thirty happy years with the railroad."

"You sum up a lifetime that easily?"

32

"It passes that fast in the lap of contentment."

"You've got to replace it with thirty years of something else."

"I know. But what?"

Michelle could answer most honest questions. That one was beyond her. Mark had to settle on his own approach to life. She could only help after the decision was made.

A waitress in a white dress sprinkled with shamrocks came to their table. "Hungry?" Mark said.

"Yes."

Mark ordered roast beef poor-boys and steins of beer, while using the pause to decide on a different approach. "Michelle, I had a job in San Francisco. The first job I ever really liked. I sold dental drills."

She was pleased to drift away from the worn-out subject of the future. "It sounds interesting."

"I met this man who invented it. He liked me. We did all right together. Maybe I could get the local franchise."

"Mark, you could do anything you wanted."

"It's a good business. There's a fortune to be made. Something I could do on my own. Michelle, you should see this drill. It sells itself. The greatest single piece of equipment I ever saw."

She enjoyed his excitement. "It sounds very wonderful."

He stopped as he remembered. A cord, a tube, a drill. Four moving parts. Smells of novocain and mouthwash. His stuttering failure. He had raced from the dentist's office. "Very big careers are built on dreams."

"Most careers are impossible without them."

"The dream's a lie. I wasn't a good salesman at all. I flunked the test."

"Mark, you could be good. Even if you had to lie a little to yourself to believe it." She wanted desperately to give him that confidence, a beginning.

But he had lost the momentum. "Maybe I'll write to Mandy, have him send a sample case."

As they ate, the conversation stalled. Michelle remembered her resolution in the restroom of the University Library. She had agreed to take the drive only to tell her secret, to spill it out without drama or sadness, to free him if he wanted to be freed.

33

Suddenly she knew she was going to sleep with Mark tonight. The tavern could have changed her mind. Its impersonal sadness seemed to attach to Mark. Insects flew in a whirlwind of specks around their heads. It smelled of cabbage, beer, and piny mops. She wanted a private place to tell him, a room where they could be alone. Perhaps she would not tell him at all, but sleep with him because she wanted him, because he was reaching so desperately for her help. "Mark, could we stay here tonight?"

He was startled. Very few people could surprise him like that. "I thought you only wanted to talk."

"There's too much to say."

"What about your mother?"

"I can tell her I stayed with Allyson in Gulfport."

Mark looked around the place. "We don't have to stay here. We could get a nice place in Biloxi. Off season they give the rooms away."

Michelle wasn't in the mood for a plush hotel. "This one will be lonelier."

Their cabin was on an oyster shell drive, floating in a puddle of chalk. Inside there was a cone-shaded light, a featherbed lumped against the wall, and a square of path-worn linoleum. They thought it a suite. Michelle became hairless as a boy in the gritty shower stall. When she had wrapped herself head to toe in towels, she took Mark's hands in hers and stated unceremoniously, "I'm going to have a baby."

The news started a strange reaction in Mark when he thought he should have felt panic. It was a surge of pleasant relief. The decision had been made for him, painlessly, irrevocably. Had he suspected, even wished for it? In the shower he had kissed the tight bulge in the triangle of her hips and groin, aroused by the new contour of her body. "I think I guessed it," he said.

"Does it make you very unhappy?"

He laughed and she was caught up in it. They laughed for a whole minute together. "I was going to ask you . . . to marry me." He laughed again, but this time Michelle did not.

"Are you sure you want that?"

He peeled away the towels, pressed his ear to her, and listened to the growl of juices under pressure. "How long has it been?"

34

"Ten weeks. I've been to a doctor."

"You must have been terrified all alone."

The truth had been plain in the doctor's tone as he eyed the five-and-dime wedding band and labeled her urine. She had been alone with it for three days until the rabbit test came back positive. "I wasn't alone. I told my mother. She cried a little but she understood."

"She must think I'm an ass."

"Not really. She likes you. She knew you'd come back."

"If I'd been a good salesman it might have been years."

"You'd have come home to a ready-made family." She sat upright. "Is that what you want, Mark? I wouldn't want it if you didn't."

Firmly and without hesitation, he said, "Tomorrow we get the license first thing," and this time he knew she believed him.

"Oh, Mark, it's perfect. I'm so glad you came home. Exactly perfect. You could be a salesman or anything you wanted. I wouldn't care. Father likes you too. He says you have potential. If only he knew how much!"

They laughed and listened to a tiny heartbeat, a synchronous echo of its mother's, and made perfect love. His finger inside her, he thought of a baby searching a purse for pennies. A baby, his and hers, all fingers and toes and gums that was them, coming into a world he could protect it from. A remarkable thing, that he could do that and yet fail at so many other things. It was like a sudden gift, a legacy he had up to now been unaware of. To Mark it was a rather pleasant feeling of accomplishment.

A startling process of growth occurred in Mark that night. He could teach things to a child, right and hopeful things. That could be what made him feel so good. He could watch it grow, see it fall, help it when it needed him. He would see a bit of himself and Michelle in it, and from today on they would be together. The future was at last defined. It was whole and had unity. With a power like that a man could do anything, drive a train, dig a ditch. While he saw it as a grave responsibility, he knew it would somehow take care of itself, that together he and Michelle could manage. These were his thoughts as they lay together listening to the drum of rain on their cottage, watching the light sway as the room rocked with the wind, feeling nothing but each other. Mark was happier that night than he had ever been in his life.

In the morning he drove to New Orleans, but much more carefully than he had come. Michelle sat glowing beside him, and he held her tenderly as he would a precious thing for fear of breaking it. Mark knew this moment of feeling could never be duplicated because he could never love anything in quite the same way again.

A clerk knocked and hastily entered the Office of the Deputy Registrar of Births, Marriages, and Deaths, and threw down a file folder. It contained a marriage license application and photocopies of two birth records. "A case you should handle personally," he said.

Pearl Marie LaCroix glared at the clerk, causing a nervous readjustment of his eyeshade. He had upset her bronze nameplate, a personal affront to her since it intruded on the dignity of her office. She allowed him to wait while she straightened it, noticing that the janitor had again left polish stains on the boldly embossed letters. She would remember to clean it later with a hairpin. "Where's the couple?" she said.

"In the waiting room."

"I will take care of it," she said, a summary dismissal. The clerk went for the door only to be stopped, "Did you check on the parents?"

"The records were in order. I didn't think it necessary to go into that."

A clerk of his ability should not have the presumptive choice of thinking for himself, she thought. She reappointed a barrette in her neatly swept gray hair and examined the application. "Tell them to wait."

The blood tests were in order, the boy and girl of age, and surprisingly, both from middle-class neighborhoods. In cases like this, she would expect one of them to give an address in Treme or Desire, the Irish Channel, Old Gentilly Road. Nevertheless, the marriage could not be permitted. The law was specific. It was her job to block it. She would manage the affair with as much compassion as she could afford.

She first needed pertinent information on the girl's parents, data the clerk had not considered necessary. Him she would take care of later. She took the folder, went into the outer office, and paused to appraise the couple. She lingered too long on the face of the very pretty girl, who smiled, and receiving none in return, shifted her gaze to the boy who held her hand. The boy almost rose in Miss LaCroix's stately presence. She waved him to his seat and entered a staircase that led her to the Bureau of Vital Statistics.

The librarian, Mrs. Thelma Petit, said, "Another one?"

"Book 199."

"Why do people try to get away with that?"

"Human nature. I also need photos on the parents."

Miss LaCroix watched while the copies were made. The operation took two minutes. Prepared to leave, she said, "Things are in order up here, Thelma. You do a good job. Ever think of working downstairs?"

"Why, Miss LaCroix—I'd love to!"

"Good. I'll talk to you about it." She thought of the clerk who had disturbed her nameplate. "My assistant has to go. He's an idiot."

Miss LaCroix returned to her office, a finger buried in the pages of Birth Registration Book No. 199. She looked at the girl but spoke to the boy. "I'll speak to you alone, Mr. Dennick."

Mark followed, annoyed that he nearly tiptoed out of some sort of reverence for official places. Back at her desk, Miss La-Croix stabbed her place in the ledger with a Japanese letter opener and indicated a chair for Mark.

He almost toppled it as he sat. "I guess I'm a bit nervous."

"An important threshhold in your life. Normal enough to be nervous." She removed her glasses, thick octagonal lenses, and massaged her eyelids. The handsome young man—twenty-two, her registrar's mind recalled—could be her own son had she not so cherished her independence as to prohibit marriage, that institution with all its unpleasant obligations. Still, she would have enjoyed a son, a boy like him. It was for them that she fought to retain her stranglehold on the Bureau of Vital Statistics.

Mark fidgeted. Somewhere in the building a typewriter tapped impersonally. His eyes dropped to the floor as if the satchel of dental drills would be there. He knew he would stutter. "I . . . if you're busy I could come back tomorrow."

38

Miss LaCroix examined the application again. There was a possibility, she thought, although a frightening one, that he might be aware of the truth about the girl. It would make her caution unnecessary. She had to find out. "How long have you known the girl?"

"About a year."

"Her parents?"

"The same." Mark sensed an impending marriage consultation. He determined to avoid it. It was none of her business. "Why, isn't the application in order?"

Then he did not know, and he would accept the truth only with absolute proof. "Yes, the application is in order."

"Good," Mark said as if to end the conference.

"One moment, if you please. The policy of this office, that is, the *law* requires that we hold original birth records in case personal copies are destroyed or altered. These are always checked against personal copies."

Mark looked at the impressive nameplate, an announcement of its owner, the Registrar. From it he duplicated her formality. "Miss LaCroix, what is it you're trying to say?"

She clapped her desk decisively. "I am trying to say your marriage cannot be authorized."

"Not authorized? But why? You have the application."

"Your fiancee . . . Miss DeJoie's birth record omits a vital bit of information contained in the original."

"What are you taking about?"

"Personal copies do not necessarily contain all the facts." She spun Book 199 until the hilt of the knife pointed to him. "Folio 837 is her original."

Michelle's birth record was fourth down on the page.

Pearl LaCroix sat quietly attentive until Mark had finished reading the document. He looked up, his face incredulous, searching hers with a plea that mounted to alarm. He read it again and slammed the ledger closed. "You expect me to believe a thing like that?"

"I'm sorry," she said, confident that her tone was edged with condolence rather than apology. "It's the truth."

BE IT REMEMBERED, That on this day to wit: the 20 of May

in the year of our Lord, One Thousand, Nine Hundred and 36

and the One Hundred and 65 of the Independence of the United States

of America, before me, Robt. J. Roberts, M. D., Chairman of the

Board of Health and Ex-Officio Recorder of Births, Deaths, and

Marriages, in and for the Parish of Orleans, and the City of New

Orleans, personally appeared ALFONSO K. DEJOIE native of

  La. residing 714 Treme who hearby declares that

on THE THIRTEENTH DAY OF MAY THIS YEAR (13TH of MAY 1936) AT NO.

714 Treme St. was born a FEMALE child, named

MICHELLE LYNN DEJOIE (NEGRO)

LAWFUL issue of ALFONSO K. DEJOIE a native of NEW ORLEANS, LA.

aged 33 years, occupation SALESMAN and

CORRINE MAY KROMRAJ a native of NEW ORLEANS, LA. aged 29

years.

   Thus done at New Orleans, in the presence of the aforesaid

ALFONSO K. DEJOIE as also in that of ADELE AUCOIN

W. J. PLOUGHWRIGHT both of this city, witnesses by me so

requested to be, who have hereunto set their hands together with me

after due reading hereof the day, month, and year first above written.

Alfonso K. Dejoie

Adele Aucoin

W. J. Ploughwright
Witnesses

R.J. Roberts M.D.
Chairman of the Board of Health
and Ex-Officio Recorder

Sworn and subscribed before me, this
  20TH day of MAY
19 . 36 .

Adele Aucoin DEPUTY RECORDER

"The truth is out there in your waiting room. You look at her and tell me."

"I have looked at her. I've seen octoroons like her in Treme, Desire. So have you. Many of them can pass. They're not above hiding it if they can."

Mark had seen them, the varied hues of "high yellows" of the city and the brown, freckled *marabou* children of back bayou towns. He thought of Michelle, her brittle perfection, a sun-polished fairness, fairer than himself. "She would tell me a thing like that," he said.

Miss LaCroix stood and cheapened her dignity by peeling her rump-sprung dress from her buttocks. "She might have told you, if she had known."

"That's a lie. How could she not know all her life?"

"Did you suspect?"

Mark lifted the ledger to measure its weight. He thought of those that came before it and those yet to come. He wanted to burn it or tear it to bits. He replaced it on the desk. "I love her very much. It makes no difference."

"Perhaps you could accept it. The law cannot."

"I don't care about the law."

Miss LaCroix lit a cigarette and paused to consider the immaturity of the young man. "Fortunately, the law cares about you. What if you'd married and found out afterwards? The law is to protect you."

"You mean to protect you."

"To preserve the races."

Black contamination was the fatuous fear in the American melting pot, like a hangnail in a leper colony. "Some people don't think like that. I'll take her to another state."

"I would give such a move very careful consideration."

"I don't have to consider it."

"Have you thought of your children?"

His thoughts of the child the night before were hardly the ones the Registrar wanted to conjure for him. His children would be assured of their place in the ledger. "We could challenge the records. You couldn't be absolutely sure of a thing like that."

Even as Mark heard his challenge, he knew by her glare that she had the proof. She set her jaw, opened the file to the photocopies, and began with the top one in a fake tone of objectivity. "Both her parents have Negro blood. Here's the certificate on her grandmother, Princess Morley. Her mother, Corinne DeJoie, is actually illegitimate. No record of a father at all. That would be enough, but there's more. Her father's father, Hernando DeJoie, has Negro relatives in Plaquemines Parish. I could have those records sent over if you insist on seeing them." As she ended the speech she gave a puff of smoke to the ceiling and watched it billow and dissolve.

Mark could only whisper, "Oh my God," as he glared at each

document, one by one as they became Michelle's doom, official proof of a damning impurity. Intended as a curse, it issued as a prayer, and he repeated it, saying it for a girl with happiness growing inside her and ignorant of the truth she must somehow face. He could not look at Miss LaCroix. "How . . . can I tell her?"

Sensitive to his moment of defeat, though not saddened by it, she said, "Perhaps it isn't necessary to tell her."

Not necessary? To be condemned and not to be told. In a moment he would greet her bewildered smile. He should boldly assure her that no more than legal trivia had trapped him. "No. She must know that I won't run out on her."

"You can say there will be a delay while I trace some . . . misplaced records. We had a fire. Things have been in general disorder. For her own good hope that she believes it. Take her home and drop it there. It won't be the first time a boy had second thoughts."

"I can't do that."

"Your loyalty is admirably misplaced."

"I can't make her hate me that much."

"In a week or a month it will be forgotten."

"It can never be forgotten."

"What do you mean?"

Yes, Mark reasoned that she was right. He needed time to think, to work it out. He must stall. He opened the door, upsetting the stale quiet of the room. Michelle was standing in the doorway of the waiting room, her face drawn and anxious. "Never mind," Mark said and walked out.

Miss LaCroix watched as he went to the girl with the forced smile, heard his whispered explanation, and closed her door. Unhappily, she had not completed the victory. She suspected what the young man would not tell her, that the girl was probably pregnant. It happened that way often enough. She feared that Mark might carry out his promise to take her away. Miss LaCroix's next move, however necessary, must be very discreet. She took a phone book from a desk drawer, leafed to the number she wanted, dialed, noting with characteristic thrift as she waited that Stephen Dennick lived on Esplanade, conveniently en route to her own home in Gentilly.

42

Michelle asked Mark to put her out at some shops near her home, making up a story that she needed materials for a dress she was making. After he had gone, she caught the Saint Charles streetcar and got off near the Registrar's Office.

The hasty explanation after the lengthy conference struck her as peculiar. *Records were missing. General disorder following a fire. A delay while they put everything together.* She could not understand the indecision in Mark; he had been so certain the night before. Now the uneasy smile, his jitters in the car, his strained assurances that all would be well, disturbed her. That woman, the Registrar, had sized her up as if she were some vital statistic. Mitchelle suspected that something had happened in that conference that Mark was keeping from her. She had to know what it was.

The clerk at the bureau was annoyed to see her. The Registrar was very busy, he said.

Michelle said she would wait.

It was her business if she wanted to wait, he said, but it would probably be a long time.

"She won't go away," the clerk said to Miss LaCroix. "Didn't the boy tell her?"

"Sad," she said. "I advised him not to."

"Sad?"

"I'll have to do it myself, won't I?"

The clerk excused himself, grateful that he had not been ordered to do it.

Miss LaCroix reviewed her choices of action. She could refuse to see the girl, but that would only cause a useless delay. She could tell the truth, the routine choice in such matters, or she could confirm the lie and hope it would be believed. She chose to try the last first. Dishonesty distressed her, but she owed to her promise of compassion at least one deception.

As Michelle took a seat opposite the ledger, she sensed its importance, stabbed as it was in ceremonial hari-kari. "I know you're busy," she said. "My boy friend wasn't very clear on the delay. I wanted to find out for myself."

"He told you we must trace some missing records?"

"Yes, but what records?"

"You shouldn't have come here."

"I had to know. It all sounds so vague."

"Very well, I'll tell you. He was lying to you."

Michelle was startled by the first evidence that her fears were not unfounded. "Mark would not lie to me."

Miss LaCroix clasped her arms over her breast, her cruciform symbol of enduring patience. By now her day had become a protracted tedium of persuasion. She disliked being cast into the role of solicitous mother. Well, on to a better lie. "Marriage is a very important step. It's not uncommon for a boy—or a girl for that matter—to have second thoughts."

"That is a lie!"

"He simply needed more time to think it over. A bit of stage fright, you could say."

"I know Mark better than that. If he wanted out he would tell me."

"To rush him is the worst thing you could do."

"It was his idea to do it right away. Something changed him. Something you said to him in this room."

"Miss—" She had forgotten the name. Misplacing a fact was a swift retribution for emotional involvement. "He wavered. He said he'd like to think about it."

"No, not that. Not think about it."

"Is it so tragic? Don't you want him to be sure?"

"He could tell me that. It was something else. Something you said to him in this room."

"A delay. A few days, a week."

"I want to know what you said to him!"

Miss LaCroix fidgeted, fondled a paperweight, scratched through the taut fibers of her hair. The girl had caused her to go too far. The deception had failed. Had the Registrar wanted it to? Had she played the role poorly so that the girl would sense the lie? The truth must be known. Miss LaCroix did not lack the courage to tell it. "All right, I invented the lie," she said. "But only to spare you from a much greater one." She spun the ledger and opened it to folio 837. "Your birth record."

A scream died as a whimper in Michelle's throat. She was a contradiction. Contrary truths were at war, Michelle in life and the Michelle of record. She was black yet white. The page offered official proof of the contradiction, hidden from her for a lifetime among the tons of statistics. She thought it must be a mistake, another Michelle in another time. A cruel joke. Everyone would laugh soon. It would be over. But no, she saw in the face of the Registrar, in the cold cinders of her eyes, that it was the truth.

Mark knew! The fact crashed down on her. Rather than tell her he had made excuses. She ran out of the room, through the halls, down stairs, into the clatter of the street. People stopped to watch her. She ran so fast from them, from the accusing faces, that she fell. She saw her knees bleed but she continued to run until she was exhausted. Then at last she could cry for herself, for Mark, and the new life inside her that she loved so very much.

Near twilight she found herself standing before the University Library. Donny would be on duty. She went inside to be alone in the quiet rooms. Donny was horrified at the sight of her and quickly dragged her back among the stacks. He saw her knees. "What happened?" he said.

"It's nothing. I fell down."

"You must have fallen more than once. Your stockings are rags. And your face. You look like you've seen a ghost. Michelle, did you quarrel with Mark?"

She wished it could be that simple. A lover's quarrel could be fixed. "No."

"Then what is it? Please tell me."

She wanted to tell him, to tell someone she could trust, to hear him laugh at the silliness of it, this awful contamination that was now part of her. But as she began to speak her voice failed her, and she began to cry. "It's nothing. Please leave me alone."

"Michelle, I want to help."

"You can help by just leaving me alone!"

Donny left and returned a few moments later with a first-aid kit. He cleaned up her knees. She stripped off her stockings and stuffed them into her purse. She felt a little better. "I'll walk you home," Donny said. "It's near closing time anyway."

"No, I'd rather go alone."

He did not want to upset her further. "As you say. But remember I'm your friend. I'll help you if I can."

She touched his hands. "I'm sorry I screamed at you."

It was long after dark when she forced herself to walk to the handsome gray house on Saint Charles Avenue. She thought it an elegant lie among the lawns and clean sidewalks and great pecan trees. It was thick and squat in its design, yet delicate in its cornice and frieze to cover the mistake of it. Her father had called it transparent antebellum. Now it seemed as contradictory as herself. Michelle had loved it. Now she hated it down to the neat gauze curtains in her mother's window, where mother would be reading a proper book and waiting for her daughter, the secret, to wander home.

Michelle crept into the house, climbed the stairs to her room, closed and locked her door. She turned down her bed and sat in the darkness. Some paintings she had made appeared translucent on the walls. She thought of Mark and wondered where he might be, what at this moment he might be thinking of her. Would he be as harsh on her as she was being on herself? In the quiet, the confusion in her mind began to clear. She knew what she must do. The future had suddenly become too heavy a burden. Finally, when she could think about it no more, she checked to be sure each window was sealed and opened a jet on a small gas heater.

The rest was as vague as a nightmare. It was several minutes before her mother smelled the odor. She came in choking, throwing up windows, screaming for her husband. As Michelle heard the siren, she saw the distraught faces of her mother and father, the knowing glances to each other. It was clear to them that their secret had come out.

When Mark left Michelle, he continued along Saint
Charles Avenue, entered Audubon Park, and stopped near the
aviaries. The sounds of the birds were like the clatter in his head.
His words to Michelle hung in his ears like the deception they
were, slippery thoughts lacking conviction. Why had he delayed
telling her the truth? Was it a vestige of prejudice in the lip-
service liberal from the deep South? All of his life Mark had
been revolted by bigotry and the kind of people Miss LaCroix
represented. But when he was suddenly involved personally, the
old way of life, the one taught to him by his family, asserted
itself. Mark had reacted like the rest of them would, in fear and
hatred of niggerness. He knew the delay could have catastrophic
consequences. Michelle must know the truth immediately if she
were to be sure of his intention. Instead of telling her and laughing it off, he had wavered, aided by Miss LaCroix, the damnable
bitch, who had sensed his weakness and led him toward merciful
indecision.

He thought of Clarey and how he might have reacted. Big
deal. The octoroons of Storyville were legend for their beauty.
Rich men raised them for their sons in the back shacks of their
plantations. This is 1957. You don't have to hide the beauties
anymore. Mark, you lucky dog, you got one by accident! Clarey
would have stalked out, dragged Michelle to airport, train, or
bus and dared the Registrar to stop him. The records would have
meant nothing to him. A favorite joke of his was to remind people
of their differences. In his way of reasoning, by making differences explicit they somehow could be laughed at. No ethnic
group escaped him. The "frogs" of Louisiana were eating themselves into the grave on "mud bugs," but he loved crawfish himself. A friend, Morey Klein, was "the Semite." Every WASP
was appointed a parochial fanatic. When he learned Mark's name
had been changed from Dennicola, he was "undewhelmed," as

he put it, to discover the son of a Sicilian soft-drink maker who never made it to the top, poor cousin of Pepsi or Coca-Cola. To Clarey Boriakoff, "Polack," Mark became "Guinea." There was affection and comradeship in that greeting. It perhaps sounded rude to outsiders, but it worked to tumble down the barriers, maybe because Clarey did it with his big cracked grin.

When they were boys, Clarey dreamed of being a middle-weight contender, maybe the champ. He trained, did his road-work, carried a rubber ball in his fist like Joe Louis did in those days. That built the forearm. To strengthen his calves he walked on his toes and seemed ever ready to spring. To fatten his punch he did push-ups, fifty a day. He wanted to be a fighter so badly he would have given his teeth into the bargain, and he did in some tough fights at Saint Mary's, to strong Irish and Italian kids who had learned to fight as a way of life. In the ring he was the gamest fighter those kids ever met. When they beat him, he asked for a return bout. If he won, he offered it. Clarey never made a great fighter. He never had quite the forearm, quite the spring or punch. What he had was heart.

Clarey failed at boxing but found the military. It was a natural find. His father had been a career officer in the Army. The day Clarey came of age, he chose the Marines. His plan was to start at the bottom like Audie Murphy did and come up through the ranks on battle commissions and decorations. Clarey knew he could do it and he never cared what anyone thought. He would do it the way he fought those fights at Saint Mary's, by putting his head down and thinking knockout. Mark had sensed the strength, seen its wonder and its fault, felt it transmit to others. He needed it now.

After dark he drove home, put the car away, and walked to the Napoleon Bar in the French Quarter. The same dozen emperors were on the walls, fat jolly ones and thin ones with sharp noses, all reaching for the classical heartbeat. The night had gained a seasonable chill, a warning of rain, but no one made a move to close the doors that opened into the banquette of Saint Louis Street.

Clarey had been drinking heavily. The cracked smile was the same, but his eyesockets were dark, his face thin and drawn. His offer of his left hand drew attention to his right. It was raw and shrunken, a claw he did not try to conceal. "Everybody sees that first," he said. "Nobody looks at my face anymore."

Gloria was prettier than Mark remembered. She had been Clarey's "sexy bitch" of the old days. She had given him a bad time flirting with other boys. Now she seemed different, grown into a woman. She wore a white dress that should have placed her at a special cocktail party. At a table, two girls, the only other patrons in the bar, chatted in breathy whispers. They seemed to be holding hands. "Hey—a drink for Mark," Clarey said. "We got a lot of drinking to do."

"Could we please sit?" Gloria said.

"A year crunching gravel she thinks I should sit. Mark, do I look tired?"

"You look okay."

"I look like hell, but I'll be okay. Gloryory won't have to feel sorry for me."

"I do not feel sorry for you."

"She could weep to look at me. Mark, don't feel sorry for me, okay?"

"Okay."

"I hang in pretty good. I can't fight the big boys anymore, but I don't have battles to worry about. Crap—I got a pension!" He laughed a cackle Mark had not heard before and wolfed down his drink. "Anyhow, they all knew I could take them in the ring."

The bartender came over and polished a glass under Clarey's nose. He knew the Clarey that liked to blow loudly at times, harmlessly really, and had had to put him out of the bar only once, the night he ripped a pay phone from the wall during a crosstown argument with Gloria. "Y'all keep it down, could you?" he said.

"I got no manners," Clarey said.

Gloria sat at the table with the girls. She saw a drunk in the street nipping from a paper-bagged bottle. She pointed to him and he pointed back. "That's you in a year," she said to Clarey.

Clarey forced Mark into a seat next to her. "Got to do what the beautiful lady says," he said. "Else she gets up tight." He introduced the other girls, a petite dark one named Silly, Gloria's roommate, and a beautiful redhead named Dede. "I bought Glory's dress," Clarey said to Mark. "You like it?"

"Sure."

Clarey cupped a hand over his mouth to whisper, but his tone was louder than before. "Want to know a secret? Nothing on underneath. Not a stitch." He hiked the dress to her knees. "She feels sexier that way."

"Why not tell everybody?" Gloria said.

"Hot. I can feel the heat come right off her."

"Clarey, please stop."

But he was entertaining his old friend. "Most times New Orleans is too warm for trusses. Think if everybody walked around naked. You'd know all about 'em right away. See, when people look at faces, they're really thinking about asses. Imagine all those no-longer-mysterious asses humping around the street!"

The barman glared at him and he got the message. "Let's go drink someplace else."

"It's time we went home," Gloria said.

The redhead kissed the dark girl, her tongue a moist red dart, and it startled Clarey. "How about the lovers," he said. "How can I permit that and not two men? Am I a latent?"

The girls, their trance destroyed, left the table and swept through the door as one body on four legs.

Clarey ignored them. He showed a wad of money. "Look, Mark. I'm loaded. People keep handing me money." He laughed the bitter laugh again. "For my rehabilitation. I thought my Top Sergeant would break down and cry. He knew how much I wanted to stay in the Marines."

"He's crazy," Gloria said.

"Don't say that!"

"You'd think he'd had enough."

"It's you who's crazy. Couple more years I could have made sergeant. You know how hard it is to make sergeant in the Marines? Ask anybody. You need balls to make sergeant!"

Gloria came to her feet. "Clarey—cut it out!"

"Want to see why they threw me out, Mark?"

"No, he does not!"

"I can show an old buddy if I want." He pushed himself from

50

the table and stood as firmly as he could. For a moment Mark saw Clarey the fighter. He tugged at his belt and his pants dropped, exposing a leg as raw as the claw hand. His testicles were gone, the penis left as a flat prepuce. Gloria covered her eyes. Mark overturned his glass. Clarey swept the room for gasps that did not come. Instantly the barman's hands lifted him, and his feet, bound by the trousers, were forced in involuntary chop-steps through the door. Outside he sprawled, laughed, and looked at the sky. "Looks like rain," he said.

"Why you do that," Gloria said. "Nobody wants to see that."

"When we were kids we didn't care if they knew our secrets."

"That was a long time ago."

"Now I got a bigger secret."

"I'll take you both home," Mark said.

Clarey managed to make it to his feet. He was wobbly. "Have another drink with me, Mark."

Mark hedged. A drink would give him time to talk about Michelle, but Clarey's eyes were closing, Gloria's face pleading. She finally made the decision. "Help me get him to my place."

Clarey rolled the claw fist and presented it to Mark. "The only time I can close it is when I'm drunk. Trouble is nobody will drink with me anymore."

They crossed Bourbon Street, turned into Dumaine, Clarey legless between them as the rain began, cool drops they could feel but not see. On the marquee of a strip house, Mark saw a blowup of beautiful red Dede, snapped at the apex of a bump or a grind and installed with pasties that lit up like Christmas tree lights. Clarey saw it too, and said, *"Chacun à son goût.* But how the hell do two girls make love?" Then he passed out completely. Mark shifted him to his shoulder, surprised by the lightness of his body.

They undressed him, put him to bed on the couch, and watched over him until the claw hand relaxed. "He always drank," Mark said. "But I've never seen him like this."

"You heard. He can close his fist and forget."

"Why did he drop his pants like that?"

"You saw what was there?"

"The Clarey I knew would never humiliate himself like that."

"Mark, he stepped on a flare and came up with his testicles in his hand. He keeps re-living it. He stands naked in the mirror and laughs that terrible laugh."

His laugh had been a happy one, infectious. Now it was a cackle before a mirror. The once proud fighter had dropped his pants for the necessary humiliation, so that Mark could know. "What are his chances?"

"He'll live, if that's what you mean. That is if he doesn't kill himself."

"I can't believe he'd give up so easily."

"Not so easily. She managed the zipper on her back and let the dress drop to her waist. Clarey had not lied about her nakedness. Black blotches, tooth-marked skin, ran from the base of her breasts to the crest of her nipples. "It happens when he fails."

"Clarey did that?"

"Oh, he was so sorry in the morning. He didn't remember. He could only look at me and cry."

"I don't understand. Why would he hurt you?"

She swam back into the dress, out of clinical nudity, but left it unzipped. She remembered undressing hourly that morning after it happened, unconcerned with the pain but anguishing over the possibility of cancer and how she would look after a mastectomy. "I don't know why. Maybe it's a way of hurting himself. I can swear to you he'll never do it again."

"We've got to help him."

"I tried that. Now I only want out. Mark, you remember us, how close we were. We made love everywhere, a park, a car, a beach—standing, sitting, swimming." She stopped, felt it inside her, weightless, water-cooled plunges. She yearned for it to be that way again. "I can't have that with him now, but I know I will . . . with someone."

Clarey stirred and said, "Paddies tong blick jump."

"Every night he talks of the war."

Mark looked at the rumpled face, the strings of his neck. The claw hand seemed to be reaching for a limb. He quivered. His breathing came with difficulty. Mark had come to him for strength, to tell him of Michelle, to hear from him what must be done. But this was a fallen fighter, all the fight gone out of him, the complete defeat the vacancy at his groin. He had asked Mark not to feel sorry for him. "We've got to help him," Mark said.

"I'm all through helping." She dropped the dress into a pile at her feet and kicked it aside. Because she knew Mark would not come to her, she took his hands and led them to her. She felt them cold against the pricking pain of the bruises. In a moment they grew warm.

Mark moved away and turned his back to her.

She sat on the couch beside Clarey, now self-conscious of her nakedness, trying to cover herself with her hands. She felt she deserved the rejection. It was a bold and selfish way to ask for love. But lately she had not had much time to think of herself. "I've got to get out of here. Damn—I've got to get out!"

In the cold light of dawn, rubbery-legged between her mother and father, Michelle could remember little of the night. It came back to her in dreamy images. She remembered the ambulance, a chrome-handled stretcher with crisp sheets, inverted street lamps passing in the darkness. Superimposed over it was her father's tearful, remorseful face. The siren was the cry of a child as she fought strong hands that clamped an oxygen mask over her mouth. The medicinal smell of the hospital made her sick. She vomited over herself and the floor. The sour odor returned to her clothing in the daylight, a reminder of what she had done. It remained until her mother changed her clothes. Then her father came into her room, removed a valve from a gas heater, and replaced it with a plug. Impetuous girl, now suicidal, was not to be trusted with a gas heater or a paring knife.

"Try and get some rest," Alfonso said and turned his tired face to the door. "I don't want you to think about what happened. It won't do a bit of good." Michelle knew it was his way of taking the blame for her, of allowing her to remain irresponsible even for her own life. The sacrificing father would take the blame for The Plague if anyone would let him. Michelle had often wondered about his self-deprecating nature. Now she knew his reason, the guarded secret, he and his wife and child in the vault of his conscience. Now that the truth had come out he was clearly ready to accept guilt.

A reverse xenophobia. Surely there was a bit of it in most people, but how tragic is the person who hates himself. You can run from a leper, but what if you are the leper? Wear woolly hoods to keep it a secret. She forgave him and she knew why. She had felt the same fear in the Registrar's office. Like her father she had tried to run from it. The shock had caused panic. It was being told she was not the self she had grown up to know, proud, compassionate of others, even a bit superior, in love with her

54

future. What had happened to that pride? Because it was false, it had crumbled like the braggart's courage. The truth was in the mouth of the Registrar and in the faces of her parents. Michelle could not change it in the slightest if she were to go on living. She decided, foolishly, that she could not live with the future. In panic, the gas chamber was simpler.

Now that she had time to reflect, she had her thoughts under control. Thinking about it had a cleansing quality. What she had reacted to with shame and embarrassment, now gave her strength. She *was* the same. Without her hackneyed pride, she could understand her parents' fear and Mark's indecisiveness. There is a higher pride in liking what you are. People like the Registrar could give out statistics on what percentage of you was what, but they couldn't hurt you if you had pride in it. The more Michelle thought about it, the more she liked the idea. She was unique, an eighth of African blood running in her veins.

She shuttered when she thought of what the Registrar would say about her baby, what *she* had almost done to it! The shock had fogged her mind. Her dominating thoughts had been of Mark. How should he have reacted? How would she if the roles were reversed? She had long ago decided that in all fairness she could not hold him to an undesirable marriage. It now seemed a very poor bargain for him.

Michelle spent the morning drafting a letter to him. She wrote it in a bold, crisp hand because she knew it would make her understand why she must give him up.

My Dearest, Dearest Mark,

I do miss you but I'm grateful for the day away from you. I want to speak to you quietly. You must forgive me. My trust in you failed me. I went back to the Registrar's office. The place has become a hell to me. That woman is evil. LaCroix, (in French, the cross) told me the truth about myself. The truth has never been difficult for me before, even frightening truths like war, starvation, disease. I was not prepared for the truth about me. I know that to spare me you chose to lie. Because I understand that I won't mention it again.

I ran home and attempted to kill myself. I was convinced I meant it. I think it was because I felt so alone. I closed my

55

windows, turned on the gas, and forgot? to lock the door. My parents rushed me to the hospital, past whispering neighbors, and all I got out of it was a sick stomach. I didn't feel ashamed when I saw my father cry. It was my punishment for him, for not letting me know the truth. I won't be cruel to him again.

Forgive me for what I almost did to myself, but I was alone and could only think of the woman and her records. Was she smiling as I ran out? Triumph? My funny face? I have a pale recollection that I fell down. My skinned knees prove it. People on the street must have thought I'd gone mad. Had I? Why do we laugh when someone slips and falls? I write badly. I kill myself badly.

I can only think it funny now. But what exactly is funny? It's an emotion turned upside down. Some people always laugh when they should cry. Some refuse to cry because it may tell something about them.

Exit and return. It is like a play. Watching it unfold and being a part player. The ending?

I've caught cold. I needed tissues and had to go all the way downstairs. Mother is in the kitchen shelling pecans. She pretended to ignore me, a pecan-pie Sunday, no different from any other. Mark, why didn't they tell me? Did they fear I would try to kill myself? They let me grow up ignorant. You were reeling from shock like me, but they had time to tell me, teach me. Leander Perez hates but not himself. It is a curse to hate yourself. I feel very sorry for mother and father. I also love them. Did I inherit martyrdom as well? In panic, I hated myself for a moment. We are all xenophobes. Would you steal food to stay alive?

Daddy has a mistress. Why am I telling you this? Am I planning to tear it up, flush it? I accidentally stumbled over his car once. He was with a woman and very self-conscious. He was wearing sunglasses. He kissed her (not a peck), put her in the car, kissed her again. I hid behind a tree. I wanted to go and scream at him. I did nothing and never told mother. I just realized why I'm telling you this. So that you can understand his weakness, a weakness I won't give in to.

My conclusions. In college I had a roommate from Bolivia. She was one-fourth what I am one-eighth of. Why can't I write it down? Negro. N-e-g-r-o. I said it several times as I wrote it. She was proud of it. She was very pretty, darker than I, smart— chemistry, physics. We became good friends. I'd never had a part

Negro friend. I felt rather proud. I had social conscience. I'd look at her as a curiosity. Am I one now? I think she read my thoughts. She'd bring up the subject and laugh and say she was proud of it, although she knew Americans could never understand that. She couldn't understand America. She'd learned English in a country school in the mountains. I remember talk of tin mines and great poverty. She spoke the language well but didn't understand why people laughed at her when she said "fortnight." I really liked Maria. I wish I knew where to find her, to talk to her, to hear her laugh at my suicide. What a laugh we would have!

Much later. It's growing dark. I cried some for you. Please don't laugh when I tell you it's because I read some Erich Fromm. He's been with me on all your travels. I can smell the syrupy pecans in the oven. I'm not hungry.

Now I must tell you. I love you. Last night I was confused, alone, hating myself like Daddy. Today I made a decision. I will not hold you to this. The child will be mine alone, like Maria and me, but mine. This is final. I will not give in. I will tell you it was another boy while you were away. It happened in his car on Lakeshore Drive. No, not there. Not in our place, a sweet bed to us, the cramped space of a car seat. No, I cannot tell such a lie. . . .

Very late. I feel I've been with you through the day. The pages have stacked up. I have so much still to say, and I wonder when I will see you. God, please love you as I do, and forgive me for being so selfish.

Yours forever,

Michelle

She folded the pages carefully and tore them into small pieces like the shreds of her thoughts. Then she sprinkled them into her purse as if she might later decide to put them together again.

Mark awoke to the sound of William's old Studebaker, the crush and rattle of its door closing. Fortunately, it stopped for only a moment to let Papa out and pulled away. Morning sunlight swept the room, illuminating swimming lint and dust. He felt cooked in the musky bouquet of the room, but he dawdled, dreading the long day ahead.

He had spent a restless night filled with thoughts and dreams of Clarey and Trudy, the two people he knew could help him in this time of need. While he felt he could discuss the scene in the Registrar's office with neither his father nor his brother, he knew he could easily explain it to Clarey or Trudy. But Clarey was defeated and Trudy was gone. Yes, he knew he would only have to speak to Trudy and the wisdom would reel out, the answers, the conviction. She had an inner strength built from a life of hardship. The boys had trusted her and taken their troubles to her.

Steamboat steamin' on a river, gonna take me on. . . . To where? Where was she now? She had packed her bag one day and left while the boys were away at school. Mark knew it was to avoid sad goodbyes. The boys had grown up. There was little need for her in the house without them. She left no hint of her destination, but she did leave a goodbye note in *The Oregon Trail*. She said simply that it was time for her to go away and left instructions on what they were to do about dinner. Typical of Trudy, he thought, to be loyal to practicalities up to her last moment in the Dennick household. Mark now placed her somewhere on a levee in a shack with billowing curtains, rocking away the moments remaining to her, peeling shrimp and shucking tubs full of butterbeans.

Even though he was alone, he knew he had only one choice of action. Miss LaCroix had made it clear to him. He must take Michelle and run. He would have to break his promise to settle

58

and take the railroad job. But how would he do it? Where would he go? Would Michelle agree to leave? These were the answers he would have to find on his own. As he dressed he thought of his conversation with Matt. The old man was going to die. Mark would have to hurt him again. Moreover, he would have to make more false promises and walk silently through the motions of a backyard Sunday.

Before going downstairs he called Michelle. Her voice was flat and distant. She explained she had caught cold. "I got it in all that rain at Pass Christian," she said.

"Take care of it," he said, an implied concern for her pregnancy.

"I'm going to spend the day in bed."

"That's just as well. I have the family all day anyway."

"Mark . . . I. . . ." She stopped as it to settle for an alternate thought. "Will I see you tomorrow?"

"Try to keep me away. I'll call early."

She paused a long moment. "I miss you. That sounds silly. It's only been a day. You were away two months and the one day seems longer."

Mark wanted to tell her everything, but he couldn't bring himself to do it on the telephone. "We'll have tomorrow together. I promise." That promise he would keep.

Papa had opened a beer and settled in a rocker on the gallery. He wore the same floppy hat, khakis, and boots. His face was creased and leathery, the look of a man who had spent most of his life outdoors. His large hands were braced on the arms of the rocker. He stood and offered a handshake when he saw his son. "Mark, you look well."

Mark tried to sound cheerful. "I got a lot of sun in California."

"California was it again? I hear it's beautiful country."

Mark thought of their own beautiful country. "You're selling the property in Saint Tammany?"

"How'd you hear that?"

"Matt left a note."

"You boys, the way you left notes when you were kids. I always figured you had a secret hiding place. Now don't tell me. No need to give up private secrets."

59

"Matt said you were selling to William."

"I expect to let him have it if he'll pay my price."

"I remember a day you'd laugh if he only hinted at buying 'Our Wilderness.' "

Papa understood the sentiment. The property had meant as much to him. But there was a greater meaning in Mark's future. Property could be bought or sold. A life needed direction. By selling to William, who was depot supervisor, Papa could guarantee a railroad job for Mark. "Property without people on it is just dirt, son. William's got kids. A place like that needs kids. When I'm up there alone there's not much to do. I make a little hogshead cheese. I don't even work the vegetable garden. Say, what about breakfast? You must be hungry."

"No thanks, Papa."

"Now you just sit there for a minute. I've got a surprise for you."

As Mark waited, he remembered the vegetable garden. They started it during the war. It was a Victory Garden. Snap beans, tomatoes, watermelons. Papa had fenced it to keep out the rabbits. He had to give much of the produce away. The garden made him a popular man in Saint Tammany.

Papa returned with a dish of hogshead cheese and French bread. "I made it just the other day. I knew you'd want some."

Mark tasted it. "It's still the best I ever ate, Papa."

The old man was pleased. He slumped in his rocker and closed his eyes. "I'm getting old, Mark. I've got to get things settled. William will take care of the place. He promised me he'd do that. I know you boys were always distrustful of him, but he's a good man. He's been good to Delia all these years. Why, just the other day he hinted at a railroad job for you if you wanted it."

The unavoidable subject at least ended the obituary on Saint Tammany. As expected, Papa lit up for it. "You could start as operations trainee, in no time move up to an executive position. Do you know what executives make when they have seniority?"

"Seniority is something you save up all your life and spend when you die."

Papa thought it rude the way Mark put some things. His

father, thirty-five years a railroad man, would only be spending that dignity by dying. "Seniority is what makes you important to the company. A member of the family. Men were standing in line for railroad jobs when I was your age. It was a lot better than digging ditches for the WPA. When nothing else worked, the railroad worked."

"Papa, that was during the Depression. There are lots of other jobs now."

"Great things were happening before that. You heard of the Transcontinental? They nailed together two pieces of the world. Two rails, four feet, eight and a half inches apart, clear across America. Those rails are still there."

"The railroad isn't all there is. A man can do other jobs if he wants."

At this point Papa knew he would have to let it cool if he were to save the conversation. He wanted desperately to reach his son, to tell him of his plan. He took a moment to finish his beer and crushed the Jax can in his hand. "What did you do in California?"

As usual Mark quickly thought of a lie. "I worked on an oil rig off the coast."

Papa seemed to appreciate it. "Steady work?"

"Pretty much. There will always be oil wells." Mark stopped. The statement seemed a mockery of his father's favorite expression, *there will always be a railroad*. "I'm sorry. I didn't mean it to sound that way."

"Son, no honest work's a bad thing. Remember the railroad carries the oil. How else would it get anywhere?"

"It would stay in the ground without men to pump it out."

"And sit in tanks without the railroad."

"Papa, a man has to do what he wants."

"That's why God gave him the know-how."

Papa, Mark wanted to say, is God responsible for the way we chop wood, mine coal, paint a house? How busy he must be. How jealous not to allow us to do one little thing for ourselves!

Like many of their conversations, this one was now lost. Mark could only sit quietly, half believing his lie of the oil rigs although he had never seen one in his life.

61

Mercifully, Aunt Emma swept through her door across the street and headed for the gallery. Her hair was oiled and swept above her head, as if it were holding up her sagging face. Mark caught her fruity fragrance as she pecked him moistly. "Mark, you got to tell me where you been, what you been up to."

"He's been working oil rigs in California," Papa said, and to make sure the statement would translate in Emma's mind as great success, he added, "He did very well."

"What it does to your Papa, you being home. Look how he brightens up. Mark going to drill oil wells here? I mean, Louisiana has lots of oil wells, don't we? I bet I saw a dozen out on the road to Chalmette." Emma either spoke in streams or not at all. Parties to her monologue were mercifully spared involvement. The family only pretended to listen to her, attributing her failing to her collision with a kitchen cabinet when she was a young woman. The unspoken opinion was that most of her brain had washed down the drain long before Dominick found her. She came out of the accident a kleptomaniac, but oddly stole only from the family, and a rather obtuse chatterbox, an unlucky combination. "I hope Mark's going to stay home this time."

They were both looking at him, waiting to hear the lie. "I'm going to stay this time."

"Well, that's just fine. Ya'll have visiting to do." She started down the stairs, stopped, and clapped her hands. "I knew there was something. Any ice in the big freezer? Dominick likes a cool drink when he comes home."

"Take what you need," Papa said.

Emma gathered a newspaper as she went through the house, emptied two ice trays into it, added two frozen packages of peas, and left by the back door so that she would pass the gallery at a distance. "I saw some paint cans in the driveway," she said. "Dominick's doing some painting."

"You're welcome to them," Papa said, making a mental note to put the full cans under lock and key.

As she disappeared into her house, Mark thought of the cabinets Papa had installed in the garage many years ago. He had known their purpose, Emma's appetite for larceny, without asking. "What did she take?" he said.

62

"Some vegetables she bought for me yesterday."

"She never was quite that open about it."

"She's become worse lately."

"Maybe if she saw a doctor. . . ."

"What's the harm? She buys the food with my money, takes it home, and the next day Dominick pays me for it."

A typical compromise solution for Papa. Sparing her feelings was simpler than the cure. To avoid the truth, they would rather permit the kleptomania. Mark wondered how long it would remain in the family, how long before Emma would strike out for new territory.

William Janin and his family arrived right after church. He carried a bundle under each arm, the fattest of the shrimps and crabs from Taliferro's Restaurant on Rampart Street, he said, and a package of tamales he had bought from a vendor. He shook Mark's hand as Papa led him to a picnic table in the yard.

Delia Janin lagged behind to greet Mark with a kiss. "You look handsome as ever," she said.

In the yard, William's four girls (still no namesake), trifled with the packages as he began a search of his pockets. "Y'all leave that alone," he said. "That's not for you. Delia, will you send them out to play? Steve and I have to talk business."

"Outside, Momma?"

She said yes and the four girls filled the alley with petticoats.

When William had turned out each pocket several times, he began to feel panic. After his careful plans, the months of clever bargaining, the Tammany Parish deal seemed to be crumbling. Mark's unexpected appearance seemed ominous. William could expect nothing but opposition from him. The deal would have been closed by now if business at the depot had not consumed two weekends. Now he had forgotten the goddamned papers. He knew he had to get them signed today or risk failure.

Delia saw him pale and said, "Look inside your coat."

William snatched them out and handed them to Papa.

"This can wait," Papa said.

"I thought you'd want to get it out of the way," William said, indicating the bundles, "before we ate."

63

"I've iced a tub of beer, Will. Help yourself. There's plenty of time."

"You made up your mind, didn't you? It's all in the papers like we discussed it. I had a lawyer. . . ." As an attorney before the bench, he instinctively withdrew, fished a beer from the tub, and flicked icy sprinkles in the air. "Just thought we could do it before our fingers got messed up."

"Mark and I want to talk it over first."

As Papa took his son aside for a private discussion of the transaction, William joined Delia for a tour of the garden, early crocuses and tulip bulbs pushing their way out of the ground. "Mark's the reason the old man's wavering," William said. "Can you tell me why that boy doesn't like me?"

"He never said he didn't like you, Will."

"He doesn't have to say it."

"You're imagining. Mark is just quiet. Take my word for it. I know the boy. I helped raise him."

William dropped it there. He saw no profit in undermining her allegiance to the boys. He sat at the table and snapped a string on one of the bundles. Delia sat delicately beside him, watching him eat, blotting perspiration from her lip with a handkerchief rolled into her threadlike fingers.

When Mark took a seat with them to go over the papers, Delia said, "It's really good to see you home again, Mark."

Mark remembered the familiar sadness in the slack print dress trimmed with lace, bought at Kress' Department Store. Delia had taken the boys shopping there before each school term. Each purchase had been a test of wise choice against cunning Jew. "Thank you, Aunt Delia," he said and tried to give his attention to the papers.

Papa stood off alone and shaded his eyes against the sun to gauge the prospects of the day. It was cool and cloudless. With luck it would stay that way through the afternoon. A clear day could help shore up his spirit. There was much more at stake than a contract of sale. Money could be spent, property sold. A solid future with the Southern Pacific Railroad was an invaluable asset. The old man believed that there was a true immortality in giving that kind of security to a son. No, it was not the kind

64

the Catholic Church preached, that the soul was all that mattered, that what a man did on earth was inconsequential as long as he obeyed the laws. Papa truly believed that his immortality was in his sons and in the life he could pass on to them.

Such was his plan for the day. He fully understood the leverage in his bargaining position. William had been after the Tammany Parish property for years. He had hinted that he might be able to arrange a railroad job for Mark. He would start with a low offer, fireman or clerk. Papa would demand special agent. They would compromise, the old man hoped, at operations trainee. Papa wanted Mark to understand these thoughts today, for as he looked at the sky he perceived, as only a man close to death is able, of the scarcity of days to come.

When Mark had finished reading the papers, Papa said, "Might as well tell you, William. Mark's against selling the property."

William's head snapped up and danced. Feigned surprise was in his plan. "Why should he be?"

One day he will get a whiplash, Mark thought, the way he does that. "Sentimental reasons," he said.

"The boys practically grew up in that old shack," Papa said, and then reflectively, "not good for a man alone though, him not well and all. . . ." He looked at Mark. "We were close to the earth out there in the woods."

"Hell—y'all come up to my place anytime," William said. "I'll have twice the earth once we close our deal."

"Please guard your language," Delia said.

William's head rolled on its spring and laughed. A younger, cocksure William had indeed been fond of foul language. He had shouted obscenities to three-year-old Mark, rejoiced as the child returned each one, adding others learned from William an earlier day. "Delia made me give up cussing. Now I have to go out in the woods to get it out."

"Now you'll have twice the woods to curse," Mark said.

William clapped his hands and bits of shrimp flew into his hair. "Right. Right!"

Mark leafed through the papers again, assuming the role of reluctant owner willing to sell but determined to drive up the price. But rather than read them, he only studied the various print sizes and William's fingerstains. William watched, nervously eating and drinking.

"Well, what do you think?" Papa said.

"They look all right to me."

William jumped in. "I had a lawyer friend over on Carondelet Street draw them up, all nice and legal." Then imitating a man too important to remember details, he asked Delia for his fountain pen.

Papa held up his hand. "Matt will be here soon."

Stephen Dennick was going to call witnesses until the jury wept, William thought, and then tried the old dramatic-pause-in-the courtroom trick. He spread his hands in a flourish and said that Stephen could show the papers to anybody in the world if he wanted to and it would be okay by him.

Jesus Christ! Mark thought. What a cornball.

Matt arrived, handling his baby like a football in the crook of his arm. Marylene brought in a bowl of baked macaroni and cheese and a tray of artichokes stuffed with Parmesan cheese. Then she sat in a patch of magnolia shade, healthfully pregnant, a preview of Michelle.

The day wore on cool and windless, a bright tropical winter afternoon. Matt had accepted the contract in his turn when Emma and Dominick burst through the gate. Dominick carried a bowl of peeled figs. Emma rode herd on Delia's girls with a switch. "Delia—they were out in the street!" Another fact charged to Emma's accident, she was childless. She insisted she had lost her only child that year she was in the coma. Mark often wondered if the absence of children was the reason she stole things, to deprive someone of something as she had been deprived of children.

As the afternoon turned into a tedium of prattling small talk, Mark wondered how graciously his family would react to the truth about Michelle. He was tempted to make a solemn confession to all of them if only to watch their reactions. He knew them well. He could imagine what each would say and do. William would go white but quickly compose himself. He would pace gravely on the grass, his hands clasped prudently behind his back. He would call on his fractured knowledge of the law, fake some wise precedents, and end with a speech on racial purity.

Papa would have some words to say. It would be a short speech, not as dramatic as William's, but as moving. It would involve honor, allegiance to family, and hard work. He would say it all without ever raising his voice, but by rolling his fists into angular balls that were his power. The answer would somehow be lumped into a railroad car, and it would somehow exclude Michelle.

That would be Delia's clue to bury her face in her handkerchief and pray that Mark would not go through with such a marriage. Emma would faint dead away and be forgotten as the others bumped about in chaotic fear and panic. Matt would hardly say a word. These images were telling things about these people, Mark's family, and he had never seen them quite as clearly before. In 1957, the Dennick household lived a long way back in the past.

The bargaining of the afternoon shaped up at last. When Matt returned the papers, Papa spread them on the table and tapped them with his fingers to indicate indecision. William read the pause accurately and offered the largesse—*lagniappe* seemed kinder—that bit of extra to be thrown into the deal. He faked surprise that Mark might be interested in a railroad job, but he was sure he could arrange it.

"It's natural," Papa said, "for a boy to want to follow in his father's footsteps."

"Of course," William said.

"As local supervisor I thought you'd be in a position. . . ."

"I could put him on as clerk right away."

But Papa laid it on him. "Mark has a good education, William. Loyola. He would suffocate in a paper job. He needs something vital . . . like special agent."

William had not anticipated the scope of the old man's ambition. He had no idea where Stephen would compromise. "Stephen, a special agent needs credentials, experience. Men of that rank have to know the business top to bottom. Mark has to start lower and work his way up."

67

"Then start him in operations as a trainee. He'll work up to an important job in no time."

William paced on the grass. He knew that Mark had majored in English at Loyola, small preparation for a technical job. "That would take a lot of string pulling. Those jobs usually go to graduate engineers. There are some things even I can't do."

"I saw that he got some science, William. Mathematics too. He can handle it."

But William shook his head indecisively.

Delia fidgeted. "Surely you can do it," she said.

Yes, he could do it. He could exaggerate the boy's qualifications. The compromise was correct. If Mark did not stand the test, the failure could only be charged to him. "Okay, operations it is."

Dominick said, "Hoo-ray!"

Delia and Emma clapped their hands.

Everyone felt something good had been done for the family.

William drew his fountain pen, checked the flow, and offered it to Papa.

With the business put aside, the family could eat and drink. They filled their plates and watched the children roll on the grass. Toward sundown, as the grassfires in the yards of the neighborhood smouldered, Mark began to put together his plan, and curiously, wondered what it would be like to be an operations trainee for the Southern Pacific Railroad.

On Saturday afternoon Pearl LaCroix had fired her assistant and hired Thelma Petit. She did both with thrift, neither a wasted word nor an excessive thought. Yet she was not pleased with the day's work. The partial victory over young Mark Dennick troubled her. She had to see personally that the matter was properly disposed of. She had tried and failed several times to reach the Dennick house by telephone. What had started as a routine matter was now turning into an emergency. Every moment wasted gave the boy that much more time to hustle the girl out of the city.

Not able to restrain herself over the entire weekend, she tried and connected on Sunday evening, right after Mark drove home with Matt and Marylene for supper. "A matter involving your son, Mark," she said to the elder Dennick.

Papa, interrupted in the middle of his goodbyes to William and Delia, was puzzled. "Is Mark in trouble with the city?"

"I'd rather not discuss it on the phone. I can be there in thirty minutes."

She arrived promptly at six, glistening a bit after the long drive from Gentilly. She carried a file folder locked under her elbow. She did not put it down until she was seated in the living room, and then, conscious of her oily prints on it, brushed it sweetly. "Are you expecting your son?"

"Not for a while. He's having supper with his brother."

"I will be as concise as possible," she said, a hint of presentiment in her tone. "Yesterday your son applied for a marriage license."

The unexpected news brought a smile to Papa's lips. Under pressure Mark had accepted the railroad job, but with less opposition than the old man had expected. This was perhaps the reason why. Marriage was his own decision, a step toward permanency. Papa was not at all offended that he had not been told. But this woman, her grave manner, that she had a reason to involve herself, distracted him. "Some young people decide to do it secretly," he said. "I suppose it seems romantic at the time. At any rate I wouldn't interfere."

"Perhaps you wouldn't . . . under normal circumstances."

"I don't understand."

"Do you know the girl?"

"Michelle DeJoie? Yes, I know her. They've been dating for a while. I have no objection to the girl. Miss LaCroix, I don't know why this matter should bring you here."

The Registrar opened her file. The preliminaries had been necessary if only to be sure of the footing ahead. She paid serious attention to the accumulation of obstinate truths, slapped the folder closed. It seemed she had said it a thousand times. "Mr. Dennick, the marriage cannot be authorized. The girl is a Negro."

It was a startling accusation, and from this nondescript head of some city bureau, hard to believe. Papa had been much impressed with Michelle. She was pretty, intelligent, from an uptown Creole family, the daughter of a businessman. There was an air of responsibility about her, a proper settling influence for Mark. He had hoped the relationship would turn serious. "How do you know this to be true?"

Miss LaCroix longed to be on her own ground, the security of her office. The man seemed actually to doubt her authority. Very well, she had the proof. She stiffened and balanced on her coccyx, affecting at best a drab pomposity. "As I explained on the phone, I am the head of the Bureau of Vital Statistics. I research records on every applicant for marriage in Orleans Parish. The reasons are obvious, wouldn't you say?"

Papa decided he disliked the Registrar. He distrusted paper people and could not read her eyes, flyspecks behind thick lenses. He checked an impulse to ask for her credentials. "I'd like to see the proof if you have any."

She handed over the folder. "I am sorry your son is involved. These cases are tragic, for the innocent party, or parties. The girl actually didn't know herself. I had to tell her. Imagine learning a thing like that after you've grown up."

As Papa read each document, he thought of his son confronted earlier by them and wished he could have accepted the burden instead. Young love could seem indestructible, yet it was fragile enough to be dealt a fatal blow, as he knew this one had. His dislike for the Registrar crystallized as he returned the folder. Her fraudulent apology, the superficial sympathy, did not hide the true meaning of her mission. He did not have to like her to appreciate it. "Thank you for telling me," he said.

She prepared to leave. "I wouldn't have come to you except . . . he threatened to take the girl to another state. I thought you should know that. I should also tell you I think the girl is pregnant. He didn't say so but they were in a rush. Blood tests and marriage license in the same morning. I've seen enough of them."

Yes, Papa thought, it would have hastened Mark's decision. He would have reacted with defiance. The boy seemed to find expression in opposition. The old man needed to be alone to think it out, to prepare a compassionate way to approach it before Mark came home. "Thank you, Miss LaCroix," he said to complete the conversation.

Aunt Emma, watching from her window, was barely able to control an impulse to streak across the boulevard and barge in on the mysterious company. Fortunately it was not a lengthy visit. She saw the woman reappear and hurry to her car. Emma rushed into her kitchen, spooned out two servings of red beans, added a slab of pork and a hill of rice, and shot through her door.

"Thank you," Papa said. "Please leave it in the kitchen."

She stepped into the house and reappeared immediately, as if she had raced to the kitchen and back, impatient to clean up the mystery. "I saw you had company."

There were times when the ubiquitous Emma was a nuisance. She would have tried the patience of a less cohesive family. But then, that was her grace, that she was family. Now she wanted the facts of the mysterious visit. Telling her the truth would be like letting it out for publication. Papa was no where near ready for that. He wanted to be alone to think. "It was a routine visit," he said. "Concerning the Tammany property. Nothing important."

Dissatisfied with the explanation, Emma stood for a while as if she expected more. Then she slowly waddled back across the street, tossing worried glances over her shoulder.

Papa knew she felt cheated out of a choice piece of gossip. He also knew she would uncover the truth in due course. That would immediately enlighten the whole family. They would react in emotional panic, a condition Papa wanted to avoid if possible. He decided he had time to approach Mark with caution. By calmly reasoning with his son, he might succeed in demonstrating the dangers and heartbreak that lie in such a union. Failing to do it alone, he thought of calling in Father Hurley, Pastor of Saint Mary's Catholic Church. The boys had attended high school there. The Pastor had taken a personal interest in the motherless boys. But would he understand the opposition of a father to such a marriage for his son? Papa thought it was at least worth a try, a better alternative than calling on William's fractured knowledge of the law, which he would turn to only as a last resort.

He went inside and flopped into a large chair. At the end of a tiring day, he often thought of death. Today, at the eleventh hour, when all seemed so neatly arranged, he felt he had been handed an unfair burden. Death could have spared a tired old man. The thought startled him. Was it a near wish that the Registrar had delayed her visit? She need not have waited long. A month, perhaps less. An old man could have passed from the world in ignorance. A young girl would not have to hate him for his last days on earth.

Papa remembered meeting her. He had thought her beautiful, fair-skinned with deep, intelligent eyes. She held her chin high and kept herself close to Mark.

Mark had corrected his father on her name. "Papa, it's pronounced *Deshwah*."

Michelle had covered a smile with her fingers, a proper young lady.

Papa had invited her for a Sunday afternoon. She came and sat in the shade with Marylene to exchange secret smiles and chatter. He thought them two fine girls, and he was pleased that his boys could do this well with their lives. That afternoon he

72

watched Mark. Beside Michelle, he seemed so different, confident, happy. He seemed more nearly a man. They walked in the garden, laughed, held hands. Emma and Delia smiled their approval. . . .

And then LaCroix. The unpleasant memory of the woman invaded the silence of his mind. She made him want to fight, to lash out. Could he make a pact with Mark? They would keep the secret. Papa would help them escape. They could be gone in an hour, be married in a distant place, begin a new life . . . of what? He was annoyed with the whim, with his storybook ending. Facts had to be faced. They were in the Registrar's file folder. No fantasy of compassion could ignore them. Papa had to give his sons the best world that he could manage. He could not permit a miscegenous marriage to mar that commitment to the future. Death had not spared a tired old man.

It was after dark when Mark returned from Matt's house. He was tired and wished he could beg off when Papa offered a chair next to him in the darkened living room. Earlier in the day he had decided to prepare Papa for the inevitable, but only to tell him as much as he needed to, to try to spare him the complete truth. "Papa, I'm going to have to go away again."

The old man did not look at his son.

"Papa, I really want to stay. I want to take the job. You've got to believe that. Only now I don't think it's possible. Something's come up. I can't tell you about it."

"There isn't anything you can't tell me, son."

"It's a very personal problem."

"Will you take the girl . . . Michelle?"

There was a kink in the way he gave it to the floor, a tossed away thought rather than a question. Michelle had never entered their conversation or his travels before. "Why do you ask that?"

Papa remembered his resolution to move cautiously. "Sometimes a boy is in love and it seems the most important thing in the world to him. Most times it isn't." The father checked his son for a response but saw none. "What I mean is you can expect a lot of loves in your lifetime. Sometimes it's just a desire for a woman. Once or twice it might be the real thing."

A curious line of conversation, Mark thought, of loves and lifetimes, all in a prosaic breath that seemed to preempt the job on the railroad. Had Papa sensed something of the truth in Mark's troubled manner? He had to find out. "Papa, what are you getting at?"

"I think I know why you want to leave. I know you applied for a marriage license yesterday."

Mark was startled. He sensed at once that his father knew much more than that, but he could not figure how. "How do you know that?"

"A woman from the city came to see me today."

Damn—the Registrar, the meddling bitch! It had not occurred to Mark that she might drag her ledgers and folios to his father's house, a reprisal for his threat to take Michelle away. It was the personal administering of her policy, deliberately sneaky, damned dishonest, and very effective. But it would not change his plan a bit. "All right, you know. But that goddamned woman had no right to come here."

"That's a matter for her conscience."

"I doubt that she has one. I doubt that she has any room in her head for anything but the official record and her own petty rules."

"She didn't make up the rules."

"She came here didn't she? Is that in the rules? It's proof she'd do anything to protect her system. Well, it won't work. I'm taking Michelle away from here."

"Where would you go?"

"I don't know. Another state. Any place the law doesn't exist. Just to get her out of this town."

Papa momentarily wished he commanded William's legal knowledge and the ability to argue it, but he remembered his intention. William would offer his services on request. "A mixed marriage. Could you run from that? Could your children?"

"Papa, Michelle is an octoroon. My children aren't going to be black, not even half black. An eighth of Caucasian blood in your veins doesn't make you white."

"But don't you see? The reverse is never a danger. Would you look for such a mate? The law is made to protect those who

74

would be so easily deceived. Yes, think of yourself. You didn't know the truth until yesterday."

"No one knew, not even Michelle. No one except Miss La-Croix."

"And by law she can't issue a license."

Mark slumped in his chair. Why did the law seem so impossible to argue against? He tried to number the places where parochial thought would give birth to such legislation. He could only think of South Africa and the antebellum South. "Papa, you're thinking like men did a hundred years ago."

"Perhaps you're right. I don't deny it. But I can't help thinking I'm grateful to those men of a hundred years ago who made laws to preserve the pride in what you are. I don't know why it's so difficult for you to grasp, but I believe a man has a right to see his children live on in his image. He has to give a part of himself to the future."

Mark said severely, "You won't stop me, Papa. I swear it. I'm going to find a place where that law doesn't exist."

"You simply won't try to understand. I devoted my life to my sons. I wanted to see that they were set when I died. That way I could feel like I was living on. That's why I extorted a railroad job for you. It's why I sold the property. The money will be yours and Matt's. It will belong to your children. I ask you once more to think of them. Would you have them pitied, laughed at behind their backs?"

LaCroix had asked the identical question. He had not been prepared for it then. He would have to learn to be ready for the smiles, the taunting of all those pure young men with pride. A hundred years ago the young Creole winked and tapped his cane on the banquettes of Storyville. He kept his dark girl in a room at the swampy edge of the plantation, while his dainty wife picked magnolia blossoms and drank minty beverages under the great columns of her gallery. In the modern parlance, the color "couldn't rub off." Such a tryst today was good for a knowing smile. It could be sloughed off because it could never approach love. Mark felt drained of further will to argue. "I'm going to bed."

"Son, will you talk to Father Hurley?"

Would Papa somehow manage to use God as his last resort? The Church had great power in his eyes. It could reduce a sentence of murder to a whisper in a confessional. Mark did not fear the priest. "Have you asked him to instruct me on the law, on pride in what you are?"

"I haven't spoken to him yet."

"I'll talk to anyone, Papa. Nobody can change my mind."

Papa listened as his son climbed the stairs and closed and bolted his door. In the drum of silence that followed, he considered Mark's stubbornness. There was a real possibility that the boy might go through with the intolerable marriage. Reason, Papa's first tactic, had failed. The mental sparring had only deepened the gulf between them. Mark had to be made to see the truth. Otherwise the carefully planned life would be thrown away. Papa could not permit that. He was committed to the future of his son as if it were his own.

He drew William Janin's number from his mind and discarded it. There was still time to follow his original plan. He had no idea whether it would work, but it was worth a try. Father Hurley had always been a fair-minded man. He dialed the rectory of Saint Mary's Catholic Church and asked for the Pastor.

Father James Hurley took the call from Stephen Dennick personally. He tried to avoid adding another house call to his itinerary, but acquiesced when the old man said, "Yes, for confession, but something more important has come up."

The Pastor had discussed the elder Dennick's sickness with Matt weeks before and promised to be available at any time. He did not know what could be more important to a dying man than confession, but he knew the old man well enough not to underrate his demand. Stephen Dennick was not a man to exaggerate the seriousness of a matter.

As Father neared the house on Esplanade, he thought of the aged Mrs. Dubuc, his next and final call for the evening. She would agonize but stay awake past her bedtime. To speed his visit with Stephen Dennick, he would try a businesslike approach. It was a large parish; its parishioners were all expert at small talk. Hurley came straight to the point. "Shall I hear your confession?"

Papa matched the priest's directness. "I told you there was something else, Father Jim. You were born in the North, weren't you?"

The use of his given name forewarned of a personal chat, the mention of his birthplace, a provincial one. "Chisholm, Minnesota. An odd place for an Irishman. You're supposed to be Serbian or Croatian or something. Anyway, I don't remember it at all. My parents moved to Ohio. That's the dullest biography I ever heard."

"Something I've always wondered about you. You seemed to fit in well down here. You understand our folkways, traditions. It's why I brought my boys to you. No one could have taught them any better."

"What is it, Stephen? What do you want me to understand? Are the boys in trouble?"

Papa calculated the proper amount of anxiety to add to his words. "Mark applied for a marriage license yesterday. The girl turned out to be part Negro." He paused for an emotional reaction, saw none, and decided to test his own on the priest. "I have to tell you I'm opposed to such a marriage."

The circumstances, the sudden discovery, shock and outrage, were as familiar to the priest as the faces of his congregation. The situation conjured the name of the Registrar, Pearl Marie LaCroix. She had made another of her odious discoveries. Father's response might put him in over his head, but he had no choice. "How does Mark feel about it?"

"He feels guilt. I think the girl is pregnant. He wants to take her away."

"Miss LaCroix offers little choice."

"You know her?"

"She's well known in the parish. More powerful than anyone would care to admit. She's no more than a clerk, yet the Mayor himself is unable to fire her."

"Why should she be fired? For telling the truth?"

"Stephen, the truth to the Registrar has become an unbelievable series of heartless indiscretions. She uses the truth to extort.

Yes, purely legal blackmail. She knows everything about everyone and uses the bureau as a weapon to insure her position. People live in fear that she might point the finger at them. The truth? She's been known to shout it across her office. It's been her crusade to dig up forgotten information. I suspect that some of it is improvised, or incorrect, or fraudulent."

"Isn't it her job to keep track of people with mixed blood?"

"Yes, a tenth of this or that. And illegitimacy, and family insanity, and I don't know what else. Keeping track of things is her power."

"She has to obey the law. The law prohibits mixed marriages."

The priest sighed deeply. "Yes, it's the law."

Papa sensed the danger of a moral discussion that might question the validity of the law. To make his approach more personal, he said, "Father Jim, I need your help."

The given name again, twice in the span of a few minutes, reminded the priest of his long friendship with Stephen Dennick. The old man was about to ask him to intercede in behalf of a law and a woman who were both personally repulsive to him. He thought of Mark and wished he knew the boy better. The older brother had grown up quiet and reserved, but he was responsive. He could be reached and understood. Mark was the distant one, seemingly distrustful of the people around him. "I don't know what I can do," he said.

"You can reason with him. Explain the impossibility of it."

"The impossibility of a sacred vow?"

"Father, we all try to do what is right. The Church tells us when we sin. I respect that and I always believed in it. I know that God will judge me for what I am and I'm not a bit afraid. You tell me, is it sinful not to want that kind of blood in my family?"

"It is a sin to hate, Stephen."

"I never hated a man in my life."

Yes, Father knew the old man was good. He was God-fearing, simple, bound to the earth and to his Church. In his mind and heart he was truly free of sin. He kept the Commandments. Father knew it was a fault of the Church, that list of laws the children are made to memorize. They were too literal; they

78

allowed a moral void. "And the girl?" Father said. "How will I deal with her?"

"The parents are guilty of that sin. For not telling her the truth. I don't know what can be done about it now."

Indeed, no one would allow the record to be forgotten, and as in the past, no one would dare to challenge it publicly. With each struggle, the Registrar grew stronger. "Stephen, I am not capable of asking Mark to forsake this girl."

"And his father? Would you have him forsake him?" The old man's face, desperate, drained of color, puffed and cracked as he spoke. "Father, I'm tired. I'm going to die. I've got a little time left. When I look back on my life, I see I've done some good things. I've made mistakes, too. At times I've been a violent man. But I always tried my best. The only meaning that life has now is in my boys. Nothing counts but them. Without them even my death has no meaning. That's about as close as I can get to defining the soul. I don't know about heaven or hell. In death I will go on with my boys. . . ."

The voice trailed weakly and stopped, as if it had ended a prayer. It was a prayer, Father knew, and a dedication of a past life to one of the future. It was all the old man had to offer. The priest was saddened that it had to end in bitterness. He resolved to speak to Mark, but he would do it in his own way. Many months ago he had devised a plan to deal with the Registrar. "Very well, Stephen. I will speak to the boy."

Papa closed his eyes and murmured a prayer of thanks. The meeting had not gone as well as he hoped. That woman, La-Croix, had spoiled it. He could not have anticipated the priest's case of personal bias against her. At least Father had agreed to speak to Mark. If all else failed, William would not. The thought was not a comforting one. "Will you hear my confession?"

"Kneel here at my side."

Wearily Papa knelt and crossed himself. He cleared his throat and began in a voice leveled in sorrow, "Bless me Father, for I have sinned. . . ."

Mark spent the night locked in his room. He watched Father Hurley come and go and listened to the muted pleas of his father's voice. Why had he promised to speak to the priest? To hear a moral judgment or further postpone his action? Perhaps it was because there were so many questions to be answered. Exactly what were the Louisiana laws on miscegenation? If he were to protect Michelle, he thought he should know them. If he were to take her away, then where? Where was the nearest place the law did not exist? Mark felt he needed, of all things, legal advice. William would melt in laughter. Mark had guarded the secret even from his brother, but La Croix, the meddling bitch, had spilled it in Papa's lap. Soon the whole family would know. He could imagine the plot that would kindle in William's head and boggle Emma's. They would stop at nothing to keep him from taking Michelle away.

After Papa climbed to his room, Mark went down and sat at the kitchen table to watch the beginning of a hot red day. He thought of an old schoolmate, Emile Prudhomme, who was now a lawyer. Emile was the bright son of a judge, the master of an old Creole family that still owned a big house in the French Quarter. In Loyola law school, Emile had looked down his nose at "Americans" like Mark. In jest he called them "Kaintucks" as in the days a hundred years ago when Canal Street was the "neutral ground" between the French Quarter Creoles and the uptown Americans. He and Mark had never become close friends. He would probably think like Papa and side with him against Michelle, but he would have the answers Mark needed. He would be in his office by ten.

Mark put in a call to Michelle. He was told by her mother, Corinne, that she had already left for the library. He decided to try to reach her there later, to reassure her that all would be well.

When he reached the business district, the bright morning was filled with billowing thunderheads speared by the building tops. A two-minute rainstorm bisected Carondelet Street as if a curtain had been drawn down its center, leaving one side dry, the other lost in a torrent. Emile was not in. Mark was given a chair. The office seemed familiar, *déjà vu*, or the lawyer's conformity to his prototype. There were shelves of leather-bound volumes, a picture of Abe Lincoln and his admonition, "A lawyer's time and advice are his stock in trade," and the usual secretary with an unhinged eyelash. Emile walked in and she said, "Mr. Osborn called several times—he's on the line now—you'd better take it—he's mad."

Emile hugged Mark into his private office, hugged him into a chair, and poked a button on a box that had Mr. Osborn's voice inside. He spoke quickly, quoting precedents, referring to correspondence, and ending with a speech, "May I remind you, Mr. Osborn, that all court decisions are open to change. The Warren Court is having its day. Someday we'll have ours. Ride with the tide. Let me do the worrying." He then disengaged Mr. Osborn and his secretary came on. "Elaine, hold my calls for now, okay? Important stuff in here." He cut her reply in half and said to Mark, "Where you been? What's been happening?"

"I've been doing some traveling."

Emile thumped his desk. "That's the trouble with being chained to a desk. Your buddies do your traveling. What can I do for you?"

"Do you remember Michelle DeJoie? She was an undergraduate at Loyola when you were in law school."

"Michelle. Yes, a little dark-haired girl. I remember. She said her father was a Creole. I even remember his name. Alfonso DeJoie. But the line ended with him. The mother is something else. North European, I think." He drew a cordless electric razor from his desk and began shaving. "Excuse me, I never have time to do this at home. Crap, we're friends. The truth is I didn't make it home last night. Elaine let me have her sofa." He clucked his tongue to let Mark know he had slept with her. "Michelle DeJoie, huh? Beautiful girl. Aloof as I remember. I never had a chance." He laughed and shaved some hairs in his nose, curious of the legal context in which Michelle might arise.

Mark had decided to tell him everything. "She's pregnant."

Not yet the master of professional disinterest, Emile grew taller in his seat. "Paternity suit?"

"Nothing like that. We applied for a marriage license. A woman at the Bureau of Vital Statistics says she's part Negro."

Emile whistled. "Sounds like Madame LaCroix's handiwork."

"You've heard of her?"

"Heard of her? She's the most famous bureaucrat since J. Edgar Hoover. And just as tough. I can tell you some very influential people are out for her scalp, and that includes the Mayor. But their hands are tied. They can't fire her without cause. Civil service and all that crap. She's got twenty-five years with the bureau."

"Never mind her. I want to know about the law, the nearest place it doesn't exist. I'll take Michelle out of here."

The razor was drilling into the desk top. Emile turned it off and blew a dust of whiskers from its insides. He put it away with care, using the time to structure his thoughts with precision. "So Michelle's got the taint. That hits pretty close to home. A half-Creole girl. It's a goddamned shame." He circled his desk, stopped to taste his lips, the unpleasant thought translating to his tongue. "Buddy, no one on earth would criticize you . . . I mean, you have to think about yourself in things like this. Your family. Imagine the shock."

"Emile, I am thinking about myself, and I'm not in the least moved by criticism."

"And the family?"

Mark did not think it necessary to lie to Emile. There was an ethic called professional discretion. But it was a mistake to assume that a one-time friend was also an ally. "Papa's having fits. La-Croix went straight to him with it."

Emile was startled. "She actually went to him personally? I didn't think she was that stupid. I bet I know a dozen people who would like to hear about a dumb move like that. What the hell does that woman think she is?"

"I don't give a damn about her. Just tell me where to take Michelle."

Emile took a long moment to estimate the situation. Mark was not the first who actually wanted to go through with it. Most of them backed out in time when they saw the opposition stacked against them. "Washington, D. C.," he said. "The Federal Government has no miscegenation laws. You could not come back here. At least not until we have a test case. That's not likely soon."

"I don't think I'd ever want to come back here."

"No, I guess not." Emile got up and searched the shelves for a book. "Criminal code," he said when he had found the one he wanted. "Louisiana revised statute, 1950, Title 14. Miscegenation. Miscegenation is the marriage or habitual cohabitation with knowledge of their difference in race, between a person of the Caucasian or white race and a person of the colored or Negro race. Whoever commits the crime of miscegenation shall be imprisoned, with or without hard labor, for not more than five years. Acts 1942, No. 43, Article 79." The reading was emotionless, almost mechanical.

Mark leaned forward in his chair. "Emile, you've seen Michelle. Is she what they're talking about in that law?"

"The law says any *traceable* amount of Negro blood."

"That's where Miss LaCroix comes in."

"That's her job unfortunately. But not for long I don't think. I told you some people are gunning for her. I think they'll get her. But that's no consolation to you." He reached for another book. "I might as well give you the whole of it. There's a civil code. Here it is. Page 33. Article 94. Marriage between persons related to each other in the direct ascending or descending line is prohibited. This prohibition is not confined to legitimate children, it extends also to children born out of marriage. Marriage between white persons and persons of color is prohibited, and the celebration of all such marriages is forbidden and such celebration carries with it no effect and is null and void. As amended, etc."

Mark let it sink in. The style was like the men who wrote it, pretentious and arrogant, long-whiskered and righteous. Had they the faintest idea what they were leaving to their progeny? Their character was null and void, their ascending and descending lines without feeling. He stood to leave. "I'll take her to Washington right away."

Emile rounded his desk and leaned very close to Mark. "You know me a long time, long enough to know I am not a prejudiced man. But as your attorney, your friend, I feel it my duty to tell you. You are not obliged to this girl in any way. There's your position to consider. The law. You could be prosecuted."

"Emile—don't you give a damn about Michelle?"

The outburst sat him down on his desk. "Yes . . . I care."

"Then you can see what I have to do."

"Won't you take a few days to think about it?"

"I don't have a few days. Papa will try to stop me."

"All right. If you've made up your mind, you'd better move fast."

Mark thought of Michelle. By late morning she would be at the library, waiting to hear from him about a technical delay on the license. After what seemed an eternity of haggling, he was right where he started—in the office of the Registrar!

After Mark had left, Emile reflected on the surprise visit. As if a third party had been witness to the scene, he said aloud, "He's quite a guy. But I really think he's out of his mind." He thought of the Registrar's personal visit to Papa Dennick. A meddling indiscretion of that sort could be just the weapon her enemies needed. The Bureau of Vital Statistics came under the authority of the Board of Health. He punched the button on the intercom. "Elaine, put in a call to the director of the Board of Health. His name is Krasner. Dr. Morton Krasner."

Michelle went to her job at the library against her mother's wishes. But when she got there, she told Donny she was not feeling well. "I'm going to sit by the lake," she said. "To breathe some fresh air. If Mark calls please tell him I'll be near the lighthouse. I can't look at books today." Donny frowned because he would have to handle the check-out counter alone.

The long bus ride out Canal Boulevard killed most of the morning. The seawall was quiet. She stopped at a place where Mark would find her, near a deserted shelter that housed dressing rooms and public lavatories. During their autumn weeks together they had often met on the lakefront to be alone, to escape the oppressive pall of the city. She sat on the grass near the water. It was a place to think, to pull her thoughts together.

Bundled against a sea breeze, she felt refreshed, a turn up from the emotional doldrums of yesterday. It seemed that she could now step beside herself and see the truth objectively as the essential piece of a long unsolved puzzle. The new insight told her a lot about the past. The cryptic years of her childhood came clear. She now understood her mother's jitters, her tracking around the issue of race in the house. "I leave those worries to the politicians, the courts." To speak out would have been to question the system, a possible self-incrimination. It was much simpler to live the lie. She remembered the apprehension that came over her parents when it came time for her to change schools. It was because she would have to show her birth certificate. She had thought it the normal anxiety of a parent for a child when an adjustment had to be made. It was fear that they would be found out!

For the same reason, grandparents were never talked about except in generalities—"Your grandmother was a wonderful woman. She worked hard all her life. She died young. Grandfather, too. He was a fine man." If her grandparents still existed,

Michelle thought they must be hidden away in Treme, where her parents lived when she was a little girl.

She clearly remembered the housing project below Basin Street, the original location of famous Storyville. She had heard people call it a *mélange*. She had laughed at their wink, the insinuation. It was a place where people seemed to be hiding from a hostile world, families in transit without ethnic origin. Corrine came to call it their "hard times." It was not the Great Depression but a long time afterward, their personal one. Michelle never understood why they had to live there. She only knew that they were poor. They lived with a threadbare sofa and ragged curtains. She remembered spare dinners of crackers and milk, *sometimes* milk, and an occasional meal of meat. They ate a lot of red beans and rice. Red beans were the roof over their heads. Michelle recalled a dress with crumbling lace worn out by repeated washings. Corrine could be clean because it cost so little. Michelle would never forget the dead-tired Alfonso when he came home from work, ashamed when he had to refuse her a dime for the movies. Nor would she forget her mother's bitterness toward the grocer who "marked with a fork." Corrine had to pay four cents when spending one because it was the only way she could get credit. But she never failed to accept those groceries. Dignity never filled an empty stomach.

Treme was a time of their lives Michelle came to look upon with pride. It was a time of building character, of acquiring social conscience. The American Dream works for some, fails for others. They had come out of it better persons, sympathetic to the impoverished ones they left behind. They were in their Garden District nest, *nouveau* middle-class escapees from a slum. They had fought their way out. The little girl had been proud of her successful father and her correct and mannered mother. A long penance had given them a proud posture. Michelle knew it had taken more than hard work to escape. To get out and stay out of Treme, Alfonso and Corrine had to *pass*. How careless of them to think she would never find out; how vulgar to allow her to hear it from the Registrar. She thought of Mark. How unfair for him to be thrown into the center of it.

It was late afternoon before Mark found her on the seawall.

Debacles had stacked up on him. From Emile's office he had gone straight to the library. He had missed Michelle only by minutes. Then he had boarded a bus with no money. The long walk to the lake had consumed most of the afternoon. He sat beside her on the grass. The wind had died and left wedges of sail becalmed on the water. "It took me most of the day to catch up with you," he said. "I wanted to tell you everything is going to be all right."

She pulled off her shoes, climbed down the stairs, and stood on a step covered with algae below the water line. Biting cold waves covered her ankles. "You don't have to lie to me."

Even in sincerity he lacked the power to convince. He must not avoid the truth another second. "Michelle, what I said the other day at the Registrar's office . . . about the delay. That was a lie."

The lie had been to spare her. There could be no more lies. "Mark, Saturday I tried to kill myself."

He took her arms and pulled her up the stairs to the grass. "Michelle, you know?"

"Oh, don't worry. I did a sloppy job of it. I had to pretend I wanted to die to get even with the Registrar. I knew my mother would smell the gas in time."

Mark felt a surge of adrenal hatred for the woman, for her diabolical cunning and her merciless arrogance. She had gone straight to Papa. Had he expected her to spare Michelle? "Damned rotten crap—to be told by her! I should have told you myself. I lacked the spine."

"I would have demanded proof just the same."

"Michelle, you've got to believe me. It makes no difference."

Of course he had to say that. She had expected it. But she knew what a difference it did make. She had struggled with that thought more than any other. "And your family? Will it matter to them?"

Mark decided not to tell her of Papa's horror and of the argument he was yet to hear, the gentle urging of a priest. He groped for a way to skirt the subject of family. "Papa is very sick. To make him worse, that woman, LaCroix, came to him. Goddamn her!"

Michelle knew that his curses for the woman were also for the condition he was caught in. She sensed it in his hedging confusion. She was the curious tragedy, not LaCroix. He would go through with such a marriage to spite the Registrar, but did he really want it? She remembered her decision to let him out. "Mark . . . I'm not going to hold you to anything."

"What are you talking about?"

"I mean I'm going to have the baby alone."

"What the hell kind of talk is that?"

"Sensible talk for a change. The end of your problem. I forget you and everybody's happy, the Registrar, your Papa, me."

"That's nonsense. I don't give a damn about LaCroix. I'm sorry I have to hurt Papa, but I care most about you and it makes no difference what they think."

Yes, he would settle for the bad bargain. Could she? A life among whispers that she had trapped him? If only there was a way to do it gently so as not to hurt him. "Mark, I've done a lot of growing up since Saturday. It makes a great deal of difference what they think and you know it."

"Michelle, I talked to a lawyer this morning. The Federal Government has no miscegenation laws. We could go to Washington tonight."

"Please stop being so damned noble. What will you do in Washington? Where will you run to next?"

"I told you I don't care!"

"I care. Saturday I wanted to die! Do you think I can just run away and have this baby and keep it a clever secret the rest of my life? Maybe in another world in another time, but we live here and I'm ashamed and I don't want it!"

She rushed down the stairs and wept in her lap, the tips of her hair curling in the foam of the water. She cried in fear of what she had said, that she did not want the child. She had the strength to give it birth, to love and nurture it, but she could not bear to watch it grow and wait for its date with the Registrar. As she shook with despair, Mark could only stand aside as the night answered with a quiet lap of the water on the steps. The grief was hers alone.

They sat in the shadows of the seawall until the lamp lights came on along the shore. The night was so quiet they could hear scratchy rock music carried on the wind from a lakefront restaurant more than a hundred yards away.

Mark saw that her tears had dried and said, "I'll take you home."

"I don't want to go home yet."

"Your mother will be worried."

She stood and stripped off her sweater. "I want to think about me for a minute. I'm going for a swim."

"Michelle—the water is freezing. Your cold. . . ."

But she had stripped to her bra and pants, plunged in, and swam straight out.

Mark rushed to the top of the stairs to watch her. She swam with a strong and steady stroke. About fifty yards out she reached a piling that marked a depth of nine feet. She clung to the shaft and waved to Mark while shaking the water from her hair. Then she started back, clearly in a path of light spilling from a yacht moored to a distant breakwater. Mark was relieved. Her return stroke was slower but steady, gracefully confident. But then she hesitated, went under, came up choking.

He had his shoes and trousers off the moment she went under the second time. He plunged in with a running dive, the shock of the icy water taking his breath away. He reached the spot where she had gone under, stopped, treaded water. All was quiet. He could see nothing on the surface in the lights from the yacht. He submerged and groped madly, digging his hands and feet in the sandy bottom. When he thought his lungs would burst, he shot to the surface, gulped air, went down again. This time he found a handful of hair and pulled with all his strength. She came up coughing and choking. He dragged her to the seawall and helped her up to the dry grass. She shivered, terrified. "I didn't mean it! I didn't mean it this time! Mark—believe me!"

"I know, I know. It's all right. It's over now. You're safe."

"Mark . . . am I crazy? I felt strong coming back. My arms turned to lead. I couldn't go another inch. I . . . was so frightened!" She finished in a choking spasm that brought up dark water. Mark held her close and allowed her to cry until she stopped.

They sat looking at the yacht. To Michelle it seemed warm

and untouchable. There were people inside who would sail it to a far-away ocean. She wished her life could be as simple, as anonymous as that. Twice in a few days she had come close to death. Death was stalking her as a solution. "God . . . I think I am crazy, the suicidal girl who can't succeed."

"It was an accident. You've been upset. You lost your wind."

"Accident or not, I came close to settling all our problems."

When she had stopped trembling, Mark said, "Michelle, more than anything in the world, I want to marry you and take care of you."

She said, "Yes, Mark," and surprised him by asking him to make love to her there in the dark shadow of the seawall. She came to him with a craving that was like a last moment taken greedily. In the quiet slap and seep of the waves, her eagerness frightened him. Although wet and cold, she did not shiver. In the darkness she turned her face away. She clung to him as if she feared he might drift away into the depths as she almost had, forever away from her. Mark felt she meant it to be their last time together.

They sat on the steps until their clothes dried and Michelle had combed the tangles from her hair. They walked to Canal Boulevard. The bus was long in coming and ahead of schedule. It crept back to the city, practically empty except for some black housemaids in stocking caps. They were a bus of strangers, swaying in their seats with the bumps and stops, unaware of their own tiredness. Michelle sat close to Mark, looking at him in a new way, as if she had settled something in her mind.

As they neared the business district, Mark thought of Union Station, only a few blocks from Canal Street. He would pull her off the bus and get her aboard the next train for Washington! "The railroad station. . . ," he said and stopped, remembering he had borrowed bus fare from her. She let the fragment pass.

In his confusion, Mark had not given a thought to the simple necessity of money. Money had not been important to his earlier travels. When he was alone it had been a matter of putting one foot after the other. A trip with a girl was much more complex. Arrangements had to be made. Normal ones on trains or buses. A girl does not live out of a canvas bag or eat sardines from a can in the cold sun of a strange town. That girl he now had to consider a part of him, and inside her was the beginning of the family he would have to care for. He thought of his brother. Mark would admit to an elopment and nothing more. Matt would lend him the money to take Michelle away.

They missed the Saint Charles streetcar in a crush of late riders returning from the theaters on Canal Street. They decided to walk. The rain began as they neared her house, but lightly and for only a moment, and with just enough wind to smear the street with sodden oak leaves. He spoke when they reached her door. "You didn't mean it. About not wanting the baby."

"I can't help wondering if it wouldn't be best."

"Michelle, all this talk about letting me out. I don't want out. Our baby is a fact. You couldn't change that no matter what Papa and the others thought. I'm going to take us away from here as soon as I can."

Michelle wanted to tell him why she could not go away with him, but she lacked the strength for the renewed argument. She watched as he climbed abroad the return streetcar and caught herself wishing she did not love him so very much.

Corrine DeJoie had been sitting alone in the darkness when she saw Mark and Michelle approach the house. The sight of them together relieved her anxiety, the panic she had felt when Michelle did not come home as scheduled from the library. She had paced and cried and wrung her hands to complete the cliché of worried mother and then slumped in the living room to re-live the horror of Saturday night.

It was her punishment to reenact it all, the spicy putrid smell of the gas, the blurry faces of the neighbors, the rush to the hospital, Alfonso's anguish. Most vividly she remembered her husband. Sick with grief and worry, he had wept in her lap, and blamed himself, themselves, for allowing the possibility that Michelle would someday blunder into the Registrar's office. For the past two days the fact had possessed Corrine like the murmur of a repeated prayer: *Michelle had almost taken her life!* The years of guarded secrecy seemed a pale emotion next to those two days of torture.

Through those years, Corrine's paramount fear had been the prospect of losing her daughter for a day, an hour, and to anything, an idea, a place, a man. Perhaps it was because she knew she would lose her someday that the thought was ever in the secrets of her mind. Yet it was something Corrine could not permit, and she had the strength to fight it. Michelle was so frail, small, helpless. She needed protection, to be shielded from the world. In Corrine's way of reasoning, the truth was the world. The truth was hard and cold and ugly. She swore Michelle would never know it. Carefully, they had provided authentic-looking birth and health records. They avoided the past with swift generalities, but they had not been so clever as to anticipate a face to face meeting with Pearl LaCroix. Corrine chastised herself for her own stupidity. She was familiar with the woman's reputation. The brutality of it had more than once made her shiver.

92

In two days Corrine had come to face some grim realities. Michelle was not a little girl. She was no longer frail or helpless. She had grown into a woman about to become a mother. She had confessed to the child proudly, almost gratefully. That she was not married to Mark moved her little. His absence disturbed her more. She worried about his happiness because he was somewhere alone in the world. As usual she was thinking more of him than of herself. But the reality of Miss LaCroix wrecked all that, Michelle's joy of pregnancy, the carefully kept secret, and struck Corrine with real terror. The truth had left Michelle abject, confused, willing to take her own life. Because the suicide attempt had failed, Corrine felt a temporary reprieve, but the next logical prospect, that Michelle might disappear from her life, terrified her. She could think of no loss that would make her life seem so completely wasted.

Corrine spoke as Michelle let herself in the house. "Your hair. Did you get caught in the rain?"

Michelle regretted her mother was up. She was in no mood for further rumination. "We swam at the lake. I think I am suicidal. Skinnydipping with a cold in freezing water. Girls are permitted most things these days. Most girls. I enjoyed being indecent for once. . . ." She stopped to protect the secret of her near drowning. "There was a yacht with honey curtains. It made me think of faraway places." The rain began very hard, and the trees shook more leaves into the current of the street. Corrine left the room and returned with teacups steaming ringlets of mist. "Mother, he wants me to go away with him. What will I do?"

"I haven't had a thought but that since Saturday."

"His father is outraged, naturally. We're a special kind of people in this town. So much to pay for such a tiny mistake."

Corrine regretted the price Michelle must pay and wondered if her daughter sensed the full impact of what was to come. In a stroke, Miss LaCroix had precluded their further existence in this town. They now had to run. "Michelle, your father and I have worked out a plan to get us away from here forever."

A simplistic answer to being found out, Michelle thought, was not being found at all. Exile was better than disgrace. "I don't know if I can just up and run away."

"You will when you see the alternatives. Miss LaCroix won't let us stay here. My father knew that a long time ago. I hated him for years for running away, but I came to know he was right."

"Mother, why is it we never talked of him? Why couldn't we ever face the truth?"

Why indeed? Why not permit a little girl to feel the disillusionment of a man whose dream it was to dig his hands in the great free American earth? Perhaps Corrine should have told of a young man with courage and determination who left a village very far away only to watch his dream crumble as he sought a pathetic living in a hostile country he could not understand. She should tell of that man's humiliation, what he believed was his sin to father a child outside the teachings of his Church, the threat of reprisal when he did, his predictable defeat. Corrine decided that until now she could have told none of it to her daughter. From a desk drawer, the only secret place in her life, she took a tattered portfolio and searched for a photograph of her father. He had forced an impish smile for the camera. His copper beard and hair were like the worn-out bristles of a brush. "This was taken when we lived in Treme," she said. "But long before the housing project was built."

"I remember the project. The buildings were so close together."

"The project. It was crowded, but we were excited to live in brick houses. Like rats in a nest, it's enough that the nest be dry. It was hateful. Even those who were alike hated one another. They took the hatred of the enemy out on one another. Yet it was better than anything we'd known before and we felt we were lucky to be alive."

"Why, mother? Who were the enemies? Miss LaCroix?"

"Who? Something much worse than her. It was the world outside and the fear within. My father was a farmer. What would a farmer do in the city? He was permitted to work in a car wash. He was humiliated to have to wash another man's dirty car, but he did it for us. I remember the coins jingling in his pockets when he came home. As poor as we were, he never failed to give me one. Michelle, he never married my mother. They wouldn't let him. Yet I know he loved her. One day he went away and never came back."

94

"You don't run out on someone you love."

Corrine wished she had not gone so far. She had lost control over the impulse to be honest, to get it all out at last. She had sworn that her own illegitimacy was a secret she would share with no one. Alfonso himself did not know. It had been her father's nightmare and hers after he had gone. She remembered the Sundays at Our Lady of Guadalupe Church praying he would return and the miserable struggle as her mother scrubbed floors and took in washing to keep her in school. The old woman, a shade browner than a suntanned WASP, never stopped believing he would come back. It was the illusion that kept her alive. He was out looking for work, she always said. It was Treme he deserted, the frustrations of it, because it was the best he could give her. He wanted to dig his hands in American earth. I remember a pathetic patch of vegetables out behind the clothes lines, his joy in growing a simple thing like a radish."

"It's all still there, those people, just as it was."

"Much worse. The clothes lines fell down and nobody cared to put them up again. Nobody plants vegetables. My mother lived and died there because of what she was. Most of them never get out. It's why I owe so much to your father. Alfonso was like me and he was brave. He swore he would get us out of Treme and he did, the same way he's going to get us out of this town now."

Yes, Alfonso would do that, Michelle thought. He would take the keel-hauling, fight a dragon or die on the rack, but first, for Corrine, he would try to run. She felt very sorry for them. "Where is Daddy? Will he come home soon?"

Corrine felt her frankness had been worthwhile. It revived a bit of her confidence, the sense of nearness to her daughter she feared had been slipping away. Michelle might as well know all there was to know. "As soon as he leaves his lady friend," she said as if to divulge a curious illness she had learned to accept. She watched Michelle for a response, and added, "I'm sorry. Up to now I didn't want you to know. Now I think it's important that you do."

Michelle knew she was expected to show surprise but could not manage it. "I know about her. I saw him wtih her a long time ago. I never understood it. I was too ashamed to tell you."

Corrine surreptitiously parted the curtains to be sure her husband would not suddenly appear from the driveway. She could not add a new problem to his burden. "I'm sorry you had to find out on your own. Now that you know, I beg you to understand. Why does a colored man, yes, if only a part-colored man, need a lily-white woman buried in the secrets of his life? Is it to prove he's good, as good as any man? Oh, I could have stopped it, but all these years I was too much in love with my home. The reason for the secret. I was afraid I'd have to give it all back. Maybe I'm wishing I had. None of it is worth what almost happened to you the other night."

Michelle had a talent for finding out things on her own, even how difficult it is to kill one's normal healthy sane self. She thought of the poor try, a child holding its breath until it turns blue. Had it been only a sham? Tonight at the lake a repeat performance? Still, it could have worked quite well. It might have been easier than taking one step into the future. Surely it occurs in the mind more often that a person will admit. Condemned by the Church, a blessed stone-cold mortal end. A coward's way to wrap up a story. She died and went to . . . heaven? Michelle did not want to be alone to be trapped with her thoughts. She was grateful that her mother had at last been honest with her. "I did want to die for only a moment," she said. "I couldn't look at the sky anymore."

"Please let's not talk about that anymore. We're going to be with you through this. We can't expect Mark to take the responsibility"—she stopped to avoid the word *alone*, for her intention was that he would not share in it. It was never more clear than now that Corrine could share her daughter with no one. "Your father's going to see about a job in Cleveland. A new start in a new place for us."

The rain had stopped. Michelle went to the door, breathed the heavy air, bundled her arms about her. She decided she would not tell her mother she had already chosen to set Mark free. But she had to say what she knew to be true, possibly because Corrine had been unable to admit it. "Mother, aren't we acting like everyone else, afraid of Miss LaCroix?"

The simple directness caused Corrine to shiver. They were

indeed running, from Treme, the Registrar, the truth. Cleveland would be no panacea, just the next facet of the escape. "I guess we have no choice," she said.

No choice. A fight that could not be won. Fear, as much as any drug, could be addictive. It was perhaps the reason she had decided to let Mark out. He did not deserve to be a part of it. At least she had the night at Pass Christian, an enduring memory of him. She understood his weakness as much as her father's. "Do you think Daddy really cares for that woman?"

"I know it can't be the same feeling we've had for each other. Nothing can change that."

"That's something like I feel about Mark. No matter what happens, I know we have something special. Even if I never see him again."

Corrine was gratified, if a bit puzzled, that Michelle was so willing to give up Mark. It would make things much easier. She wanted to say so, but she dared not approach the subject. With improper handling, it could become a tinderbox. "Such things are important to a woman," she said.

"I wish Daddy would come home."

"He will very soon now."

Clarey was huddled in the doorway of the Half Moon Bar, directly across the street from Gloria's apartment, trying to reconstruct the details of an unpleasant dream. As images formed into settings with faces and shadows, he concentrated, but he had been drunk too long. The state following drunkenness was full of aches and dry bitter tastes, and he desperately needed a drink to clear his head. He tried to forget the dream. He closed his eyes and laid himself down in a cool field of grass. He could hear the sound of a brook and feel leaves curling in his ears.

Still the dream persisted. In it he was drunk and naked. Not a pretty picture that one, the drunken, emaciated Clarey the doctors had managed to put together again. Gloria was in the dream. She was in her bed, wrapped in a sheet, cowering from him. Gloria afraid of him! His hand held why. It was a thing like a whip, a belt. He was whipping her. He was cursing, mad with anger. But why? The first thing in life he wanted was Gloria. The last thing to hurt her. Then suddenly it came clear. It was not a dream. He had beaten her!

Cars were hacking by in the afternoon sun. The bar opened. Clarey went inside and ordered a glass of wine. The drink was cool and sweet. Slowly he began to put the scene together, agonizing over each newly remembered detail. Mark had been with him at the Napoleon House. Gloria had called him crazy. He had dropped his pants. They had been thrown out of the bar. They had gone . . . where?

Next he remembered climbing into bed with Gloria. They struggled. He pinned her arms. She turned away her contemptuous scowl. Then he *failed*. Was it her rejection? He thought not. The failure was somewhere in the circuits of his mind, the parts of him he had left on the battlefield. It was the reason for his madness, the animal response to frustration. He had never failed so miserably before. He had fought and won most battles, the result as predictable as daybreak. She laughed at the prepuce

98

that was left of him. It was too much for him to bear. In a fit of anger he had beaten her! Clarey screamed. The barkeep looked up from his mop and winced a recognition. The man was accustomed to the sight of delirium tremens.

Because Clarey loved Gloria, he knew he must try to earn her forgiveness. He must find Mark, too, and apologize to him. He would make a comeback. He had done it before. At a clothing store on Rampart Street, he bought an out-dated seersucker suit for seven dollars. The sleeves flopped to his thumbs, but it was clean and dignified by the initials of a former owner sewn into the lining. He bought a shirt, a tie, and underwear, changed into everything in the store, and left his old clothes behind. He wanted a drink, perhaps several of them, but he forced himself to pass the Half Moon. For his mission he needed all of his senses. It was late as he reached the Dennick house. He was suited as a badly wrapped package, but sober, and he was content that the improvement would sufficiently impress Mark and Gloria. He would dazzle them with his footwork.

Mark had come home famished after delivering Michelle to her door. He was in the kitchen eating the remains of Emma's gift of red beans and rice, by now a delicious lumpy paste, when he heard Clarey's whistle. It was a sharp, shrill note, his way of avoiding doorbells. "I'll take you for a drink," he said as he clasped Mark's hand.

But Mark pulled him into the house. "Come in, Clarey. We can talk in the kitchen. Keep your voice down. Papa's asleep upstairs." There was a decanter of red wine on the table. "Want a drink?"

Clarey handled the bottle and pushed it away. "Mark, I've been drunk for weeks. I want to apologize for the way I acted the other night. It must have been embarrassing for you and Gloria. I guess I am crazy like she says."

Mark remembered the humiliation of the broken fighter. "Forget it. You were feeling down. Good God—I know the feeling." He tossed his empty plate into the sink. It rattled but didn't break. "I've never been so screwed up in my life."

A friend in trouble made Clarey come alert. "Mark, what's screwed up?"

He had wanted to tell Clarey that first night to gain his

strength, to hear him laugh at the Registrar's secret. He could still use that support. "Michelle and I decided to get married. We went down to get the license. The Bureau of Vital Statistics . . . her birth record says she's part Negro." He said it all flatly. It was old news by now.

Clarey showed no shock, but he paused for digestion. He needed a moment to conjure Michelle, the pretty, quiet girl he had sought out in order to find Mark. He cursed himself for being drunk when he met her. "Uh-huh," he said, smiled, and turned serious again. His reaction was predictable. He wanted to know Mark's.

"Papa found out about it. He's very upset. Clarey . . . he's a sick man. He's going to die. Now this race thing pops up. I hate to have to hurt him, but I see no other way."

Clarey was relieved. Mark was not asking to be talked out of hurting his father. He wanted to be talked into marrying Michelle. "Is there really a race thing, Mark? I mean, nowadays?"

"There is to Papa. He sees his whole world falling apart."

"The old people would act like that. But who knows what we all are a hundred years back. Apes I would think the way we treat one another. There's some kind of black in every one of us I bet. Anyway, it's outdated thinking even for this town. The old folks have to swallow that because it's the way it is."

Mark wished he could have been as affirmative in the Registrar's office and in his later conversation with Papa. Even Michelle had recognized the wavering indecision. It was the reason she was so afraid that she was willing to let him out. He would not make the same mistake again. "Papa could never swallow it."

"Then it's his loss because *we* will."

"I'll have to take her away. That might kill Papa."

"Sure, you could marry her somewhere else where they don't have her vital statistics." Clarey laughed. To him, the expression had always pertained to a girl's private measurements. "I mean, Mexico or someplace where they have those marriage mills. I always thought it a little silly to stand up in church anyway. Then you could come back here."

"We could never come back here. Here the marriage would be null and void. We could be prosecuted under the miscegenation laws."

Clarey sucked in air, now fully understanding Papa's opposition. The old man would lose his son for the short time remaining to him. "Well, I don't see anything so great about this town. The air smells bad. The rain comes down hot as piss. I don't even like seafood. I stayed away a long time. I wouldn't have come back except for Gloria." He fell silent for a while, remembering the beating he had given her. He hoped Mark would not find out about it. He took a bank book out of his pocket. The account was dismally low. "Mark, I get my pension on the first. I could let you have a loan."

"No need for that. Matt will let me have some money for my *elopement*. That's all he knows, at least for the moment."

"Matt would be on your side."

"Perhaps he would. I don't know."

"Where will you go?"

"Washington, D.C. There's no law there."

Clarey thought again of Gloria. An old dream of theirs was to travel around the country. He could do it now on his pension. "Maybe I'll see you up there sometime. I'd like to see it. Washington sounds great. Better than here."

The crisis put aside, friends could talk of old times, of Clarey's best fights. The one they remembered best was against a tough red-headed kid named Delaney. It lasted ten bloody rounds before the towel was thrown in. Clarey remembered it had a big shamrock on it. The Irish kid was a game fighter and a good loser. "He came to my dressing room. Cuffed me on the chin."

Sober, Clarey could even talk about the war without grief. He described a war fought on the slopes of hills and in paddies and in the sky at night. The fireworks of air raids, the freezing cold, men dying silently beside him. It was a miracle that he had come out of it at all. He turned sad only at the end when he remarked bitterly that they had put him out to pasture. He quickly brightened. He was going to have fun now that the fighting was over. Mark was pleased to see some of the old charm and spirit return. Clarey could have talked all night, but

Mark had to cut him off. "I've got a big day tomorrow. Maybe the biggest of my life."

"Will I see you before you leave?"

"I don't know. I'll keep in touch."

Clarey was reluctant to part with him. He held his hand firmly. "Mark, all good luck. If you need help—"

"Thanks. You have helped. I won't forget it."

As Mark watched him leave, the list seemed less painful. The gait was strong and purposeful. The soul of the fighter was still there, ready for the comeback. He would win back his Gloria with pure will. At least, Mark sincerely hoped he would.

The shrill, flat whistle woke Gloria from a sound sleep. Her roommate, Sylvia, was asleep in a mat of black hair beside her. She knew Clarey was on the landing, now sobered, tidy, remorseful, ready to spread out his cloak for her. He would be armed with resolutions he could not keep. Because she ignored the whistle, he said, "How does a dumb bum try to say he's sorry? I came to tell you the great news. I quit drinking. You believe that? Gloria . . . I know I hurt you. I don't know why I did it. It upset me so much I decided to go away and leave you alone . . . forever."

Gloria was exasperated by the artlessness of the lies, but she was moved by the sincerity of the apology. It was not the Clarey she had known, this imploring liar. She supposed she owed something to her earlier memory of him. When she heard the marktime stamping of going away feet, she threw open the door. Clarey seemed startled that he had actually been talking to her all along. He waved and dropped into a chair. "Thank you, Glory. I don't know why you put up with me."

She was pleased with the way he looked and said so. Then she thought of the past. "Maybe I'm sentimental. I keep thinking I can return to the past, which I can't, which no one can."

"We could if we tried!" he said loudly as if it were the only wish he had in the world.

"Please lower your voice. Silly hasn't slept since I don't know when."

Clarey remembered the two girls from the Napoleon Bar. The

redhead had kissed the littler girl on the mouth, startling him. "Silly here? Boy, you're running all the bases."

"She's my roommate, remember? And if you talk like that you'll have to get out."

"I'm sorry."

"She and Dede had a fight is all. Dede's husband blundered into her dressing room without knocking. He started breaking up the place, calling them freaks. Silly had to get out. Imagine— Dede's husband accused her of being unfaithful—for sleeping with a girl!"

The thought of two women making love disturbed Clarey. He had enough to cloud his mind, but he had trouble avoiding the picture of them locked in an embrace, unable to commit a crime. To Gloria, fidelity depended on biological polarity. He wondered if the heart were not involved in such a generic union.

Gloria continued, "Anyway, it's all over with them. Silly wants to be straight and leave here forever."

"Will you go with her? You always wanted to go to California."

They once had a dream of California, of the white beaches and grassy hills. It had evaporated long ago. To Gloria, California was now a faraway place where she could discard the memories of the life they once had. She had talked it over with Silly, who in her hysteria, was willing to go anywhere. Gloria was not particularly fond of Silly. Up to now she had tolerated her as a split-rent necessity. A time of desperation is not a time to quibble. Gloria needed a companion, for she could not bear to go alone. She had no intention of giving her plan away to Clarey. "Oh, I gave that up," she said transparently. "I'm going to stay here."

Clarey's face hardened for the lie. "Mark's going away, too. To Washington."

"Oh? How did you hear that?"

"Mark told me. I spoke to him. He has to take his girl away. They can't be married here. There's a law against it. Michelle's part black."

Gloria was startled by this unfolding drama that she knew nothing about. She had tried to forget the night with Mark, her bold offer to him, his rejection of it. She had cried herself to sleep. "What else did he tell you?"

"That's all. His Papa found out. To the old man, a little bit of black blood is like being black to your toenails."

The rehash seemed to sadden Clarey, but to Gloria it was like a plunge into an icy stream. Gloria was blonde and fair. Michelle was fairer. The thought was inconceivable. "Couldn't it be a mistake? You can't tell it by looking at her."

"It's no mistake. They have the proof down at the Bureau of Vital Statistics. Gloria, I've got to help him somehow."

Her heart was pounding. "Right now I need help. I need a drink." She fixed two tall whiskies and drank hers quickly.

Clarey dawdled with his. "Dammit—I've got to help him!"

"What can you do? He's going to take her away. That settles it. I don't know what I would do if the same thing happened to me."

He knew she would not have the strength of character to deal with such a crisis. It was difficult to explain to her the simple concept of binding friendship. Whenever he tried, her self-interest prevailed. Gloria had no abiding friendships. He had often wondered if she even liked herself. "Maybe . . . I could reach his father, make him understand. Mark could go away in peace."

"I think you ought to mind your own business. It's none of your affair." She gathered her robe around her and went to the door. "You'd better go now."

Clarey took out his bank book. It was tattered and bent. His mother, a prudent woman, had insisted he open an account so that he might grasp the reality of the future. It had only cost a dollar to start. He had added little to it. "Did you know I had a bank account? I got a pension, too. I could travel if I wanted. I mean, with little worries about money. We could always be together, have lots of fun."

Why was he so incapable of giving up! A hundred times since his discharge he had begged her to with him to California. Each time she refused, he started over, a broken record. He could sack the enemy by brainwashing! But patience would end the conversation quicker. "I told you before. I gave all that up."

"Gloria, I can take care of us."

"Clarey—you can't even take care of yourself!"

Her quick arrogance was insulting to him. He had come to

beg, to accept any scorn if he could sway her. Now he sensed the uselessness of further argument. To her he was a decrepit nuisance, but a petty one, a mole in a crinkle of her skin. "I'm sorry I bothered you," he said. He returned his glass to the kitchen, made a noisome display of washing it, dried it carefully, and crashed it to the floor. "I'm going to help Mark if I can. You can go to hell."

He heard the bolt on her door come forward behind him.

The Half Moon Bar was crowded with seamen, filled with the brassy murmur of their voices and the smells of their bodies, flat beer and urine. Clarey ordered one drink and sipped it slowly. Customers watched a prize fight on a flickering television set. LeBlanc, the barman, a thick and stringy Cajun, weaved silent punches in the air. Everyone was bored by the way the boxers danced and tapped each other with indecisive blows. Clarey decided he could have taken either of them in a couple of rounds. Finally it was over and someone switched off the set. The men began to talk among themselves. Clarey was glad for the company. In a quiet place he would only dwell on Gloria, and he wanted to concentrate on a way to help Mark.

His thoughts took him back to the time of their childhood. There was a memory of Mark as he would always know him. Theirs had been an untouchable friendship, difficult for others to understand because they were so unalike. Clarey was the kidder, the fighter going about life as if it were a punching bag. In Mark, Clarey saw a quiet, spiritual quality of gentleness. People admired it. Although he said little, when he did speak the words were important. Most often, none were needed. He preached no cause, but there was no doubt of his opinions on most ideas. You could expect a fairness, that gentleness. Now he had a great trouble, and it was Clarey's fight as well.

Clarey had trouble picturing exactly whom he would be fighting and disliked himself for mentally mowing down little old ladies and men, aunts and uncles armed with hairpins and rakes. To shake the image, he turned his thoughts again to Gloria. In spite of her denial, he was certain of her plan to go to California. He resolved to follow her, but first he must do what he could for Mark. He knew what it had to be, a proper visit with Papa Stephen Dennick.

Mark called his brother early to ask for money. Matt laughed and said, "You're becoming practical in your old age. Yes, even romance costs money." He agreed to leave five hundred dollars in cash with Marylene. With the call completed, Mark felt better than he had since the scene in the Registrar's office. The beginning outline of a plan increased his confidence.

During the night, after Clarey had left, Mark had called Union Station to check the schedules. There was a morning and an evening train to Washington. He would pick up the cash and head straight to Michelle. They would be on the seven o'clock train. He would then worry about what he would do when he got there. It was the nearest he had come to a certain future for her.

But other developments weighed heavily on his upturned spirits. Several times he had dialed Michelle to tell her of the plan. The family was out or not answering. Her mood at the lake the night before troubled him. He had dismissed her outburst about not wanting the baby and her pledge to set him free as emotional reactions to a feeling of despair. The attitude would pass as he proved his intention. Now in her silence, the threats carried more weight. Moreover, his desire to rush to her was preempted by a note from Papa telling him of his appointment with Father Hurley. He had promised to speak to the priest. What was in that promise? Blessed rhetoric or a simple delay? He decided he could and must spare the time. Father Hurley could become the liaison, the man to explain to Papa Mark's only course of action.

At the rectory, Mark was told to wait. Father was in chapel.

Father Hurley was praying an odd prayer for a priest. He had prayed it many times. In it he asked for the Registrar's dismissal. The need to change the law, and hopefully to eliminate her in the process, had first come to him in the cold reality of crisis. He had been called to confront a young prizefighter who had killed a policeman. Johnny DiPaolo wept in the arms of the priest. His career and his life were ruined. That day he had learned from the local newspaper that he was part Negro. It had been discovered by accident, he thought, by a clerk in the Bureau of Vital Records. Under Louisiana law, he could not fight a white man in the ring. Father Hurley had not heard of the law, nor until that moment, of Pearl Marie LaCroix.

He first tried to reason with her. He implored her to help him change the laws, and until they were changed, to apply them with restraint. The public had little reason to know the truth about all the Johnny DiPaolos. She answered bluntly, "You administer to their souls, and I'll take care of their statistics."

With the help of a young lawyer, Emile Prudhomme, and the Deputy Director of the Board of Health, Dr. Mort Krasner, he had worked out a plan, the only one available to them. They would force the issue into the courts. The plan had not succeeded because it lacked a catalyst, a test case, a Mark Dennick. Father was not sure the boy had the courage to accept his own and the girl's humiliation. It was much to ask of him. Yet he must ask and perhaps be refused, and hope for the next opportunity while praying for its victims. The thought was uppermost in his mind as he strode through the rectory to his office, one hand clamped to Mark's shoulder, the other leafing through a wad of telephone messages. He offered Mark a chair and sat on his desk. "Thanks for coming, Mark."

"Papa insisted I see you. Papa gets his way most of the time."

The priest examined his fingers as if the digits were an outline for the forthcoming speech. There was more depth in this boy than in his brother. A hostility, true enough, but a depth of feeling shielded from outside forces. It made for a difficult character to judge. Beneath the facade, Father hoped to find great strength. "Mark, I need your help to change the miscegenation laws of Louisiana."

It was a sharp corner, and Mark did not turn it well. "I'm confused. I expected to hear you tell me to forget Michelle. To tell me not to take her away."

"I might be the one to *ask* you to take her away after you've heard my plan."

"Father, Michelle is pregnant. I've got to help her. Marry her or not marry her or take her away or something. I've got her and a baby to think of."

"The whole situation would be much less complicated if that were not true."

"You're telling me? Look—I've been all through the what-ifs. I've been living with them for days. What if the Registrar was wrong? What if Michelle wasn't pregnant, wasn't . . . alive? Why did I have to meet her, love her? But I did. I do. I've got to start living with reality."

Father slammed his fist into his desk. He would not fool with words or spare the truth. "All right—I'll tell you about reality. What are you young people thinking when you fornicate behind every bush? Yes—the sweetness of love and the beauty of it. Reality is what you put inside her while your head is swimming in glory!" He stripped off his coat. It was stained with sweat. He rolled it into a ball and thrust it into a chair. "Well, it's done. It'll be a bit harder on her, but we can work it out. Perhaps the baby will work to our advantage."

Mark accepted the wrath and settled deeper into his seat.

Father went on, "My plan is an action *in mandamus*. It's no more than a writ to force an official to do his duty. In your case, issue a marriage license. LaCroix will refuse, of course. The law forbids it. The courts will take it from there. The law will be found unconstitutional. Hopefully, the Registrar will try to expose those responsible and make mistakes. She's been very outspoken in the past, to the point of telling the Board of Health, her superiors, where to get off. They would love to fire her. With the right ammunition we could do it."

The priest had done his homework. He had wrapped himself in a crusade. He seemed dedicated to it and had a list of prominent confederates. While the legal aspect had merit, striking out the laws was but a premium to his true ambition, the elimination of Miss LaCroix. Hatred, as much as love, was kinetic. "You don't have to make me hate the woman, but she doesn't sound like she makes many mistakes."

"She does. When you threatened to take Michelle away, she went straight to your father. If we could prove one indiscretion like that she'd be in trouble."

108

The mention of Michelle made the disposition of LaCroix and the law seem trivial by comparison. How long would it take for the wheels of justice to move such a distance? Perhaps for years Michelle would be doomed to wait it through, become a mother and a martyr, accept the hatred and outrage to save all the Michelles yet to come. "It would be so much easier to take her away."

It was the course all the others had taken. Father could not fault Mark for longing for it. "Yes, but it would accomplish nothing. Not for the future."

"What do you want to accomplish, Father?"

"Complete reorganization of the bureau. Top to bottom removal of all discriminatory notations on race, legitimacy. Out with all the old Jim Crow laws so that a person can be what he is rather than what's written down by the Registrar. If it takes legislation, we'll get that, too. We'll get this woman if we have to prove she accepted a bribe. I would fear no conscience for it."

It was desperation, but it was also the new pragmatism, as old as the Republic, to make change by force if necessary, but make it. The rules be damned. Violence, deceit, ruthlessness could be essential to the most lofty crusade. That the priest was willing to surpass the malice of a Miss LaCroix was in a way admirable, a sin as venial as a spoken obscenity. Father knew where he stood. God could forgive—even a Miss LaCroix. The priest could accept purgatory to save another from hell. "I think you hate the Registrar as much as I do," Mark said.

"Hate her? There was a time when I could not allow myself to hate. I've watched her too long, watched her manipulate her private register of Negro families to force people to live in terror. Do you know how many times she's shouted it across a corridor? 'So and so's a nigger. Tell 'em to go home!' There's a movement under way to withhold welfare funds from unwed mothers. Do you know who's behind it, how many times she's cried bastard? It's her personal vendetta."

In turn, the priest had created his own. Mark was sickened by all of it. He wanted to escape it. The sounds of a ball game in the schoolyard drew him to a window. The boys conjured a memory of himself, of balls and bats and feet slapping on a macadam court. He wanted to be with them to copy the way the pros knock dust from their cleats, among them to wander home in a gritty sweatshirt. It was all they had to think about. Would he have one like them out there soon? No, for his son there would be a schoolyard far away. "I can't do it," he said.

"Mark—you must. It's the only way we can change it."

"Frankly, Father, I don't care about changing it. I don't care about getting even or whatever you're doing with Miss LaCroix. I'm sick of the hatred of this town and what it does to men like you. I'm going to get Michelle out of her before it happens to me."

Father slumped behind his desk. It was the answer he had expected, the choice of all the others. No one would challenge the law or the woman publicly. He could not fight the hordes with a paper spear. He wondered if he himself would have the courage in Mark's place. The game ended and the schoolyard disgorged its players, their laughter an innocent mockery of his moment of defeat.

Sensitive to that moment, Mark spoke gently. "All right, you can say it. I'm a coward because I can't destroy Michelle by taking on the world. Maybe I don't give a damn about the world. It's all too complicated and stupid and dishonest."

"There are stupid and dishonest people in it."

"Sure, and I hate myself a little more every day because I'm a part of it, the whole cheap ignorance of this town. Because I only care about me and a little girl who tried to kill herself when she became a horror she had been taught to hate."

"No, you are not a coward. You're a young man with a great burden. I can't fault you. But the world will change. We will get the Registrar and all the others like her. We will break their laws into pieces. We'll win because we will fight until we do."

Mark felt deep admiration for the priest because he was also a man and could permit himself a fault. For his children he could hate a law so repulsive as to make him fighting mad. Mark knew that men like Father Hurley would have to make the changes, suffer any humiliation to lobotomize the fastened-down minds and free the children of the future. Somewhere along the way, a Michelle would have to suffer. Mark did not have the ruthlessness to do it to his own. "I'm sorry, Father. I'm deeply sorry."

110

Father took his hand and saw him to the door. There was no spring in his walk. His head was lowered in dark thought. He was a man who had waited a long time to see a dream come true and seen it fail many times. "Will you be leaving soon?"

"Tonight, I hope."

"God speed."

"Father, I want to ask you to speak to Papa after I'm gone. He will be terribly hurt. If you could try to explain to him . . . that I had no other choice. Somehow make him understand . . ."

The priest did not think it possible to make Stephen Dennick understand, but he nodded. "I'll make him understand."

There were tears of gratitude in Mark's eyes. "Thank you, Father."

In the schoolyard, the shadow of a spire bisected home plate. The cheers of the children hung in Mark's ears. The rooms of the school were filled, the blackboards splashed with sunlight. His days in those rooms were warm in his mind, filled with bells and books and friends. He was saddened, for he felt he was seeing the school for the last time.

Inside the rectory, Father Hurley leafed through his pile of telephone messages. There was one from Stephen Dennick. The priest thought for a long moment on how to structure his reply. He had to take care not to give away Mark's plan.

"We talked for over an hour," Father Hurley said. "I'm afraid we didn't resolve anything." It was the priest's intention to be purposely vague.

"Did he talk about his plans?" Papa said.

"No, he didn't. I'm sorry, Stephen."

Papa put down the phone, hedging on his next move. William would be irate for not being told sooner. Papa hated to bring him in at all but knew he had no choice. He dialed the number with great deliberation.

Clearly in a state of panic and exactly twenty minutes after Papa phoned him, William rattled up in his Studebaker. His face was flushed and his eyes jittery as if he saw spirits lurking everywhere. "I'll be damned!" he said, his eyebrows dancing in apprehension. "I've got to say it, Stephen. I'll be goddamned!"

"Please calm down, William."

"Jesus H. Kee-rist. Do you know what this would do to me on the railroad? I got niggers working on the railroad!"

"Nothing's going to happen to you on the railroad."

William stopped for breath, sucked in a lungful of worry. He was piqued that Stephen could remain so calm looking such a cataclysm in the teeth. He was an old man. Senility fogged the brain. Age met emergency with faked control. "Stephen, what have you been doing all this time?"

"I tried to talk him out of it. I failed. Father Hurley also failed. Mark's determined to take the girl away."

William paced, socked his palm, rolled his sleeves, damned himself again. "You should have called me immediately. Yesterday I could have set up a long session with Judge Prudhomme. Now I'm lucky if I get ten minutes." He glanced at his watch. "In an hour from now."

"There was time. I wanted Father to talk to him."

In William, frustration and horror blended to make the sound of a huffing rhino. "What did you expect the good father to do? Hear his confession? There's no better way than the law."

"I had to try reason first."

"Yes, reason. They preach it every Sunday. Make my fellow man richer while I get poorer." Receiving so little support from Stephen, William knew he would have to rely on his own cunning. He drew an impacted hankerchief from a pocket, pressed his face into it, emerged dry but puffed with anxiety. The linen in his sleeve, he became a barrister and assumed a jurisprudent posture. "The Mann Act. He took her to Mississippi over the weekend, didn't he? We could scare the pants off them, and we're sitting here quietly while they're planning to slip away."

Papa considered the Mann Act a desperate stab, but he fully understood William's feeling of personal horror. "William, please listen carefully. I want you to approach Mark with great care. Talk to him earnestly, explain the law. If you can frighten him into backing out of his commitment to this girl, fine. But I will not have him persecuted."

The speech could have come out of the mouth of a Mafia don. To William Janin, a Cajun, it seemed an Italian trait to order people around. He detested the subordinate role. Why did he let the old man dominate him? Surely he was made of sterner stuff. He was younger, stronger, a leader on the railroad. It was for Delia, he decided, that he let Stephen rule the family. He comforted himself that it was only a temporary condition. The old man was dying. "The wound can only heal," he said, pleased with the implied compassion, "after the cut is made."

"Perhaps the cut isn't necessary."

Clearly, William was to save the family honor with his hands tied. "Stephen, you've got to trust me to handle this as I must."

"I do trust you. But as repulsive as this situation is to me, I won't have Mark's future ruined trying to save it. Read the law to him. Present a strong case. Tell him what he is doing to me. Leave it there." The old man reflected a long moment. "In the end, every man has the final say on what he is to do with his own life."

William was appalled that the old man had actually prepared himself for a possible defeat. He rankled that Stephen's sentiment dictated the cards to be played. He pictured the myriad of black faces at the depot, watermelon smiles spiced with giggles. A social disease in his immediate family would be less humiliating. He knew he must maintain control and carefully devise an argument based on any evidence he could collect to defeat Mark. He had some shocking cards to play. "I hope you're not making a costly mistake."

"I know what I'm doing."

William probed his knowledge of the boy. Mark was stubborn. He had opposed the property deal to the last moment. He was idealistic. Yes, given favorable circumstances, he would go through with such a marriage. "Stephen, if they should run away, he could never come back to Louisiana. Such a marriage would be null and void here."

"I know that."

And to lift his brother-in-law to the plateau of horror he had reached, he said, "You know the railroad job would be impossible, of course."

"I've thought of that, too, William."

Clarey was much too sober, he decided, for his mission. He had the jitters and a dull ache in a corner of his head. He ducked into the Half Moon Bar, threw down two ounces of whiskey, and topped that off with a cold beer. He felt better immediately. He left the bar and walked toward the Dennick home, but when he reached it he continued on around the block. Rather than lack courage, he was without a plan, a way to approach the old man in Mark's behalf. Abstract argument was not his forte. Clarey's fights involved action, not words. Yet he had to try. He had promised to do that much.

Eventually he found himself before his own home. In a window, the star representing his military service hung, a testament to his mother's celestial pride. His mother was one reason Clarey had not spent a night at home in more than a week. While her compassion for him was genuine, her constant doting had turned to pity. A week was not long enough away from the pitying embraces, the tedium of the invalid—hot broth, rocking chair, pension check—the whole deceptive battle he was expected to wage against himself. To the distress of his mother, who thought of him as a war hero (bronze star!), and his stuffed-colonel father, himself at the end of a military career, he could not live out his life as a cripple. To Clarey, the only proof of a vital future was a fight. Then on to the one at hand, he thought, and walked in the direction of the Dennick house.

As he neared it, he saw William Janin come out and drive away fast. He hoped the old man would now be alone. Papa was long in answering the doorbell and startled when he saw Clarey's maimed hand. He looked shrunken, worn out by life. "Hello, Clarey. Mark isn't home at the moment."

"I really came to see you, Mr. Dennick. Can I come in for a minute?"

In the kitchen, Papa opened beers for them, using the moment to conjecture on the meaning of the visit. He remembered Clarey as a child. He and Mark had been inseparable. But a social call on an old man he had not seen in years? Papa was sure he had come to discuss Mark. He would probe carefully and hope for an ally. He handed Clarey a frothy mug. "I'm glad you dropped by. It gives me a chance to say how proud we were of you boys in Korea. I heard you were wounded."

Clarey did not want to discuss himself. "I'm okay now. I came to talk to you about Mark."

"I thought you might have. He's in serious trouble."

"He told me about it."

"The family is very disturbed. Mostly I'm sorry about the girl. I blame her parents. If she'd known the truth from the start, this whole mess could have been avoided."

"I wonder about that, Mr. Dennick. If Michelle had known the truth, would it have kept her from falling in love with Mark?"

"Surely she would have been able to approach her life more realistically."

"You mean she'd have kept her place?"

Papa correctly interpreted the tone and at last understood the purpose of the visit. "I don't think that's a very nice way to put it."

Clarey knew that if he were ever to successfully explain Mark's feelings to the old man, he would have to use plain language. "Mr. Dennick, this whole race thing has been in our craw for centuries. The Negro in America is no longer a savage living in a house of dung. We've given him our civilization but refuse to grant him dignity. The only way we're going to solve the problem is by facing that fact."

"Clarey, I don't want to get into a racial argument. I've heard it too many times. I sympathize with some of it. You're young. When I was your age, it didn't amount to much."

"That's my point. We're supposed to be enlightened now. We brought the black man a long way. Still we go on thinking of him as something less than human."

"I regret that. But it has nothing to do with Mark's problem. What about my rights? Is it wrong for a man to want his children to have a certain future? That includes marrying well in the tradition of the family. That's what I want for Mark. It's a long way from the anguish he wants to choose for himself."

"I mean no disrespect, Mr. Dennick, but isn't there a higher law that says a man has a right to marry anyone he wants?"

Papa remembered his own words to William. In the end, he had said, every man has the final say on what he is to do with his own life. That included throwing it away. "I believe in freedom of choice. But the children. No one ever thinks of the children. What are their rights? A man has an obligation to have them in his own likeness. I wonder if the girl could change it, would she ever let the truth be known?"

It was the old line, and it was persuasive. Clarey had heard it all before from his father, the colonel. No black man in his right mind would not lighten his skin, straighten his hair, screw the white girls. That was the trouble with him. Everybody wanted him to be white. "Mr. Dennick, my dad was a career Army man, a colonel. He was passed over twice for brigadier. He was crushed in his last year of service to see a Negro promoted over him. He thought he was better than any black man on earth. Is that possible, that every white man is superior to every black one?"

"Of course not."

"Then what is all this fear of having some black in you?"

The presumption, that the old man could become accustomed to the fact of Michelle and accept the child she carried, was abhorrent to him. In deference to a war veteran, he said gently, "I sincerely believe it is wrong to mix the races."

Clarey knew he would never penetrate that bias. He had doubted it from the start. The old man would take his belief to the grave. Clarey hoped he could at least make Mark's feelings clear. "Mr. Dennick, when we were kids you were always a fair man. You taught Mark to do the right things. I learned from you, too. Most of the time my dad was in Timbuktu. You were our example. We looked up to you. Mark always admired you for getting the family out of the Irish Channel."

"I worked hard. I did what I thought was right."

"Don't you see that's what Mark's doing? All he wants is to do the right thing. He's another generation, Mr. Dennick. He isn't bound by the old thinking. He loves Michelle but he's your son." Clarey stood up to put the thought into action. "Dammit—it's killing him that all this business will hurt you. He can handle his head when it comes to Michelle, but he can't keep from hurting you in the process!"

The speech left the room in a drumming silence. The old man made no movement. His eyes, open sharp sockets, were fixed in a stare at the ceiling, his hands clamped to the chair. He began to choke. Clarey feared some sort of attack, but soon the coughing turned to sobs. Papa was weeping for his son.

Clarey felt uncomfortable. The room was hot, locked tight in the mid-afternoon heat. His mouth was dry. His headache had returned. He wondered if he should have come at all. "Mr. Dennick, I know you're sick. I'm sorry I spouted off so much. I guess it's none of my business, but Mark is my best friend. I had to help him if I could. I had to try to make you understand."

Papa held up a large hand. "I'm grateful for your help. Please believe that."

Clarey smiled his cracked smile. His mission had not failed after all. He left the house with a spring in his walk and had no thought of going into the Half Moon Bar.

Papa's thoughts were all of his son and the conflict that was driving them apart. For the first time since the visit of the Registrar, he realized that he had seriously miscalculated Mark's love for the girl. William's law was a frail weapon indeed to go against it.

The old man tried to stand but fell helplessly back into the chair. He felt dizzy and nauseous. His vision blurred. His arms and legs weighed heavily, turning numb. He felt cold. "My God . . . I can't die now. Not like this . . ." He lost consciousness at the moment Emma was coming through the front door to get the gossip on the visit from young Clarey Boriakoff.

Mark drove from the rectory to his brother's house to pick up the money. Marylene was in the kitchen amid piles of laundry. She greeted him glumly, as if afraid to look at him directly. Her eyes were puffed and raw, evidence that she had been crying. Mark knew that the truth was out.

"Emma called," she said. "She's calling everybody. I told her Matt didn't have a phone at the office, the busybody. I didn't have the strength to call him myself. All I could do was cry."

She started to cry again. Mark took her in his arms. "It's going to be all right. I'm taking Michelle away."

"She's not answering her phone. I called and called. I . . . wanted her to know how I felt."

"I'll tell her for you. I'm going to her now, as soon as I get my things together. Tell Matt. . . ." He remembered his promise to his brother to stay home and take the railroad job. The commitment seemed so small and distant. "Please try to explain to him."

"Matt will understand. You must hurry, Mark."

The money was in a wad, wrapped in a rubber band. He thrust it into his pocket and drove to the house on Esplanade. The sight of William's car, ticking as it cooled from a hot race across town, affirmed Mark's expectation of trouble. Inside the house, like a war party pow-wow, Emma, Dominick, William, and Delia formed a solemn circle. Accusation marked their faces. This would be the last battle.

William began with an excuse for their presence. "Your Papa had an attack. Emma found him unconscious. The doctor's been here. . . ."

Mark rushed to his father's room. Papa was asleep, bathed in his own sweat. His lips were pale and taut in a face pumped with blood. The old man sensed his son's presence and opened his eyes. "I guess I had a dizzy spell. I just passed out. I feel better now. The doc says I need rest is all."

In spite of William's ominous tones, the attack had apparently not been a serious one. Mark was relieved. There was no time for further delay. "Papa, I have to say goodbye. I'm leaving New Orleans tonight. More than anything I want you to understand why I must."

The old man stopped him with an outstretched hand. Mark gripped it firmly. It still had good strength. "Clarey Boriakoff came to see me today. We had a good talk. It made me remember how it was when you and Matt were boys. They were good times. We had 'Our Wilderness.' We had one another."

Mark had not expected Clarey to be so bold. The fighter could not resist a good slugging match. Papa had probably given him one. "Clarey's a good friend, Papa."

"I know how good. He's a fine young man. How quickly you've all grown into men." His eyes closed. The grip relaxed. Mark thought he had fallen asleep when he continued, "Men have to make their own decisions. I know you'll do what's right because I taught you to do that."

"Yes, you did."

"Mark, I asked William to talk to you. Will you listen to him? Do this one last thing for me. I want you to understand the trouble you're facing."

"I'll talk to him, Papa."

The grip relaxed again as the old man drifted to sleep, sweat standing in the folds of his brow. Mark thought the short talk had been an honest one. Papa had tried hard to understand, to put aside the old way of thinking. Clearly, he had prepared himself for whatever decision his son made. Acceptance had somehow made the possibilities less painful. Because Mark felt it was the last time he would see his father, he wept silently as he watched over him.

In his room, he slid his canvas bag from under his bed. Although he had been home only a few days, it was covered with lint. He packed his shaving gear, a pair of rolled socks, and two yellowed shirts that could have been laundered by Trudy. He checked a clock on his bureau. It was three-thirty. He had just a few hours to get Michelle to the station. But he had promised to talk to William.

The sultry confinement of the room recalled days too warm and windless to remain indoors. He opened a window. There was not wind enough to stir in the trees. He could hear voices from the living room. The words were vague, but he could not mistake the modulated tension as his relatives discussed their plan. The bayou legalist, William, would be elected to deliver it. It could possibly be funny. His knowledge of the law was spotty, his technique less than polished. He would be tired after a day of collecting evidence. He had possibly missed lunch, and nothing unnerved him as much as hunger. Bubbling smiles would accompany trite flourishes that made the fat man look ludicrous. Mark thought of climbing out of a window to escape him, but he remembered his promise to Papa.

The smile bubbled as William knocked and entered the room. His tie was askew, the points of his collar turned upward under the mass of his neck. He glistened in the heat. "Can I speak to you a few minutes?"

"I've been expecting you, William."

"Mark, I'd like it if we could be friends, trust each other for once. I've a feeling we've never really been friends."

The boys had disliked him from the day Delia brought him home for their approval. Mark could never explain why. William was not fat then. He had a fine car and Delia loved him. Perhaps it was his transparent sweetness, his self-serving rule. It soon became the habit to ignore him.

William continued, "I'm sorry I have to go over this whole nasty business, but it's very important to your future. It's most important, therefore, that you comprehend it."

He had been drinking his secret lawyer's potion again. Mark hoped he would not pile up a mess of so forths and therefores. The visit would be tiring without them. To hear an ignorant man pepper his speech with worn-out words, the fakery of the pedant, would make it unbearable. "Speak your piece plainly, William. What do you want to say?"

Since entering the room, William had kept his briefcase at his feet. It held his store of energy, absolute proof of all the views dear to him. He had spent years collecting it, and today he had the need to lay it out to build an airtight case. It had earned him a special appreciation from his friends, and he wished he could do as well with Mark. He had already failed at a cordial beginning. He lifted the case to his lap, took out a paper, and announced, "Civil Code of Louisiana. Article 94. Marriage between white persons and persons of color. . . ."

Mark cut him off. He remembered it verbatim from Emile's office. ". . . Is prohibited, and the celebration of all such marriages is forbidden and such celebration carries with it no effect and is null and void."

"All right. You know the law. Do you know its meaning?"

"I'm not stupid, William."

As a result of his effort to tread lightly, a sweat had appeared on his brow. He scrubbed it and wiped the oily residue on his pants. "I didn't mean that. Please don't misunderstand me. I mean do you know the reasoning behind it? Somebody was doing some mighty smart thinking. They knew that the Negro race was defective, mentally and physically defective."

"Where did these reasoning beings get their information, William?"

"They didn't have the proof we have today, but they saw the diseases that came over from Africa. Diseases like *sickle cell anemia*. I have the proof right here." He took out a newspaper clipping he had underscored entirely in red ink.

TEST DETECTS

BLOOD DISEASE

Sickle Cell Anemia Afflicts

One In Ten American Negroes

About ten per cent of American Negroes are genetically disposed to a disease they may not know they have that can debilitate or kill them, sometimes under bizarre conditions.

Sickle cell anemia is a hereditary disease in which the normal round red blood cells curl up to form crescents or sickles. This prevents the cells from carrying oxygen to the heart, lungs, and brain. The twisted cells clog up the blood vessels.

Centuries ago the genetic mutation responsible for the sickling trait evolved in malaria-ridden Africa. Malarial parasites preferred to invade blood with normal cells rather than defective ones, so that individuals having the sickling trait were better

122

able to ward off disease. They lived longer and had more children who themselves carry the sickling trait.

If both parents carry the trait, their offspring have only a fifty-fifty chance of being born and surviving the first year of life.

The sickling trait problem, which has been known for more than fifty years, has no cure. . . .

William read it dispassionately down to the last word and paused for reply. Receiving none, he exploded. "Mark—a fifty-fifty chance of being born and surviving the first year of life!"

Mark looked at him hard. "William, so what?"

Annoyed that Mark did not share his horror, William scooped up a handful of clippings and spread them on the bed. "Read them. Unless you're afraid to learn about Tay-Sachs disease. It causes a degeneration of the nervous system and early death. Have you heard of the Lesch-Nyhan Syndrome? Little children compulsively mutilate themselves. Lots of others. All hereditary. They all came over from Africa and Asia. Read and learn what I've known for years, that the Negro is physically and *mentally* inferior to the white man."

"William, there's no proof for such a thing as that."

"Oh, no?" He tapped the briefcase confidently, for he had saved the best for last. "You ever hear of the XYY syndrome? A smart young man like you should know about it. I have an article from a Shreveport magazine, written by a Dr. George Mason Parker. A *doctor*. A man respected in his community. The article's about heredity, probably the most advanced article ever written on it. Dr. Parker is certain that many Negro males are born criminals."

"That's stupid. Nobody's a born criminal."

"Do you agree insanity, simplemindedness are carried from father to son?"

"We don't know that for sure. Retarded children are born in the best of families."

"I'm talking about something quite different from retardation. Dr. Parker has proved an inherited capacity in the nigger male for violent antisocial behavior. Let me explain further. See, every male has an X and a Y chromosome along with lots of others. The Y determines the sex of the baby. But the *extra* Y, when it

123

appears alongside—that's the catch. It causes antisocial behavior. The factor has been isolated in very tall, pimply-faced males who are low morons. Now what does that describe to you? I mean in most cases?"

Mark had underestimated William's dedication. The bayou legalist was expert at digging up shreds of fake evidence to support his cause. But he would have to wait a long time for Mark to concede a point based in hatred. "It describes your Dr. Parker as a screwball fanatic," he said.

William rooted for a photocopy of the article. It was tattered as if fingered by a hundred readers. He had underscored every word and sprinkled exclamation marks in the margins. As he examined it, an insect persisted over his nose. He was too excited to notice it. "Here's the study. Out of a thousand nigger males examined, thirty-one percent are over six feet tall, below average intelligence, and have bad skin. I don't see how you can argue with the facts."

Mark pictured a Watusi tribe of Shreveport Negroes, standing about like fenceposts while the good doctor measured them, tested them, and probed their pimples. "I suppose they also have an extra chromosome."

"Dr. Parker thinks so. But it will take more money and study to find out. Try to get money out of our government for a study like that. They'd rather bribe the niggers to keep them from burning our cities."

"William, this is racist propaganda."

"It is a scientific study."

"Then let me ask you a question. How many white men are over six feet tall, below average intelligence, and acned? Why is Doctor Parker studying only the Negro?"

"Because he believes them defective, at least a large percentage of them. Did you ever hear of the prognathous jaw? Apelike, the prehistoric man. One simple proof that niggers are behind us on the ladder of evolution. You believe in Darwin, don't you?"

"Did Darwin say that?"

"No, Dr. Parker said it. Oh, what's the use? Look at your crime statistics. Who commits most of the violent crimes? I have them here. Would you like to see them?"

124

The Registrar's heart would twitter at the word. She and William had a common cause. Their scientific evidence was based on a group of black rural men who performed probably at the level of their educational opportunities and had bad skin because of a poor diet. Mark thought he saw in William's face the scars of an adolescent acne. "William, you're over six feet tall. I bet you once had a pimple or two. I think you'd better go check out your own chromosmes."

William puffed himself up with outrage. "That was uncalled for. I am not the subject of discussion here."

"William, I think you're a goddamned bigot!"

He poked a finger at all the lurking liberals. His face turned hot. He huffed and puffed. "This is the youth who want to give away a country and its economy to a race that would only wear it on Saturday night and throw it away on cigars and candy. I'm going to show you that your permissive attitude will destroy you. Crime is on the increase, violence against innocent white people. Still the government keeps bringing them in by the thousands, mixing with them. You are putting your life in your hands. We intend to stop it."

"You can go to hell."

William shook visibly, barely able to control his temper. He searched his case for another paper, a precedent under the civil law. "In the case of Hibbert versus Mudd, Louisiana Court of Appeals, to establish legal succession of children of a miscegenous marriage. The court ruled and I quote: 'No acknowledgement of children was possible if the union was miscegenous.' The children were entitled to not one speck of property. Your children would be bastards, plain and simple."

"Bastards with an extra chromosome. This is becoming indecent. I don't want to hear any more."

William had not often in his life felt true horror. It was possible that this young man could compromise his honor. "Legitimacy is still important to honorable men. Whatever you think of me, I wouldn't do that to my children. Will you at least listen to the criminal law?"

"Why don't I recite it to you?"

Very well, William thought. He had none but a desperate

move left open to him. It was a bold one he wanted to avoid if at all possible. "All right, Mark. You leave me no choice. Since you know the law you must also know that you can be prosecuted if you cohabit with her in this state. Judge Prudhomme was very positive on that point."

"You told him?"

"I spent most of the day with him," William lied. Actually he had been granted a four-minute audience with the judge, who listened carefully and explained that unless Mark and Michelle lived together or married, there was no case. A clerk had typed the applicable laws. William knew it would leave Mark no alternative but to flee the city with Michelle. As a last resort, it was exactly what he wanted.

"You and the judge don't have to worry," Mark said. "I'm taking her away."

"I think that's stupid. It would be easier to dissolve your relationship with this girl. But then it's your life."

Mark felt anger crawl on his neck. He decided he hated the phony amateur lawyer for his arrogance and ignorance. He stood and rolled his fists. He wanted to hit William in his fat stomach and watch the blood drain from the worms of broken capillaries in his cheeks. He seethed but kept his fists at his sides. It would do no good to fight this man. His corruption was beyond any help that fury could achieve. "Get out of here, William. Get out before I knock your fat ass down the stairs!"

William was frightened by the anger and pretended to arrange the papers in his briefcase. He closed it and pondered its awesome contents. "I think it only fair to tell you. Her house will be watched. You cannot live with her here." He finished the speech while backing away in fear and farted, a dyspeptic editorial. Mark decided he could not have succeeded as the most primitive of backwoods charlatans. Loyola must have been bored even to flunk him.

The summation to the family, interrupted by a squawk from Emma or the drone of a passing car, took a quarter of an hour. Then William drove away with Delia in his rattletrap. Next Emma waddled across the boulevard, leading Dominick by the hand as if he were a child. It was nearly five o'clock.

126

Mark thought of stealing the car but dropped the idea. Grand larceny would be too sweet a weapon to give William on top of everything else. The streetcar to Michelle's house took half an hour. He used the time to evaluate William's arguments. The motives were clear—to intimidate and defile. Perhaps to root out a trace of bias left in a boy's indoctrination? The evidence was false, the reasoning childishly thin. While the odd diseases were plausible, they applied only faintly to Michelle, like the widely scattered genes of hemophilia. The rest, Dr. Parker's asinine research, was as absurd as William's fears of a degenerate race. Yet William had succeeded in one way. Mark was frightened. A dangerous potential in the fat man disturbed him. How far had he gone, would he go? Plainly, he wanted Mark to flee with Michelle.

The first rap brought Corrine and Alfonso to the door. They greeted him coldly with worried faces. In an effort to hide his panic, the words shot out. "Get Michelle packed. We're getting out of this town tonight."

Corrine had only a moment to decide to fight. It was a moment she had prepared for long ago. She had no intention of allowing her daughter to rush out of her life and had a plan to prevent it. In the past, she had been too cool in estimating Mark. His affair with Michelle seemed to have gone stale. Given the opportunity, she felt he would quickly give her up. She would test his determination. She said calmly, "Please sit down."

"There's no time. The train leaves at seven."

She waved her husband into a chair. He sat on her command. "A train to where?" she said.

"Washington. We can be married there."

Alfonso stood uncomfortably. "Corrine. . . ." He had given thought to the boy's position and sympathized with it. He had secretly hoped Mark would step forward to take Michelle away.

He would give a lot to see it done quickly, but he was certain Corrine would oppose it unless they all left together. "Maybe it's not a bad idea that they get out of town right away. We could help them." The effect of the statement was wasted as it trailed weakly. Alfonso bowed his head as if he knew it.

Corrine could swiftly deal with her husband and knew she must if she were to win the fight with Mark. "Al, we've been over this time and again. Where would they go? How could we help them in a city as far away as Washington? No, Michelle is not strong enough for that. I want her near me where I can help her."

"But the job in Cleveland. I'm almost certain of it. We could give them money, meet them later."

Yes, she had decided on Cleveland. She could hardly allow her daughter to go in another direction, to a strange city with a young man who roamed irresponsibly around the country. The thought of Michelle trapped alone to have her baby caused her to shiver. "I could never send Michelle away to a strange city. Never. Don't fight me, Alfonso. If the job works out in Cleveland, we'll all go together."

"Look—we're wasting time," Mark said. "Michelle and I can't stay here. I just had a long lecture from the family. They made threats, came up with a lot of lies about black people having diseases, about a crackpot doctor in Shreveport named Parker. Because they knew they would fail with that, they went to Judge Prudhomme. They will prosecute if I stay here with Michelle. Don't you see we have no other choice?"

Corrine's face hardened. "There is a solution. You simply stop seeing Michelle."

Mark looked to Alfonso for support. He got none. "Do you seriously think I could give up Michelle that easily?"

Corrine realized she was going to have to be tougher than she wanted to be. She had learned how to be cold in Saint Mary's churchyard, where she had first glimpsed a copy of Dr. Parker's article. Palm Sunday, ladies fanning themselves with their sacred fronds, lacy doilies tacked to their hair, prepared to worship their Lord in a church of Madonna lilies. The Palm Sunday motto— beware of tall, acned, moronic Negroes. Was it anger or revul-

128

sion that pricked her? She had read the article, passed it along to the next eager reader, and filed with the ladies into their pews to share their missals. She bowed her head like them and struck her breast to the purest tinkle of bells. *Mea culpa.* Her friends never dreamed she was praying that she would not be found out! The experience had hardened her in a way she did not like. "And I suppose you're here to tell us you weren't at all moved by Dr. Parker's report?"

"Corrine," Alfonso said.

The implication in her tone and in Alfonso's plea was clear. Mark had patiently listened to the evidence. Like the rest of the people in this town, he wanted to hear it. Was there, as Corrine suspected, a doubt in him? Mark did not hedge. "I don't believe a word of it."

But they had judged him. Their faces were turned from him and from each other, blankly to the walls and the floors, unable to make a direct accusation. The outsider could not be trusted. There was no way he could prove his sincerity to them. Their shame, their self-deprecation, favored William. Mark decided to give them Father Hurley's drastic alternative. He would jolt them out of their self-pity. "Listen to me, both of you. There's another way. Father Hurley says we could force them to issue a marriage license here."

Corrine's head snapped up in disbelief.

Mark read it correctly. "Yes, that horror. A public case. Maybe a long time public. Your church bazaar ladies, your nice Garden District neighbors would all look at you with those sly, knowing smiles. Would you rather that?"

A thousand times Corrine had imagined how it would be. Her neighbor, Charlotte Naquin, would weep pity from the depths of her liberal blue eyes. She would offer the comfort of her very white hands. Corrine could not bear the thought. She would rather the whispers in the churchyard, the article passed in the pews. Never the grieving smiles on the faces of her friends. "You would do that to Michelle?" she said.

"You mean to you!"

"Yes, then, to all of us!"

Alfonso stood, opened his mouth, closed it, and sat down.

Mark said. "You see why I have to take her away."

To look at him would be to transmit the truth, her cowardice. "No, Alfonso is going to see about the job in Cleveland. We'll leave here together. That's the only way it can be done. You can join us there later if you wish."

If you wish! This is your way out, if you wish, she meant. The protective mother could not let her daughter go even to save her. Better to skirt the truth and live the lie, a petticoat shelter in a storm. Mark said very loudly, hoping his voice would carry through the house, "I said I'm taking her away from here to-night!"

"No, you are not!"

As Mark tried to push past her, Alfonso wedged himself between them. Pressed together, the bodies shoved and grunted about the room, a comical dance of three partners. Mark lost against the weight of them both, and like an off-balance clump of drunks, they crushed a lampshade, knocked over a table, and spilled in a tangle on the floor. Mark struggled to get up. Corrine was strapped to his throat. Alfonso lunged in her defense. His mouth met Mark's fist, a light blow that made no sound at all. Alfonso cried out and went down. The battle, the idiotic tug of arms and bodies, was over as a red button of blood appeared on his lip. He touched it, tasted it, and looked sourly at his fingers.

Corrine sat frozen in a spread of daisies. Mark dropped into a sofa. He had wanted to hit William for the hatred and ignorance. Instead he had picked Alfonso, who was guilty of nothing but fear. Unable to strike out at malevolence, he had fought impotence. As he looked at Alfonso, the comma of blood on the weak line of his lip, Mark felt intense despair. He had lost. The only true fight of his life, against the meanness of a town, he had lost in one blow. He could fight them no more.

Michelle had appeared at the doorway, secretly in time for the struggle, avoiding a creak of the seventh stair from her room. She had heard part of the argument and judged her parents wrong. She wanted to tell them and rush to Mark, leave with him and run to Washington or anywhere. But she knew she could not. "Mark, I can't go away with you. Please try to understand. You could never come back."

130

"I don't care about coming back here."

"You will one day."

"Will you go to Cleveland?"

Cleveland was the next facet of the escape. There would be new birth and health records. A new place to hide from the Registrar. She had no intention of running from anything. "I don't know," she said.

Mark could fight weak men like Alfonso. He could kill William and suffer no conscience for it. He could fight Papa's dream of immortality, and even wage Father Hurley's great spiritual crusade. But he had no power at all to fight Michelle. "You must believe me. I want you very much."

She said softly, "I believe you."

When Mark had gone, Michelle sat beside her father. Corrine had found a tissue for his lip. It was dotted with blood. The cut was small to bleed so much. Alfonso took her hand but did not speak. As Corrine gathered up the flowers, she strangled her middle with the belt of her robe, gaining strength from the constriction. Michelle had nothing more to say. She sat quietly as she went over her plan for tomorrow.

Mark walked a slow, foot-dragging walk along dim streets and around blank corners. He felt suspended in time without tense or sense. With no future there was no longer any need for either. If he could feel at all, there was relief in the simple act of giving up, a catharsis, as if the fibers of his nerves had been stripped and cleaned. And he never felt more alone in his life.

Eventually, he found himself before the only place left to him, Clarey's house. He wondered why. For condemnation? Or the will to go on? Mrs. Boriakoff crushed a handkerchief in the heel of her hand and explained that she had not seen her son in days. The Colonel had thought of calling the police and hospitals. Clarey was sick; he had no idea how sick. They were afraid he was stranded somewhere helpless and alone. Mark agreed to try to find him. He would look in all the probable places and report back to them tomorrow.

He checked the Half Moon Bar and crossed the street to Gloria's apartment. She was asleep. Her face, pressed with a grid of wrinkles, brightened when she saw him. Without makeup she was freckled and depthless. She rushed to put on her face and returned combed and painted, self-conscious of her soggy robe and slippers. "I didn't expect to see you again."

"I didn't intend to come back. I have to find Clarey."

"The last time I saw him was the day after you carried him home. Mark, he beat me that night with a strap. I think it's because he failed. We're finished." Her eyes dropped to his bag, ran up his arm to his face, and saw the sorrow in it. "Are you going away?"

"Yes. After I find Clarey."

Unable to conceal her satisfaction, Gloria paused to approach the subject with caution, searching for a way to reinforce his decision. Had he possibly come to hear her talk him out of it? Was it the reason he was searching for Clarey? A careless reaction could botch it. "Perhaps it's best you do leave. They would persecute Michelle if you stayed."

"You know about her?"

"Clarey told me."

"All I can think . . . Gloria, she'll have the baby alone."

She curled into a chair, thinking she must phrase her speech delicately. "Mark, there are quite a few things a girl can do alone. One of them is having a baby. Women know what they're getting into when they decide to have a baby. And that's just what they do—decide. So it turned out to be a shocker. You'd marry her if you could. It's just one of those dumb, unfortunate things about life."

A frightening explanation, Mark thought. The child had been conceived deliberately, however lovingly. Because Mark had not shared the decision, the sole responsibility could be laid to Michelle. One day Gloria would have a baby as casually as a trip to the supermarket. "Damn—I wanted to take her away!"

"There must be a reason you decided against that."

"It was decided for me. Everyone fought it. My family, hers. When the fighting was done, she refused to go. She gave up on me."

"There you are."

There he was. The solution had wondrous economy and precise fact. He couldn't take her away because she refused to go. In one minute, they had completed his days of anguish in a tossed away summary.

So as not to let the moment die, she said, "Mark, I have a car and some money. Will you take me with you? Silly wants to come along. We were planning to leave right away."

"I don't know. I have to find Clarey first. See if he's all right. Find out what he's going to do."

She stiffened and frowned. "You're not going to ask him to come along, are you? Mark, he'll be drunk all the time. He'll wreck everything."

Mark was not surprised by the proposition, although it was not as explicit as her first one had been. It would, of course, exclude Clarey. Silly would tag along to increase the kicks. He permutated the ménage. Silly and/or Mark, Gloria and/or Silly,

Mark and/or Gloria. Clarey's wildcat bitch was reaching out for new thrills. Mark seriously wondered what his friend had ever seen in her. "Gloria, don't you understand I could never leave here with you unless Clarey came along?"

She said, "Shit," and bit her lip as if she wished Clarey had somehow vanished from the earth.

Mark was tired. He asked Gloria for a drink. She made it solemnly. As he drank, he tried to see himself as Clarey would now, the sorry son of a Mediterranean soft-drink peddler. He was not the Mark of his given name, King of Cornwall, uncle of Tristram, husband of Isolde. This Mark was not made of that stuff.

As he slumped in the chair, his eyes rested on an ornate clock on the wall. It said ten o'clock. The train to Washington was long on its way.

It was close to the time of the Mardi Gras, and the city was preparing for the holiday. Workers were building reviewing stands on Canal Street and on Saint Charles at City Hall. Each year, Michelle looked forward to the festivities. Her father's membership in the Boston Club allowed them choice seats in the stands. It was a day the family spent together, catching loads of loot from passing floats, and ending with dinner at Kolb's or Antoine's. This year, Michelle would not enjoy the Mardi Gras.

The only dividend to her plight, if there was one, was that she had given up ballet class. Not that she disliked the dance. She rather enjoyed its ritual, grace, and discipline. She was annoyed by the instructor, Mrs. Pleasance. The woman made the class unnerving with her contralto wails—"The spine is a REED in a GENtle wind. We are gaZELLS. Ready now, up-and-down-and-up-and-down-and . . ." Michelle phoned in her resignation, disliking herself for blaming Mrs. Pleasance, and aware that the true reason for quitting was that her pregnancy could no longer be concealed in a leotard.

In the time redeemed from the class, she arranged a meeting with her friend Donny. She called him during his shift at the library, told him what she wanted, and covered her panic with a joke about the lost ballet class. Donny protested but she insisted. He cursed and asked if she was out of her mind. She coolly assured him of her sanity and made him agree to meet her later.

Among the private stacks, she chose *Forensic Medicine* as their meeting place, along a dark aisle, where she found a book she had sought in the card catalogue:

Subject: Forensic Medicine
Author: Dassin, Eugene Erastus, M.D. (Fr.)
Title: "Mostly Murder"

Argument on morality in medicine, the
value of man, with reference to the measure

135

of self-inflicted or consensual damages to
any part or parts of the body.
(Intro. by S. Albert Smith)

TDO p.v. 24x

As she waited for Donny, Michelle skimmed the chapter on
euthanasia. Dr. Dassin was pro in the best French polemic tradition. He suffered for all the old people who were denied the
blessing of merciful death. Michelle's too vivid imagination,
stirred by the descriptions of unbearable pain, caused her to clap
the book closed. She hoped the doctor would not be so convincing
on a subject she planned to read about next. She checked her
watch. Donny was late. Librarians are almost never late for anything, she thought, a tribute to their dullness. He arrived breath-
less and just in time to save her from a chapter entitled, *Criminal
Quackery and Abortion.* "I've been waiting almost an hour," she
said.

He nosed self-consciously over a shelf and said in a sharp
whisper, "You ask me to do the illegal—the *impossible,* and expect me to do it yesterday."

"I explained it was urgent. Do you have the information?"

Donny sighed. Michelle felt the tension in this place where
none should exist, in the familiar wormy-musky smell of books.
His eyes dropped to the volume she held. He frowned disapproval. "What are you reading *that* for?"

"To learn things I need to know."

He took up her hands. "Michelle, I touch you and you're cold.
You're never cold. I don't know you today."

"Please, no lectures. I don't have time for it."

"I think I have a right to ask. Remember, I'm an accessory.
So I'll ask. What are you doing to yourself? Do you know?"

"I'm correcting a little mistake."

A little mistake, a pus pimple. Donny thought it sad that life
itself could be a small mistake. He felt he owed her an argument
if only that she might see the enormity of her decision. He had
been shocked by her call; she had glowed happiness with the
prospect of becoming a mother. He knew the trouble had to be
with Mark Dennick. "Michelle, why do it at all? Can you tell

136

me? This is 1957. While it isn't yet fashionable to have illegitimate children, it isn't exactly a curse upon the house."

"I don't think you're very funny."

"My attempt to lighten it is meant seriously. This is a dumb, important thing you choose to do. What about Mark?"

She answered by not answering, by turning her face away. The book in her lap had opened itself to the chapter on abortion. She saw why. For the several minutes she had glared at the title page, the paper had withered under her moist fingers. To the touch she was cold and her hands were sweating.

The absence of a reply told Donny the truth. She had not told Mark her decision. This was supergirl, Joan of Arc. She was in it alone. He felt guilty in part because he, the liberal thinker, was a part of the mentality that permitted it. "I think you should tell him."

"Oh, damn, sweet Donny! Why was he tormenting her? She wanted to tell him to shut up, to give her the information and go away. "Don't you think I've considered telling him? I can't because he would try to stop me. I started this whole mess myself and I can finish it. Please just give me the information and go."

She had clearly made up her mind. Mark had refused or not refused her, but she was now alone. Further argument would only intensify her panic. "Yes, I'll give it to you. Because I know a little more about shame than most people care to learn."

The implied confession, because it was unnecessary, made her feel ashamed. "I'm sorry Donny. I don't want to hurt you. I'm just tired of talking about it."

"You'll need two hundred dollars."

"I have the money."

Donny thought bitterly of the affluent society. Include in a girl's mad money the price of an occasional abortion. Had he a doubt that the operation was less than morally correct? He wondered if he should keep the slip of paper in his pocket, swallow it, walk out and have her never speak to him again. Instead, he crushed it into her hand. "The top numbers are the address on Carondelet Street. The woman's name and phone number are next—Mrs. George, a sort of code name. You have to call to set up an appointment. I'll go with you, of course."

"Thanks, but this is not your trouble. I'd rather be alone."

"Michelle, that's insane. You might be too weak to walk. If anything happened. . . ." What horror had crossed his mind? That she might bleed to death in the arms of Mrs. George? The little girl was thinking like a soldier, ready to die if she must. What grim facts could inspire such cold courage? Rubella? Something worse than that. Fatherless shame. She would go through it bravely and alone, without a hint of self-pity. Aware of his own sibilant sound, he said weakly, "Please call me if you need me. I'll drop everything," and disappeared from the aisle.

Michelle sat at a table in the study room. She opened Dr. Dassin's book to the fearful chapter. The first sentence gave his stand with the proper invective, "Abortion, except when a pregnancy is a clear danger to the life of the mother, is a heinous crime against mankind, infanticide. . . ." She shivered at the passage, closed her eyes, and thought of her dance class. She wanted to be back there now, worrying over the not quite firm flesh of her thighs, enjoying the sweaty bouquet of the gym.

Mark awoke on the couch, his unfinished drink beside him on the floor. He woke Gloria and asked for the use of her car. She consented reluctantly and rolled over in her bed, interrupting the rhythm of Silly's breathing. "Silly and I are leaving tonight," she said, meaning the car must be returned by then. They would leave with or without him. The keys were on a hook in the kitchen. He drove to a counter restaurant, had a plate of eggs and grits, and began his search for Clarey.

Most French Quarter bars are open day and night. Mark crisscrossed the grid of the Vieux Carré from Canal to Esplanade and Rampart to the river, checking each one, wondering what he would say to Clarey when he found him. Was it to hear himself condemned or to gain support for his failure? No, it was because he needed to tell someone who would understand, not slough off Michelle the way Gloria had. He also felt that Clarey might be in trouble, perhaps drunk and helpless, unaware of his own sickness.

When he had covered the French Quarter, Mark parked to think. He remembered an exhibition gymnasium where Clarey had spent most of his afternoons after school. For a dollar, a boy could watch professional boxers spar in the ring. The place was on Poydras Street, a few blocks on the other side of Canal. Someone there might have seen Clarey.

A half-dozen spectators were lined up at the door. Mark questioned each one, giving a description of Clarey. Their answers were cautious; if they had seen him, they weren't telling. Mark paid his dollar and sat with them on folding chairs. He watched four rounds of poor boxing between two middleweights who were saving their muscle for more serious gains. Mark remembered one of them from Saint Mary's. The boxer had beaten Clarey, but not easily, in three rounds. He was Moose . . . something.

"Moose Hagen," the fighter said in a room of lockers that smelled of dirty socks. "You a friend of Clarey's?"

"Yes. He disappeared. His parents are worried."

"Sometimes a guy likes to stay lost."

"Moose, he's sick. Somebody has to take care of him."

The boxer ripped tape from around his fist. "He's sick all right. He came in one day sober, looking better than he had in weeks. He sat in his regular chair, right in the first row, punching the air like he always did. When the show was over, he couldn't stand up. He'd lost his legs. He could talk, but he wouldn't tell anyone his name. Somebody called an ambulance."

"Do you know where they took him?"

"The ambulance was from Charity Hospital."

Mark started to rush out, but Moose stopped him. "You going to tell his folks? He didn't want that."

"If Clarey's sick they have to know, Moose."

Moose stretched out on a table, clutched his head in his hands, and yawned. The four rounds had failed to warm him up. "You let me know about Clarey, hear?"

Mark phoned the Boriakoff house from a booth outside the gym. The Colonel was not surprised. He barked an order for Mark to check the hospital and said he would meet him there.

The receiving nurse said, "We have two unidentified patients. One is an old woman who doesn't know who she is. The other's a young man suffering from malnutrition. He won't give his name. He has a maimed right hand."

Mark said he could identify the man.

"He's in the psychiatric ward, second floor. A nurse will have to accompany you."

A nurse wrote down Clarey's name and address and left them alone. A tube coming out of his nose was taped to his chin. He was being fed intravenously. His face brightened for Mark. "How the hell did you find me?"

"Moose Hagen is your friend, Clarey."

"The Moose is a pretty good middleweight, but he got me with a lucky punch."

"I'd like to know what the hell you're doing to yourself. Jesus Christ, Clarey—the psycho ward!"

"Mark, don't be mad at me. I guess I gave them a little argument. Look, I'll be out of here in a couple days good as new. I just forgot to eat. I throw up everything anyway. Mess hall chow screwed up my stomach. I can't live on cornflakes. So I lost my legs for a minute. I couldn't have the Colonel come stand over me with a face full of pity. You can understand that."

"Too late. I called him. He's on his way here."

Clarey seemed relieved that it had been done for him. "Okay, I guess you're right. I don't know why I'm so down on the old man. Most times he seems like a stranger." He stopped to conjure a time when the Colonel was a strange man who came home for visits. He and the war had seemed synonymous, distant and impersonal to a little boy. Papa Dennick had been more of a father. "Mark, I went to see your Papa. We had a great talk. You know, I think he really understood. Hey—what are you doing here? You're supposed to be in Washington."

Like Clarey's unhappy reality, Mark's also had to be faced. "It's too late for that. She refused to go. I think I know why. I could drag her a million miles from here and it wouldn't make any difference. She's built up a case against herself, afraid I could never come back home."

"But you've got to take her away."

"I can't fight her. The others, her parents, my family I could win against. Not her."

"You've got to fight for her. No matter what. The only way is to fight!"

The outburst brought a nurse, wary of Clarey's behavior, to the foot of his bed. Mark indicated that the situation was under control. "Clarey, I can't camp on her doorstep. Should I starve myself, the broken-hearted lover? Her father's taking a job in Cleveland. Maybe." Until now the distant future had been an unbearable thought to him. "Maybe I'll join her there later if she'll have me."

Clarey was greatly disappointed that his friend had weakened and lost the fight, that he could not mount the insurmountable. How many times had he fought against the odds, at last thrown his life into the battle? "I'll be out of here in a few days. I'll help you fight for her."

"In a few days I'll be gone. I can't stay in this town another day. Too many bitter memories here."

"When we were kids we fought to get what we wanted. We never gave up."

Good fighters had feared Clarey's talent, the eye and the brain to stop time and compute the counter blow. He had loved the game of it, the winning and the losing. Mark had never understood the endless competition. He could only think to say, "When does all the fighting stop?"

Clarey reflected on the question. He seemed confused. It had never occurred to him that the game might end. Nor could he accept the fact that it had for him. "I was always the kid who wanted to pull the beard off the fake Santa. You were the deep thinker. You tell me the answer."

A flattering accusation from Clarey, that Mark was a thinker of depth. Perhaps he had appeared to be in all the times he had so little to say. At this point in life, he understood neither Clarey's fight nor his own. He had sought a changing world. There was no rule against a good life being made better. Was it why he had bolted the system, the imprisonment of the mind Papa had so carefully prepared for him? The prescribed life was based on outdated laws issued by men of the past. Clarey had given his vitality to it, and Mark was helpless to explain why. "I wish I knew the answers, Clarey, for both of us."

"Well, I'm not very smart. Maybe I'm running on instinct, but I think it's up to us to pull off the disguises and show them up for what they are. I get mad when they don't fight fair. The way to win is to crush the people in your way."

His arrogance equaled that of Father Hurley's. The priest had put aside spiritual purity when there was a battle to be won. They had to meet hostility with more hostility. They should now give Michelle to the legal process and watch it dismember her spirit. Mark could never go through with it. If the alternative made him a coward, a coward he would have to be. "My fight is over," he said. "I'll be clearing out of here tonight."

Clarey thought of Gloria and her dream of escaping to the beaches of California. "Gloria wants to leave, too. Everybody's going on a trip but me."

Mark knew that the truth was a necessary matter of trust. "Clarey, I spent the night on her couch. I didn't have any place else to go. I know that she's planning to leave tonight with Silly. If you want my advice, you'll let her."

The advice was wasted. Clarey could never give her up. He was alarmed that she was leaving so quickly. He thought of a way to keep track of her at least for a while. "Mark, please go with her, keep track of her until I can get out of here. I'll catch up to you as soon as I can, I swear it."

Mark doubted that he wanted to get involved with Gloria. Travel would be much less complicated alone.

Clarey saw the indecision in his face and began to panic. He tried to sit up, the tube in his nose drawing taut. "You've got to do this for me. I'll lose track of her otherwise. You've got to promise. . . ."

The Colonel appeared in the ward, puffing sourly. Mark held Clarey down by the shoulders until he relaxed. "All right, Clarey. I'll try."

Colonel Boriakoff had the carriage of a military man even in a chair. He began his lecture in slow, sonorous tones, ignoring Mark and punctuating the air with an outstretched finger.

Gloria was storing dishes in a box. She was angry and glad to see Mark. "Where've you been? It'll be dark soon. I have to get the car packed."

"Gloria, Clarey is in the hospital. He's very sick."

"I'm sorry to hear that. You saw how he was drinking. He did it to himself."

"I told him you were leaving tonight. He asked me to go with you to keep track of you."

The thought that Clarey would be tracking her sat her down, a dish hanging from her fingers. "He'll never let me go, will he?"

"It's impossible for Clarey to give up on anything."

"Well, he will on me. I can promise that."

Gloria spent the next hour packing tins of anchovy paste, hearts of palm, endives, *fillets* of *thon blanc,* and other essentials to her diet. Pressed by time, she prodded Silly to help but preempted her in every chore, linen, toiletries, until Silly became exasperated, packed her own things, and settled in the car, the pupils of her eyes like buckshot.

"Moody," Gloria said, but Mark saw a forecast of trouble. If this was Gloria's good mood, her happiness in leaving "Noo All-yens" once and for all, what was to be her temperament during the long trip ahead?

Feeling useless, Mark crossed over to the Half Moon Bar, ordered a beer and a po-boy, and asked for his change in nickels. He watched Gloria pack her car as he ate. Dressed in sun shorts that displayed her dimpled behind, she moved like a quivery crook, darting back and forth, glancing over her shoulder as if she feared the landlord might suddenly appear to demand the next month's rent. Her car leaked at the curb. Someone had written, "Wash me," in the dust of its trunk. It had opened its seams to tropical summers, but it had good tires and the motor was sound. If they drove slowly, Mark thought they would make it to California.

He then spent an indecisive hour in a phone booth, sitting before the pile of nickels. Each time he dialed Michelle's number he cradled the phone before it rang. What would he say to her? To speak he must hear his own voice. He feared it would lack conviction. He thought of calling his father and his brother. Either conversation, as the one with Michelle, would become an abject apology, for Mark had managed to please no one but William Janin. He scooped the change angrily into his pocket and returned to Gloria's apartment.

Near twilight, when Gloria indicated she was ready, Mark carried the last suitcases to the car. As they drove west, Gloria matched each Cajun village to its place on a map, LaPlace, Gareyville, Prairieville, dismissing each one sourly. She was happy to escape New Orleans for the Mardi Gras, calling it a holiday for drunks and homosexuals. They used the same floats every year anyway. Outside Baton Rouge, in the moonlit stubble of harvested canefields, she took the wheel and spoke a commentary on Louisiana. It was scummy and full of rats and alligators. Silly sat quietly, her fists rolled in her lap. Mark fell asleep watching lightning flashes open cracks in the sky.

Dr. Morton Krasner, deputy director of the Board of Health, strode into his office like a man relishing an important success, as indeed he was, for in a last bold stroke he had accumulated enough evidence to fire Pearl Marie LaCroix. He had only to write the final letter of dismissal. As he wound a sheet of paper into his typewriter, he reflected on the long, frustrating struggle.

His relationship with the Registrar had begun more than a year ago, when he was appointed to head the board. He had thought it an unacceptable burden and wanted to refuse. He had a thriving practice, a growing family, a neglected wife, and as his friend, Ben Fruchart, put it, "A need for roller skates to speed his calls at the hospital." A possible television series—"Doctor on Roller Skates!" He would not have accepted the job had the Mayor not called personally. "I need you, Mort," his Honor said. "The former board never met, not once. The whole department's in a terrible mess." As Mort listened, he divided his day into minutes and seconds, searching for moments to spare. When the call ended, he was committed. Well, if he must, he must. A standing physician in the community could not shirk civil responsibility.

"By the way, Mort," the Mayor had said, "There's no pay for the job," and hung up. The Mayor was a very busy man.

Splitting the divisions of the department among the new members of the board was like slicing up a rancid pie. The room shuddered when the Sanitation Bureau was brought up. Dr. Murray Nossiter said, "What do you do, go around telling women a sanitary belt is not a shot in a clean glass?" Everyone laughed. The bad joke frankly summed up what they knew about the Health Department.

Mort was made deputy director by acclamation. He decided the fairest way to assign jobs was to draw lots. Ben Fruchart drew the Bureau of Communicable Disease Control. Murray suspected a plot when he got sanitation. Mort sighed relief when he took for himself the Bureau of Vital Statistics. Every doctor resigns himself early to a quagmire of paper work. Mort was something of a whiz at it. While Murray was all over town inspecting public latrines, Mort would be looking after a tight little bureau of records. He could possibly get by with a semi-annual look-see. Or so he thought. That was before he met Pearl LaCroix.

It took a full month to arrange an appointment with her. He was offered a chair and told to wait. In minutes, his dream of a tight little bureau crumbled. The office operated near the efficiency level of a traffic jam. With only a handful of people in line for documents, the office force seemed unable to handle the work. Clerks jostled one another rushing from typewriter to filing cabinet to counter in a frenzy. Telephones went unanswered. Questions were answered in a common shriek. At one end of the counter, a black man who obviously could not write, hunched dumbly over a form, frustrated by the show. Over this chaos stood the Registrar's assistant, a man in a green eyeshade, ordering his troops about as if he were a general. Mort heard him address a young couple requesting a marriage license. "Your birth date is not filled in," he said and thrust the application in the boy's face. "I can't research your records without the correct date, can I?"

"I'm not sure of the date," the boy said. "Mom says the tenth of April, but Dad says the eleventh."

"That's not my problem. Put down the date or get out."

The boy looked bewildered and frightened.

Then the Registrar swept through her door. "I'll handle this personally," she said and faced the boy squarely. "You know perfectly well why you don't have the correct date. Your birth certificate got conveniently misplaced. You also know that everyone born in White Castle is a half-breed." She left him gaping, said to Mort, "Come in," and stalked into her office. Mort followed, grateful that she had closed her door.

Her desk was a clutter of papers, photocopies, today's lunch, old telephone messages. He looked at her over the rubble. "Yes, it's a mess," she said, "because I have to handle every detail in the office personally."

146

"Did you have to be so rough on the boy?"

"Dr. Krasner, I know why you're here. The Mayor gets complaints. Well, I'll tell you I run this office by the rules. Where race or legitimacy are in doubt, I can't issue a document without precise information. The law is very clear. Sometimes my own files help, sometimes not."

The Mayor had mentioned the Registrar only briefly, calling her an irascible old woman. Mort saw that she was much more than that. "Your own files?"

She opened a drawer and took out a steel box. "My private register. Every scrap of it has been cross-checked against records in this and other parishes. It's a list of names I know to contain mixed blood. Like that boy out there. They leave it to me to tell him the truth about himself. It's what they pay me for." The Registrar stopped short of telling him she had planned the encounter to demonstrate the distastefulness of her important job. She pushed the box over to Mort. "It's privileged information, but now you're a member of the board. Have a look. You may need it when your children begin dating."

Mort did not open the box. "If the records ever disagree with your personal file, do you correct them?"

Meddling sawbones, she thought. Correct them indeed. Change them, he meant. "I have never altered a document in my life. Nor would I if my life depended on it. Besides, it isn't necessary. Look up the names yourself. DiPaola, DeJoie, Brown, Realtor. . . ."

"I'm talking about the human factor. Someone could correct a record as far away as White Castle or Calcasieu and swear it was true because it was based on their own private register."

The doctor was implying that someone would actually *change* a record. The forces opposed to her would stoop to such treachery to crush her. Looking for fault, he could invent one. She nearly hissed, "Doctor, you tell the Mayor I do my job by the rules. If he wants to change them, fine. In the meantime, I don't need any meddling from the Board of Health. Now if you don't mind, I'm busy."

A few days later, Mort got a call from an exasperated funeral director. "I've got some bodies I can't bury without death certificates," the man said. "The Registrar won't issue them until she finishes her research. I don't know what on. Tell that to the Mayor." The woman clearly had the bureau in a stranglehold.

Mort wrote a report recommending her dismissal. The Mayor received him warmly but seemed deeply troubled by the matter. "Some important people have been speaking up for her, Mort. If you could prove she did something illegal, an indiscretion. . . ."

"The way she tells those kids off across a crowded room. Is that indiscreet?"

"The kids have to be told. It's a civil service job. I can't go to the commission with anything less than proof of incompetence. They'll look at her twenty years of service and tell me to go run up a tree."

Mort left the Mayor's office angry, embittered that the Mayor had called on him in a time of need but refused to take action when the roles were reversed. He would have given up on the Health Department except for a catalyst that appeared to renew his efforts. Father James Hurley approached him with the *mandamus* plan. With young Emile Prudhomme as legal aide, "willing to take the case for free," they worked out the details only to watch it fail repeatedly. Father himself, after months of trying, admitted that the plan would not work. He was unable to find a young couple willing to make the sacrifice. The Registrar was secure on her throne. Eventually, Mort concluded that the one way to get LaCroix was to build a slick case against her. It would be based on her arrogance to the public and her insolent treatment of her superiors. With luck and some help from Ben Fruchart, he hoped he could charge her with insubordination.

He arranged a second meeting with the Registrar but did not mention that he would bring a witness. As expected, it was a repeat performance. Ben's presence failed to surprise or impress her. She made them wait to experience the chaos of her office. Once invited inside, Ben could only watch with disbelief as she made her speech on rules, laws, and meddling officials. When Mort brought up bad public relations, she scowled, "This is the Office of the Registrar, not City Public Relations." He ordered her to cooperate fully or face disciplinary action. She dismissed them rudely. It was the dare they had hoped for, the substance for the charge of insubordination. As they left, they saw a cartoon posted on the bulletin board, a grinning doctor with the caption, "Big Brother is Watching You."

"Write your letter of dismissal," Ben said. "I'm sure the Mayor will back you. We can only hope the Civil Service Commission sees it our way."

But Mort stewed on it for days. Important people, the Mayor had said, were speaking up for her. Did the charges seem trumped up—bad public relations, delaying the issuance of official documents, rudeness to the public, lack of leadership, insubordination? There would be publicity, possibly a sympathetic outcry demanding an appeal. He could predict her argument. She was obeying the law; goddamned doctors were meddling outside their sphere.

Then came the surprise call from Emile Prudhomme. Miss LaCroix had actually interfered personally in a case by invading the privacy of a family involved in a miscegenation dispute. She had moved out of *her* sphere, a serious mistake if Mort could prove it. He decided to make a play as bold as the Registrar's own. He drafted a formal complaint, implying in it that Miss LaCroix's visit had caused great distress in the family. He addressed it to himself and worded it strongly, demanding immediate disciplinary action. At the bottom of the page he typed the name Stephen Dennick.

Papa received him warily, expecting a repeat of the LaCroix visit. But as he read the complaint twice over, he remembered his whimsical dream of a pact with Mark and Michelle. Yes, he had wished that the Registrar had delayed her visit to spare a dying old man. Her faked compassion had irritated him. "You have no idea how much the matter has distressed me. My son is gone."

Dr. Krasner recognized the signs of approaching death. The old man feared he would not see his son again. "It's what we'd like to prevent in the future, Mr. Dennick. The woman is completely out of order. She had no right to come to you. It's none of her affair."

"If she had not come . . ." Papa left the thought incomplete.

"I think I should also explain there might be some unpleasant publicity. Miss LaCroix will appeal to the Civil Service Commission. Your name might be in the papers."

Papa considered the thought for a long moment. Then, surprising Mort, he signed the paper without further urging.

Back in the office, Mort rejoiced. A complaint from a private citizen on what the Mayor would call an indiscretion, on top of all the other charges, might just stick. He called Father Hurley to give him the good news. "I'm really surprised the old man signed it," Father said. "He was dead set against the affair from the beginning."

"He's deeply hurt that his son left town. Maybe he feels a bit of conscience for driving him away."

"Yes. Stephen Dennick is a good man."

"Anyway, I thought you'd enjoy the news. I'm firing the Registrar today."

"Mort, are we simply hatching another LaCroix?"

The reference was to Thelma Petit, who was in line to succeed the Registrar. The point had nagged at Mort. The woman had been trained by a master whose footsteps were impressive. He refused to dwell on it, feeling that the new Registrar would have learned something from the demise of her predecessor. "Father, please. One problem at a time."

"And there's still the law."

"Yes, sadly. But there's no reason we can't go through with the *mandamus* plan. We'll get our test case yet. This is at least a beginning. Rejoice, Father."

As Mort structured his letter of dismissal, rain lashed at his window, the start of a violent storm. He dwelled for a moment on his last words to the priest. It was a beginning. He would indeed like to be present to witness the ending. The rain came down harder as he hammered at his typewriter.

Matt Dennick met the full force of the storm as he turned his car onto Veterans Highway. He pulled to the side of the road. In moments, water overflowed the center trench to make the street impassable. He relaxed as his breath fogged the windows. His game leg ached. He lifted it and spread it gingerly along the seat. He was grateful that the rain would cancel the parade of the Crewe of Hermes. It was Marylene's favorite. He had promised her they would go downtown to see it together. But handling a small child in a crowd was exhausting, and he was already tired from a day of thinking dark thoughts of failure. Matt believed he had failed his brother, his father, and himself. As he sat alone in his car, he was saddened because he felt he could not tell the whole truth to the closest person in his life, his wife Marylene.

On orders that morning from Papa, Matt had spent several hours searching for a clue to his brother's whereabouts. He had little to report. The delay would give him time to frame what information he did have into words of encouragement for his father.

He had first called Michelle, the hoped for solution to Mark's disappearance. As he talked to her, he pretended ignorance, hating himself for the deception, able to think only of the insults Emma's report had delivered to him. The old woman had related every detail over the telephone, embellishing the story with tales he could only describe as lore. William's arguments became a muddle in her head: "He says they're diseased. Got cycle cell amenias in their blood. Did you know it's catching? They're criminals, too. Exits and whys all over their chromosomes. He has proof. I know one thing for sure. Color crops up every third generation." Matt told her not to call again, explaining that the baby was sick with a cold. Emma prescribed a potherb broth of sassafras and parsley and blessed them with silence. Marylene wept and he was unable to console her.

At the top of his list of failures was his ignorance of the situation until it was too late to do anything about it. Why had Mark not told him the truth? The fact spoke sorely of a brother's trust, if indeed any trust remained between them. Matt felt responsible for the loss. He had allowed them to drift apart, content in his own narrow world, impatient with Mark's lack of responsibility. Mark was the subject of conversation. He was getting the railroad job. He was the one with a future. Irritated, Matt had cut himself off. The result was clear. He had not been told because his brother expected no support from him. In the midst of crisis, a severe blow had been dealt to an already tenuous relationship.

Had he been told, would he have taken a stand in favor of his brother? Should he now? He knew something of the lies they were using. He had heard them many times from William. He should have been in the room beside his brother to counter them. Was it too late to do it still? He would have to endure Papa's disapproval, William's contempt. He decided against it. It was useless to run up the warning after the storm has passed. He felt guilt even for that. It seemed a bit of evidence of a remaining spark of his own careful indoctrination.

With the day's investigation completed, he knew he had lost the chance to help. Clarey had made it clear. Matt had called the Colonel, learned about Clarey, and rushed to the hospital. Clarey welcomed him with the left-handed shake. "I think you missed him by now," he said. "He left last night with Gloria."

"Do you know where?"

"I don't think they had an actual destination. Maybe California. Too painful to stay around here."

Matt sat rejected. "Clarey, he should have told me he was in trouble. I could have helped."

"It wouldn't have made a difference. It was his fight. He fought them all but lost in the end because he couldn't fight Michelle."

"If you hear from him, please let me know."

"I know he'll keep in touch. Matt, you might try Gloria's apartment. She's fairly unpredictable."

The apartment was stripped of personal belongings, but

Gloria's name was still on the doorbell. A neighbor directed him to the landlady, a woman beside a pool two doors away. She was oiling her skin with paste and cursing the cool February sun. "I knew the girl all right. The racket that came out of there at night. I could hear them all the way down here."

"Did she leave a forwarding address?"

"Nope. She just drove away with a boy and another girl. She didn't say where. I'm glad to be rid of her. Lucky the rent was paid." She swam out of the straps of her swimsuit, using them to correct her pendulous bustline. "You a cop?"

"No. I think the boy might be my brother."

Her eyes dropped to his braced leg and back to his face. It was the familiar reaction of a stranger to a cripple. "You look like him. But he was darker, with very brown eyes. He looked at me and I thought he looked like Jesus."

Matt crossed to the Half Moon Bar, certain that Gloria's companion was his brother. Papa would consider the information worthless without a specific destination.

Leblanc, the barman, was sucking on a cigar, the smell of burning rope. He did not know Mark. Gloria, he remembered with a leer, "Had a real fine built. She was always talking about California. A girl like her could do pretty good freelancing in a place like California." Matt assumed that Leblanc thought her the kind of girl who was not above earning a living in the ancient way.

As Matt drove home, the rain began with large drops that splashed like asterisks on the banquette. He discussed the details of his investigation with Marylene but did not mention his feelings of personal failure. With dread he thought of the report he must make to his father.

Papa and Emma were in their usual places on the gallery, bundled against a damp chill in the air. Matt hobbled from his car, managing what speed he could through the dregs of the street. He declined Emma's offer of a rocker and sat on the bare floor. He did not want to make his report in her presence. Papa did not open the subject. He only looked into the rain-washed street, watched as an oily residue flooded the lawn, aware that the sludge would inhibit the spring grass. He looked shrunken in the dimming light, the threads of his neck straining to hold his head aloft. Matt hoped he might fall asleep and postpone the report. There was so little to tell.

Emma began in a monotone that suited the mood. "Matt, your Papa hasn't eaten a thing in days. I bring him every kind of food and he never touches it. He hasn't the strength to get out of bed mornings. Can you do something with him? I tell you one day it'll be too late . . ." She stopped, regretting her blunder. The thoughtless reference to his illness had been unintentional. She began rocking swiftly in her chair. "I just think he should take better care of himself is all."

"I feel all right," Papa said. "You don't have to worry about me." Papa had known the truth since his trip to the hospital. He knew that everyone, down to the littlest of Delia's tots, also knew. Yet he continued to pretend robust health as best he could in their presence, even enduring the morning sun to hide the blotches on his arms. Death, he believed, was a private matter to be accepted with dignity. His chief fear was that it was closer than anyone had guessed, and that there might not be time to settle things with Mark.

They listened to the rain until it became apparent to Matt that Emma intended to stay for the gossip. He thought of Marylene and the baby alone in the storm and wished he were with them. He started with a fact he knew would please his father. "Mark didn't leave with Michelle."

"Thank heavens for that," Emma said.

"William called to tell me that," Papa said. "Did you find out where he went?"

"I talked to some of his friends. Apparently he didn't tell any of them."

Papa slumped in his chair, his worst fear confirmed. "He loved his home, Matt. I know he wouldn't have gone away again if this terrible thing hadn't happened to him."

It had been a proud home, Matt thought, made so by the strength of a prideful man whose home was the most important thing in his life. It was warm, bright, clean, made of stone and wood like the rocks and slats of that pride. It was a house of gleaming furniture, good food, starched fresh clothing. Papa saw

154

to it all with great care. But was it enough? There had been so little laughter. "It's a fine home," Matt said.

"He's a good boy. I raised him in the church so he'd know what's right."

The boys had learned it well. The Commandments, the Sacraments, the Golden Rule. Matt remembered Latin prayers set to memory. They learned to genuflect when lighting beeswax candles, to walk the Stations of the Cross, to honor their father and their mother while they also learned: The black man is inferior, eats garfish and cats, is diseased, and is good for little more than hard labor. It was a strange mixture of dogma and legend, the wisdom of the Church and home, but no boy was permitted to doubt it openly.

Emma said, "I believe it's a sin for a boy to leave his sick Papa."

Matt wondered what trifles Aunt Emma carried to the confessional. Her kleptomania? Had she ever committed a mortal sin knowingly because she was weak? Never one covetous desire or one false witness? One profanity in the name of the Lord? He did not have the anger in his heart to ask the questions.

"It's over now," Papa said. "I can do no more."

The storm had diminished. The wind handled the trees gently. The rain came down in spears against the lamplights. Matt stood and felt the blood rush with prickly greed into his bad leg. "I've got to go, Papa. Marylene's alone with the baby. I'll check on some more leads tomorrow."

As he hobbled to his car, Matt again felt great despair. He was much like his Papa in his pride and his house of gleaming furniture, his perfect world of contentment. According to the teachings, a man was required to make the good life for himself if he could. He had to go on doing it until he died. Matt felt grateful for the rule. He could go to his wife and say nothing to her. They had discussed Mark and Michelle at length; helpless rumination had laid the problem to rest. It would grow cold in the routines of life.

When Matt had gone, Emma blew her nose. "Dominick will be waiting for me. Can I get you something to eat?"

"Please go home, Emma."

Inside Papa sat quietly, listening to surviving thrusts of rain on the rooftop. The sound conjured voices for him, and he remembered his boys as they were when they were young. They were happy children with bright smiles and hair tossed in their faces. He longed to be back in that time and place. The words he would say to them would somehow be different now. He had a lifetime of experience to draw upon.

At his desk, he began a letter. The words came with difficulty, for in his lifetime Stephen Dennick had not been a man of sorrow. His hand faintly trembled as he wrote.

My dear son Mark,

I am very sorry that you are not home today. I do not fault you, aware as I am of my part in driving you away. I must tell you that I did not approve of William's tactics. I had no idea he would bring up all that old racial propaganda. I told him only to instruct you on the law. When I learned the truth, I nearly forbade him from entering my home again. He is very sorry, or at least he pretends to be. I will leave it alone. William has his own conscience to face one day.

The property deal will come out of escrow very soon now. The money is yours and Matt's to do with as you please. It is not a great deal that I leave you. I wish I could do more. All my life my ambition has been to provide a future for my boys. You were good boys and I swore I would do that. Never have I had the slightest doubt that you would both turn out fine, carrying on for me the way you are.

I spoke to William on the phone this morning. He believes you did the right thing in leaving as you did. I am not as sure it was the correct action. While it is true that you have dissolved a difficult relationship and spared the parties involved, I am not at all sure in the aftermath that the conflict should not have been faced squarely and resolved courageously. Now we can only hope that it will soon blow over. My only wish is that we could have discussed it more before you left. There are many things left to be said. The written word fails me. Let me just say that you have had more than your share of bad luck. That fact weighs heavily on me.

There is a bit of good news. William assures me that the railroad job is yours any time you want it. I made him promise that. I know he will stick to it. He also said he would do all in his power to compute your seniority to the date we signed the Tammany property deal. I think that's fair, considering you would be starting about now if this other situation had not developed. So take note. No one holds bad feelings for you. You have your job and home whenever you wish. I'm sure there will be happiness in it for you. Until then, may God be with you in all your travels.

With deep affection,

Papa

He folded the letter into the pages of *The Oregon Trail* and smiled, for he had known of the secret place for years. He replaced the volume upside down on the shelf, pausing to regret not having read it. Then he stored the thought along with the rest of the world he had not experienced. There was not time to do everything. He thought of his wife and sons and the total of their years together. It had been a good life but not without hardship. Instinctively, he knew it would be better for his boys.

In the darkness, he climbed the stairs and went into his bed. As the dawn lighted the rain-washed streets of New Orleans and all living things paused in memory of the storm, Papa Dennick died.

Pearl LaCroix received Dr. Krasner's letter of dismissal by special messenger. Attached to it was an apologetic endorsement from the Mayor's Office. More than shock, she felt contempt. She rang for her assistant. "The bastards," she said. "They finally got up the nerve to do it. Thelma, the Mayor actually regrets having to let me go in this way. Isn't it a pity?"

"Can they get away with it?"

"They wouldn't have gone this far if they expected to fail. Oh, but will they get a fight. I have good friends in this town. My appeal will be widely publicized. They're meddling with the law. The Civil Service Commission *and* the Mayor have to answer to the public." Her relish turned into a scowl. "One thing puzzles me. Stephen Dennick signed a complaint. Didn't he know that this action would expose his son and the girl?"

"Who knows? Maybe he was intimidated."

"It's possible, of course, but I don't know. The old man seemed strong-headed. I don't think he would be easily frightened."

Thelma Petit remembered an admonition to herself. From the time of Krasner's first inquiry, she had thought it a mistake to make enemies of the members of the Board of Health. While she admired Pearl's courage in opposing them where the law was involved, she thought her at times foolhardy, unnecessarily obstinate. "Damn them!" she said.

"Never mind them. They will pay their dues. There's something more important for us to consider here and now. Under the seniority rules, you will succeed me. Have you given it any thought? They expect you to be soft on the law."

Thelma had considered the possibility. She had secretly coveted the top job. But she was startled by the sudden turn, off balance. She knew what Pearl wanted to hear. "They won't sneak anything past me."

"You can expect pressure. That priest, Father Hurley, will be the first to visit you. He'll expect you to play the stooge."

The priest, Thelma thought, could have been Pearl's first blunder. Then the Mayor, Krasner, Fruchart—the mistakes had piled up. Had the Registrar purposely forced the test? Thelma said, "Yes, to save my soul from the eternal fires of hell. Don't worry, I can handle him."

"He's skillful, as they all are. The Mayor, the doctors. . . . You'll be dealing with tough men. You'll have to be tougher."

It seemed that Pearl was groping for an assurance of loyalty. "Please believe me, Miss LaCroix. I won't run the bureau any differently than you have all these years. The only right way to do it is by the law."

Yes, Miss LaCroix could be sure of it. She had hand-picked and personally trained her successor for precisely this moment. Privately, she wondered if she had wanted to be fired, weary of the abuse. No, she had foreseen the public appeal, sure she would win and at the same time expose some people in high places for their hypocrisy in interpreting the law. Thelma would only be a temporary replacement. The Registrar would return in glory. Satisfied that her successor would hold to the right path, Miss LaCroix took out her private register and reverently slid it across her desk. "It was given to me a long time ago by a very fine man. He made me promise to treat it with care."

Thelma thought it a sad moment. She squared her shoulders. "I swear to guard it always," she said and gave in to sentimentality, hoping her boss would not disapprove. "I'm very, very sorry."

"Just remember to watch for the half-breeds."

"I will."

"Now please leave me alone. I'll be out of here by five o'clock."

At the door, Thelma suppressed a sniffle. "The bureau won't be the same without you, Miss LaCroix."

Of that fact the Registrar could be sure, but she disliked the show of emotion. It was a sign of weakness. It could be a fatal one in the temperament of a Registrar. But perhaps not. Thelma had clutched the private register as if it were a treasure.

Miss LaCroix spent the afternoon alone in her office. In temporary defeat, she felt detached from the loneliness of the position she had held for so many years. She felt relief in her sudden freedom. That Krasner might win his case distressed her, but she was consoled by his failure to change anything. The bureau would go on functioning as in the past. The laws remained. The private register was still useful.

She also reflected on the curious motive that would make Stephen Dennick sign the complaint against her. The old man had seemed so grateful for her visit. Yet in a stroke, he had made his family secret public, creating circumstances that could drive his son away with the girl. She dismissed the old man as probably addled, for she knew in his senses he could never do a thing like that. She hoped he would not choke on tomorrow's newspapers.

When her personal things were packed, Miss LaCroix dialed the number of the New Orleans *Item,* a newspaper that delighted in ruffling the City Administration. "I want to speak to the managing editor," she said. "Mr. Joseph Deschamps. Yes, it's important. I'll hold." When she had held the line for several minutes, she said, "Why the hell is it so hard to get anything done around Mardi Gras time?" Deschamps came on the line as if he had heard her and did not want to incur her wrath.

For weeks Alfonso DeJoie had planned indecisively to go after the job in Cleveland. He was a cautious man. In challenge there was risk. While the financial rewards were great, a move would disrupt his well-ordered life. So he hesitated as circumstances piled up. Michelle had learned the truth about herself in the crudest possible manner. Her attempted suicide had terrified him. The fight with Mark and the news of his father's death left Michelle sickened and confined to her room. She felt she was to blame for everything.

Then Alfonso read of Miss LaCroix's dismissal. He was both pleased and shocked. The end of the woman's reign was comforting, but the newspapers mentioned a complaint from a private citizen, Mr. Stephen Dennick. The Registrar had visited him to warn that his son had applied for a marriage license with a girl of mixed blood. Fortunately, the girl was not identified. Still Corrine became hysterical. Miss LaCroix was appealling her case. Michelle might be dragged into the controversy. Alfonso knew he must take his family from the city without further delay.

With his desperation under control, he put in a call to Vosbien Toys, Inc., and booked a flight to Cleveland. He was greeted by Leon Vosbien himself, who spoke non-stop from airport to office on his fall line, while kneading a wad of last year's top seller, Peppy Putty, in his fist. "We're going to take some of the toy business out of Cincinnati," he said. "I'll show you how."

Vosbien's son Dean, a replica of his father except that he had hair, brought out a Superman comic book. Vosbien opened a plastic Easter egg and took out another glob of putty. "Everything is born from an egg. Dean thought of that. Children can understand it." He bounced the glob on his desk and sculptured an aardvark. "Think of all the young sculptors growing up." Then he pressed it against the comic book and thrust it into

Alfonso's face. The impression of the man of steel was clear to his curly forelock. "I've got the goods. I need the men to get them in the stores. The reason you're here."

"I'm a good salesman, Mr. Vosbien."

"You wouldn't be here if you weren't. I checked on you. Discreetly, of course. I need good men, family men. Men who understand children. Men like that inspire integrity. Know what I mean?"

"I have a child, a daughter."

"I know. Al, when you look at a Vosbien man, you know he would never sell a dangerous toy to a kid. He'd quit first. More than that, I need men of ideas."

As Vosbien talked, his son demonstrated some of the other new toys. There was an Eskimo yo-yo, two leather pouches attached to strings of different lengths. He skillfully spun the pouches in opposite directions, smiled like a little boy, and the pouches collided in mid-air. Vosbien predicted it would be bigger than the yo-yo if they could only find an imaginative name for it. When Alfonso suggested "bopper balls," Vosbien came to his feet. "Dean, put that in your notebook with the rest. That's the kind of thing I want, Al. Men of ideas."

Alfonso listened attentively, thinking of the New Orleans newspaper in his briefcase, while Vosbien built up Cleveland. There were figures on median income, industrial output, gross toy sales. He explained his theory that extra money is usually spent on the kids. The right product could nab a hunk of that cash. Vosbien Toys expected to double last year's sales. He only needed the men, new members of the family. He symbolically included Alfonso in his group when he said, "Can you keep a secret? I'll show you my real ace in the hold." From a locked drawer, he took out a ray gun. He aimed it and pulled the trigger. It made a drivel of smoke and a squawk like a sick chicken. He whispered, "The Ionization Nebulizer."

Like the ending of a corporate fairy tale, they would all live happily ever after. His enthusiasm out of control, Vosbien resolved to tier his company with slabs of concrete accomplishment. Alfonso had to hold back a laugh while wondering if Vosbien had ever employed a Madison Avenue cast-off. Yet he liked the man.

There was sincerity in his ambition and his loyalty to his people. Alfonso would have no trouble making the transition from advertising to toys. Even the jargon was interchangeable. It would be a fresh start. Cleveland was a good long way from New Orleans. When at the airport Vosbien clasped his hand firmly, Alfonso knew he had clinched the job. "I only have to take it to my board," he said in a way that implied it was his decision alone, and added that he would call to confirm on Friday.

Only one thing about the man disturbed Alfonso. "We have a large colored population here in Cleveland," he said. "Naturally a crime problem. But don't let that disturb you. The city's moving ahead just the same." Alfonso knew he must successfully conceal his past to endure at Vosbien Toys. Rather than anxiety, he felt relief, for that was precisely what he wanted to do.

Aboard the return plane to New Orleans, Alfonso felt better than he had in days. The situation was resolving itself neatly. They could pack and leave almost immediately. Corrine would be thrilled. He decided to withhold the good news until the family sat down for the Friday meal, after the call from Leon Vosbien.

"No, I can not wait until after Mardi Gras," Michelle said to Mrs. George on the telephone. "I'm in my twelfth week already. You have to do it now."

"All right, honey. Don't panic."

Michelle timed the appointment to coincide with her father's trip to Cleveland. Since the attempted suicide, he eyed her suspiciously. With him out of the house, she could make a feminine excuse to her mother that she needed some private things, to be alone to think some private thoughts.

She had spent two days with Dr. Dassin's book, *Mostly Murder,* and now considered herself very pregnant. The doctor had told her as much about her twelve-week-old fetus as she cared to know, and she was confused on only one point, what he called the "Quickening," that time when the mother first feels the baby move. It happens about midway in the pregnancy, but Michelle thought she felt him kicking every day. She charged it to her vivid imagination and put aside a question to ask an obstetrican somewhere out in the distant future. More urgent matters had to be attended to in the present.

For her appointment, she decided to be anonymous. It was a daringly illegal thing she was doing. No one must recognize her or remember her later. She dressed in a plain coat-suit more suitable for spring, but aptly concealing. She made up her face vaguely, a dusting of powder, a hint of rouge, and piled her hair like black ropes. Through dark glasses she approved of the result. A neat and plain appearance for her date. She was sure that no one who knew her would recognize her at a glance. At her bank, she withdrew two hundred dollars and rolled the money in her handkerchief.

"Vacation?" the teller said and flirted.

"A rainy day," she said, pleased that she was still outwardly attractive and walked out holding her breath to de-emphasize her middle.

On Saint Charles, she hailed a taxi, using the rolled handkerchief to cover her face. Secretgirl would leave no tracks. She gave the address in Central City, and the driver appraised her curiously, unable to place the neat pretty girl in the neighborhood. Michelle checked her face in the rear-view mirror, aware that the powder did not cover the parched redness under her eyes. She had done a lot of crying lately. A result of her father's habitual thoroughness with the *Times-Picayune,* she had learned of Papa Dennick's death. Alfonso had read the obituary and broken it to her gently, apologizing as if it were his fault. Locked in her room, she had cried for hours for Mark, for his father, and for her plan to set them free. Then she read of Miss LaCroix's dismissal. The event had enforced her decision. No child deserved to grow up looking forward to its date with the new Registrar.

The driver found the address on Carondelet without trouble. He turned to his passenger as if to question what business she might have there. The house was old and tilted, a single column holding it up like a crutch. Its wormy gallery had never seen paint. Michelle wondered what sort of ogre could possibly lurk inside it. She tipped the driver poorly, hoping he would not remember her, and turned briskly from the house as if afraid someone would sprint through the door to snare her.

After a block, she felt foolish. What was she afraid of? Mrs. George had been sympathetic on the phone. She had offered understanding. A girl in trouble was her business. Michelle walked back slowly, feeling lonely on the littered street. Black children playing in the gutters watched her curiously. Central City had been a shortcut to town, one she had always driven with the car doors locked, ignoring the dark faces that warned she was out of her place. She was not afraid but wished she was not alone. She thought of Donny, his sweet concern for her and his offer to help. She fought an impulse to call him. His sympathy would make her cry. She had cried enough.

Michelle forced herself to think clearly. In the two days with Dr. Dassin, she had struck down his arguments one after another, beginning with his opening remark, "Abortion is a heinous crime against all mankind, infanticide. The expulsion of a viable fetus is performed illegally in some countries, usually by an outlaw quack untrained in basic medical techniques, and generally for an enormous sum of money." She had an answer for that. Perhaps the most viable argument against him. Why illegal and why a quack? A simple act made complex. Dilation and curettage. A table, stirrups, speculum, probe. Why clothes hangers and knitting needles? She pictured Mrs. George standing over, the quack comforting her. Then a scrape, a prickly pain, and a gush. Easier than a date with the Registrar.

The doctor continued, "The only justifiable abortional act is one committed upon a female by a duly licensed physician acting under a reasonable belief that such is necessary to preserve the life of the female." The statement was stiff, the law laid down, and hardly acceptable to modern woman. When must it be necessary that the female die? Immediately or in a week or a month? Who is to make the life or death judgment? The decision that a woman was denied, holy medicine was granted.

Still he continued, "Any other abortion is a crime, with the seriousness of the offense depending on whether the operation was performed before or during the final trimester of pregnancy." That put it on an academic plane. Gladly, she picked up the thread. He spoke of crimes, but what of rights? The right of privacy and liberty in sex. Surely the right to conceive extends to the right not to conceive. Abortion is a sure-fire contraceptive. A woman should not be deprived of her right to plan a family simply because contraception fails or has not been used. If we are trading lives, then who has the best right to do the trading but the one who conceives it? Modern woman refuses, Dr. Dassin, to be the incubators of the human race.

Finally, the doctor had asked, "When does life begin?" She had the answer to that, too. The truth is that it does not begin. It began. Something happened a billion years ago to turn inanimate sludge into living cells, and it happened only once. Since then, life had been continuous. The human person is not continuous but an individual. The early fetus is not an individual but a mass of protoplasm, less than a fish, no more trouble than a toothache. It was her right to see it handled in dishwashing gloves, discarded, a simple mistake. Think of the social implications, doctor. Read the statistics on malformed infants, simplemindedness, insanity, mental deficiency, starvation through over-population. The loss of healthy effective human beings is a small problem by comparison. Michelle looked at the money through the gauzy handkerchief, at the famous faces of presidents of the United States, all great men allowed by old-fashioned women to live. . . .

As she neared the house, Michelle thought of the one quirk in her argument. It was Mark. She had thought of him during the doctor's discussion of fetology. When a doctor treats a pregnant woman, he instinctively knows he is treating two persons. It was enough to make her understand she was thinking for three, herself, her twelve-week-old, and Mark. What of his rights? He had half the job of making the zygote. If he could see her now, here on this street, would he be repulsed and do to her what she was about to do to it? It was her last thought, and completely unresolved, as she knocked and said, "I have an appointment with Mrs. George," surprised by the calmness in her voice.

An old black woman said, "Yass. Come in."

On a narrow Louisiana road that seemed a canyon walled by tall pine trees, Gloria tired of the driving and asked Mark to take over. She piled into the back seat and stripped off her blouse. "I'm bored," she said and sat proud and unashamed. Mark was momentarily distracted; Silly was irritated. But to Gloria it seemed quite the thing to do to break the boredom, there in a Louisiana parish where Christian state troopers were legendary for their rectitude.

To further lighten the tedium, she recited a poem taught her, she said, "by a famous Noo All-yens poet."

> "Little girls are made of
> Pre-pubescent boobs and pubes,
> And milligrams of fallopian tubes.
>
> Little boys are made of
> Stops and stalls, stumbles, falls,
> And hairless little bebe balls!"

She laughed and made up several others as she sat half naked. Silly glared silently out of a window. Mark was grateful for the cover of darkness. He pretended to listen while he could only think of Michelle among the stacks of the library, reading Ruppert Brooke or Gibran. Finally, Gloria said, "Y'all have no sense of humor," and slumped in her seat to count passing telephone poles.

Later she dressed and ate a midnight meal of canned goose paté and sliced celery knobs, which made her thirsty. She demanded a beer. Mark tried to explain that country stores did not remain open all night to accommodate travelers and she would have to wait until they found one open. Unhappy with the explanation, she cursed the state of Louisiana, crank teetotalers, and hard-nosed Baptists. Mark at last bought three quarts of beer. She drank one quickly and fell asleep, creating a longed-for silence.

As they crossed the Atchafalaya River, a tire exploded. They had no spare. Mark drove to a gas station in Krotz Springs on the rim. He chose a replacement from a used group and helped an attendant mount it. He also bought a spare, gaining Gloria's disapproval as he put it in the back seat next to her. "There's no room in the trunk," he said and she frowned.

When they were on their way again, Gloria stamped her feet and cursed the wind that matted her hair. "I can't stand it. I won't go another mile until I get some sleep in a real bed." She gathered her hair in her fists and checked her map. "The next big town is Shreveport. We'll find a big motel. I want a bed with cool sheets and enough water to sit in."

As a futile practical gesture, Silly said, "We haven't been on the road but a few hours. If we drive through the day, we cover most of Texas by nightfall."

"Oh, Silly, what's the hurry? I tell you I'm exHAUSTed. What do you say, Mark?"

"I don't care. We can stop if you want."

"Good. We'll get a nice modern motel, the kind with a heated swimming pool. I brought my bathing suit."

Gloria was clearly on a holiday, but she would not be granted her wish of comfort. The car died with a scalding hiss in a small town miles from Shreveport called Grand Bayou, a long way from a nice modern motel. The best accommodations they could get was a rotting bungalow hidden from the highway by tall grass, on a driveway clogged with mud. But it had a bathtub. Gloria went straight for it as Mark inquired about repairs on the car. The motel manager, a large Cajun man with ill-fitting false teeth, assured him that Grand Bayou had a first-rate mechanic. Sonny Chauvin was down at Bayou Pierre on a fishing trip. He would be back any day now. They were stuck until he returned. Gloria had some curses for the rotten luck, but she was too tired to make an issue of it. The sun had risen on a bright day before she settled into her promised sleep.

Mark awoke at sundown. Gloria was gone. He scrambled to the window. The manager was standing in the parking lot, as if waiting for the young man's reaction when he discovered the girl missing. "You slept all day," he said. "Folks sometimes do that when they're on the road."

"The girl with us. Did you see her?"

"She stood out on the highway about an hour ago. She caught a ride pretty quick."

"Did she say anything? Where she was going?"

The manager checked his pocket watch. It was a large one like Papa used to have. "Shreveport's about a two hour drive. You going to stay on overnight? Grand Bayou has a good eating place. We have a picture show, too."

"I have to get the car repaired."

"Sure. I'll let you know when Sonny shows up."

Silly had anticipated the possibility of being left behind. She was glad that Mark had been deserted as well. As Mark went inside, she was working herself into a quiet rage. "The bitch," she said. "I'm not a bit surprised. I know the way she uses people and then drops them." She took a folded wad of money out of a shoe and handed it to Mark.

He gave it back. "I have enough to fix the car."

"Mark, why fix it at all? It's her car, filled with her own junk. We could leave it and get on a bus."

"She'll be back. I promised Clarey I'd look after her."

"How long do you intend to wait?"

He did not answer. She would not ask again. As she dressed, she pondered the thought of setting out alone, planning to do just that if she had no other choice. Through the evening she watched Mark as he sat staring out at the empty parking lot. He seemed betrayed, deeply disturbed. She could not have known that his thoughts were all of Michelle as he remembered her at Pass Christian, the day she told him of the baby.

Sonny Chauvin returned from his fishing trip the following day. In less than an hour, he mended a ruptured radiator and replaced a manifold gasket on the car. Mark took Silly to the restaurant to celebrate. The food, *pot-au-feu* and soft-shell crabs, was good, the coffee strong. But she only picked at her plate, aware that she was being inspected by two middle-aged women. She got the message and attended a conference in the restroom. Later she made the excuse that she was going to the picture show. Marilyn Monroe was playing. She did not ask Mark to come along. He watched as she crept across the highway to be whisked away in a brand new car. In her bedclothes he found an apology, a hastily scrawled note. Silly was going on to California with some friends she had met. She had left the folded wad of money. He thought it an odd transcation. She had bought her freedom. She thought like that. Wondering if Gloria had fared as well, though not really caring, Mark bought a bottle of whiskey and settled into his room.

The motel had additional guests that night, a couple in faded denim with four small children. They all piled out of an old car. The children were cranky from the day on the road. They fought and rolled on the parking lot. The man worked on his car, while the woman started a cooking fire in the lot. The manager rushed to put it out and went away with a scorched boot that filled the air with the smell of burnt rubber. Mark finished the bottle quickly, vomited, and laid in the close air of the room, listening to the squeals of the children. The family was miserably poor, but they had one another. As always when he was alone in a strange place, he felt depressed, numb, his spirit disembodied, as if he could step beside himself and look at his life with indifference. Studied by a drunkard, it seemed a wasted, witless existence. At last the alcohol took over to permit him a drugged sleep.

Gloria's shrill falsetto, the southerner's faked enthusiasm, woke him at noon. She came in correcting the rump of a new silk dress and said in that high pitch, "Hi. Where's Silly?"

Mark had made his decision not to go on with her if she returned, but he was relieved to see her. The presence of someone familiar, even self-serving Gloria, banished the loneliness and turned his mind away from himself. His head was clogged. His skin ached. "She found some friends to take her to California."

"Funny, I expected you might be gone, but not her."

"Another day and you'd have missed us both. I was planning to drive out tonight. I'm going home."

"The car's fixed? How nice of you."

"You can have it back for eighteen dollars. That's what it cost me. I'll take a bus."

Gloria had anticipated the coolness. It was to be her punishment. She suffered patiently for a moment. "Mark, please don't be angry with me. Look, I'm with a friend of mine, out there in the car. He owns a bar in Shreveport. He gave me a job." She took a roll of bills out of her purse and spread them on the bed. "Two hundred dollars. We can go to California in style."

Mark's silence betrayed his thoughts.

"It is not what you think. I am not THAT kind of girl. That afternoon I woke up . . . well, I just couldn't stand being stuck in this dirty little town. This motel—the whole place smells of stale pee. I thought the car was finished for good. So I hitched a ride to Shreveport. I wanted to call you when I got there, but I couldn't remember the name of this place. Look for yourself. It doesn't have a name."

Gloria had found evidence of her intended good will. The place had no identification but the word, "Motel," handpainted on a hanging shingle.

The morning was unseasonably warm. She fanned herself with her purse and twisted her hemline above her knees. "It's so damned hot. We can have a cool drink. I want you to meet Drews." She called out and a head appeared from the car window, a mottled brown globe. "Drews, you got that vodka? We'll need grapefruit juice for salty dogs. Can you go and get some? Mark, I want you to believe I didn't mean to run off on you. I'd rather you threw me out right now than to go on thinking I'd do a thing like that. I wanted to come back right away."

"Gloria—stop! The talk is giving me a headache."

"Okay, don't let me make it up to you. I'm a dirty word. You can throw me out if you want. I'll even admit I deserve it."

"For Christssake shut up!"

The outburst sat her on the bed in sad contrition, her fingers picking nervously in her lap. The offer to make it up to him was in her posture, her thighs exposed up to the white pad of her crotch. She pleaded with outstretched arms, "Mark, please, let me make it up to you."

Mark felt intense contempt for the harlot's offer to pay a debt when none was owed. Angrily aroused, he wanted to hurt her with cold indifference. He pinned her roughly on the bed, threw back the dress, stripped off her pants. He entered her and finished

172

in a dozen thrusts, scattering the cash on the floor with his knees. As he tried to withdraw, she clung to him. She had not removed her shoes. A lock of her hair was dislodged. She was crying. He had not thought her capable of crying.

At the sound of Drews's approaching car, she rushed into the bathroom and came out, her makeup obviously corrected. Drews glistened after the hot drive. He said, "Day-um, it's hot," as Gloria introduced him. Standing his tallest, he was less than three-quarters of a man, gnomelike next to her.

They drank the grapefruit and vodka with ice borrowed from the motel manager. Drews recited what was no doubt an earlier speech of Gloria's on plans for fun on the way to California. They would see the Painted Desert, the Petrified Forest, the Grand Canyon, Tijuana. "Day-um," he said. Gloria wanted to swim in the Rio Grande, see a bullfight, eat a tortilla, and drink from a wineskin. She sat quietly through the speech, glowing content-edly, nearly wallowing as she stared respectfully at Mark. He had meant the rape to hurt her. It has chastened her instead.

Mark's mind drifted to thoughts of Clarey. Clarey would paint a desert for her, petrify a forest, his beloved Gloryory who had copulated with a gnome and a trusted friend. Why had Mark violated the trust? Simply to hurt her? He suspected the truth was more damning than that. He had done it because he needed her.

Gloria took the silence as further rejection and prescribed more penance for herself. "Drews, please go wait in the car. Mark and I have to talk private."

"Ah'll wait in the cau-er," Drews said.

"All right, Mark, go ahead and say it. You're thinking I'm a tramp. You think I slept with Drews for that money. It's why you wanted to hurt me."

"Yes, I wanted to hurt you. That makes me something close to what you are."

"Will you at least listen to why I did it? So you can maybe understand? Yes, I slept with him. He was nice. I needed some-one to be nice to me. As much as I wanted you, you never liked me. I was drinking . . . thinking about it. It was funny and sad. I thought how many times I'd given it away. Ole Glory was

173

always an easy make. She liked it too much. I . . . thought of you back here, how you didn't want anything to do with me. Then I decided, but when we got in bed I couldn't go through with it. I got sick. I threw up in the toilet. The toilet seat fell on my nose. Drews took care of me. He was kind. Mark, I was unconscious when he . . . well, I mean, that's just the same as not doing it at all, isn't it?"

Mark had witnessed her talent for rationalization before. How quickly she had disposed of Michelle as the cunning female determined to get pregnant. Mark had been cleared of any wrong-doing as easily as Gloria was now absolving herself. A toilet seat had caused her to stray from the path of decency. The proof was there on her nose, a nick, the corrupting blow of a toilet seat. "I don't think it matters now, Gloria."

"But it matters to me. I don't want you to think I'd do that with just anybody. What happened with Drews was biology. He doesn't mean a thing to me."

Mark began stuffing personal articles into his bag. "I'm going home."

"Take me with you."

"I can't. I've got to straighten out my life."

"But I can help you."

"Nobody can help me but myself."

She chewed her lips, trying hard for control. "Mark, I know you wanted to hurt me. I don't care about that. Maybe I wanted to be hurt. But I felt something awful wonderful. I thought about you, how sad you are. I wanted to help you. I'd do any-thing in the world for you, Mark."

He was moved by the genuine plea. It was a Gloria he had not experienced before. But he had made up his mind. He touched her cheek. "Goodbye, Gloria. I hope you find what you need."

She waited until he disappeared behind the tall grass along the highway. Then she threw open the door and screamed as loud as she could, "I need you!"

Drews came running. "You all have a spat?"

"No. He wanted to go home. He wouldn't take me with him. I guess he hates me. Sometimes I hate myself."

174

Drews slapped his thighs, an attempt to lighten the mood. "Well, there's our trip to California to think about, the Painted Desert and all those other places. I promised I'd take you."

"Drews, honey, you have to understand I can't do that now. I have to go to him. He'll be needing me."

"Uh-huh," he said and wiped the dome of his head with a handkerchief. "I figured something like that might happen when you asked me to drive you down here to Grand Bayou."

Early Friday morning, the day of the scheduled call from Leon Vosbien, Alfonso called in sick on his job. He lied that the gout made any activity unbearable, wondering why he thought an excuse was necessary. He was an executive in a large advertising agency, a prominent, substantial business man. Then why the symptom of insecurity? He resolved to start the job in Cleveland with a new confidence. He would simply take a day off whenever he wished.

His wife and daughter were still asleep. He left a note for them explaining that he expected a long-distance call, added that he would take care of the Friday shopping, and left the house on a secret errand. Enroute downtown, he was delayed by trucks placing barricades on Saint Charles Avenue in preparation for the evening parade. He would remember to return home by way of Tchoupitoulas Street along the river to avoid traffic.

Alfonso considered the distasteful task before him. He must break the news to his mistress, Josianne Fontanet. He disliked thinking of her in that way. It smacked of a bourgeois snobbery, the style of the semi-literate college girls who used the words *rendezvous* and *liaison*. Josianne meant more to him than that. For more than ten years they had been completely involved. He was certain he loved her, and despite periodic feelings of guilt brought on by an equal loyalty to his wife, he was helpless to break with her. She was younger than Corrine, and prettier, with a voluptuous figure and perfect white skin.

Was that fairness the true measure of his attraction, a whiteness that he had to possess? He knew there was much more. There was tenderness, understanding, mutual respect in their relationship. There was also sex as Alfonso had never experienced it. They experimented with positions Corrine would timidly call a bit unnatural. Naked dancing on a darkened gallery and nude dashes into the yard at night. They discovered oral things that

176

were quite nice, mirrors, and ice. Josianne did it all happily and willingly. Corrine would have paled at the suggestion. Alfonso had never known such fulfillment in his life.

He had borrowed a theory, probably a justification, on why he required a mistress. He had read a psychiatric report on the reasons married men stray. The report hypothesized the "Pedestal Complex," that adoration of the American man for the purity of his woman. How could the male animal, all erected and burning for a fresh approach, subject his bride to a mount from the rear? The bride, because she had been taught to do so, would gag at the thought of cunnilingus or fellatio. Plainly, sex was for making babies. Therefore, the frustrated husband had to look elsewhere for the real thing, while diligently using the missionary position in the bed of his helpmate. It was a rather bold hypothesis for careful Alfonso. He believed the author of the report a man acutely aware of the sexual nature of man.

He had discussed his thoughts with Josie. She had smiled and blushed and said she understood. She possesed a rare quality in women, the ability to make a man believe in himself. He had told her all his secrets. She had accepted him without question. Now he had to tell her he was leaving New Orleans for good. Would she understand that? The move would keep them apart for weeks until arrangements could be made. She would demand to know why the change was necessary. He was not sure he could successfully lie to her. Then why lie at all? Why not tell her the truth about Michelle's pregnancy and the possibility that his secret could be made public? She would understand, but he feared she would encourage him to stay and face the humiliation on his own ground. Alfonso could never do that.

She was still in her robe, brewing coffee, the strong aroma permeating the small apartment. "Shouldn't you be at work?"

"I felt tired this morning. I said to myself, why shouldn't I take a day off once in a while if I feel like it. I told them it was the gout, but it wasn't necessary. I'm not worried about this job anymore."

"Al, you have to have a job."

"I will have a new one in Cleveland."

Josie was stunned. She had thought it a routine trip to Cleveland. Now she realized he was planning a permanent move. It was the first time he had deceived her. "When did you decide this?"

"Some time ago. It's a good opportunity. A step up. Vosbien Toys, one of the biggest manufacturers in the country. The boss, Leon Vosbien, has been trying to get me for months. He's a wonderful guy. Sort of strait-laced and corny, but honest as a judge. I'm sure I'll do very well."

She sensed a lie in his causal disposition of an important move, as if he were holding something back. Last evening he had been similarly preoccupied with thoughts he was unwilling to share with her. She felt that he might at last be prepared to end their relationship but unable to do it boldly. It was like him to be indecisive. "Al, is it too difficult to say what you really mean?"

"I'm telling the truth. It's a job I can't refuse."

"I see. You will take your family to Cleveland and I'll stay here."

"No, not that. We'll be together again very soon. I just don't want you to follow me right away. As I said, Vosbien is very strait-laced. He wouldn't understand. I want to get settled first, be secure on the job. Then I'll send for you right away."

Still she did not believe him. If Cleveland was his plan to break with her, he was being too kind about it. "All right. If you can't say it, I can. I guess I always expected to become a part of that mysterious past of yours."

"But I don't want that. I promise we'll be together soon. I'll write to you, take care of you as I always have. That isn't the problem."

"Al, what is the problem?"

She knew him too well. How helpless he was in an argument with her. She had made him admit that there was a problem. "The problem is I'm going paranoid. I hear whispers everywhere."

"So that's it. Don't you realize you'll have neighbors in Cleveland? You'll still be a man with a very big secret."

"It's bigger now. Bigger than you know."

"What do you mean?"

Through coffee breath, he said, "I didn't want to bother you with it. New Orleans is no good for me anymore. Michelle is pregnant. She applied for a marriage license and found out the truth about herself. Josie, the boy's father signed a complaint against the Registrar for meddling. We're lucky we're not already in the newspapers."

Josianne now fully understood. She had read the reports of Miss LaCroix's dismissal. Alfonso feared a public disgrace. "You're a fool to run away."

"Am I? Am I a fool to be thinking of Michelle and the child she is about to bear?"

The birth of a child was an event to be cherished. For Alfonso it only inspired fear. She recalled the endless wishes that Michelle were her daughter. In her fantasies, she resolved time and again to tell a little girl the truth about herself so that she could learn to be proud of it. Alfonso and Corrine had seriously erred in holding it back. She knew enough of Alfonso's self-deprecating nature to understand it. "Al, someday it's going to come out. I hope when it does you'll have the good sense to know it isn't so ugly as you think."

"No. It will never come out. Not while we're here. Corrine could never stand that. We've suffered too much to let that happen."

Yes, they had suffered and were willing to hand down that life of suffering to their child. "How does Michelle feel about leaving?"

"She says she won't go, but she will. She can only think of the boy at the moment. His father died in the middle of all this. He's left town. Perhaps he will meet us later in Cleveland."

The boy should be brave, less horrified than Alfonso was of himself. He should show strength when Alfonso had none. "All right, Al. Go to Cleveland. I have to think about whether I'm willing to meet you there."

"But you must. It won't be long. We'll be together again very soon."

He kissed her and left her with her thoughts. In Cleveland, there would be another bright apartment, a kitchenette behind louvered doors, nights of loving and days of loneliness. Running away was no answer to anything. She knew that if she were to continue to respect him, he would have to face the truth. She made a difficult decision swiftly, a cruel one necessary to save Michelle from her father's fate. She lifted her phone and dialed the operator. "I want Vosbien Toys of Cleveland, Ohio," she said. "I'd like to talk to Leon Vosbien personally."

During the long pause, she almost recradled the phone. Finally a voice came on, "Vosbien speaking." It sounded strait-laced.

"This is Alfonso DeJoie's mistress . . . Yes, I said mistress. . . ."

Josianne ended the call and said a prayer that Alfonso would somehow find courage.

Along South Claiborne Avenue, Alfonso remembered his promise to do the Friday shopping. He turned back to Rampart and headed for Taliferro's Restaurant. For the evening meal, Corrine had decided on Creole gumbo, the seafood potpourri, seasoned with filé, the pulverized leaves of sassafras. He bought dozens of crabs and shrimps and slid the package away from him on the seat. The smell of it and the aftertaste of the clumsy conversation with Josianne made him pause for breath. Fear had caused him to deal hastily with her. He had planned to break it to her properly over dinner at Antoine's, to assure her that it was only a temporary separation. Events had backed up on him. Time had run out.

To escape the odor of the seafood, he rolled down his car windows. Alfonso had never learned to enjoy Creole cooking as his family had. It always conjured a picture of his father, Hernando, propped against the bar at Taliferro's, eating raw oysters in horseradish sauce. Each payday was the day of the feast—stuffed artichokes, French bread, giant draughts of beer. When Hernando could eat and drink no more, he found his way home with enough money left for beans and rice until next payday. Alfonso started his car roughly, annoyed with himself. Out of possibly a hundred places to buy seafood in New Orleans, he always came back to the outskirts of Treme. Cleveland would be different. There would be no Treme, no whispers, and no Creole dishes.

"No Creole dishes," he said aloud, remembering the original meaning of the word, the marriage of the early French and Spanish settlers. Creole became corrupted among the poor people. It came to include the "high yellows" of New Orleans, people like Hernando. In ignorance, he had snapped to attention at the mention of the word. He was Creole down to the grit under his fingernails, as were all his ancestors back to Bienville, who

181

founded the city, and DeSoto, who discovered the Mississippi River. Poor dreaming Hernando. All he ever had were those ancestors. He neglected to tell his son he was also part black. It was why a cocksure Alfonso rode the bus up front, while his neighbors sat in the rear and spat out of the windows. He was Creole like his father—full of shit! Not until he was almost grown up did he learn that his light skin and a necktie did not make him white. Oh, he could fool the driver of a bus but not those like him. He continued to pretend even after he knew the truth because he could not accept it, not with all that crap Hernando was dishing up about ancestors.

It was his passion for anything Spanish—Carmen Miranda on a wind-up Victrola, hot peppers, words memorized from a plaque at the Cabildo Museum. He drank Spanish wine and held dish rag bullfights with Alfonso in the role of the bull. He had seen a bullfight somewhere, or read about one, or dreamed it up as he had his Castilian ancestry. It was set in a stone castle in Spain with a "whole bevy of servants," and fancy ladies drinking wine from tinkling crystal. It was an exciting dream until Alfonso's mother tired of the lie.

She was in her eternal place in the kitchen, busy among the pots of stewing pork and collard greens, one day when he came home from school. He asked her what Spain was like. If she knew, she cared little. She stirred a kettle, capped off the steam. "I'd like to go there someday," he said. "Maybe I could learn Spanish. I could take it in school."

"You could learn it."

"Pop could help me. He knows all about Spain. Did you know they have bullfights there?"

"I heard about them."

"Pop saw one once. I sure would like that. Bullfights and fiestas and a castle with servants. A whole bevy of servants." It was Son of Hernando talking.

The mother smiled sadly at her boy, unable to share the childish dream, planning secretly to deal later with its source. "You have to work mighty hard for things like that."

"Sure, I know. I don't mind working. I'll get a job as soon as I finish school. I'll save all my money."

"Alfy, try to understand. Those things don't come to all folks. You have to be rich to have those things."

But Alfy had a slant on the American Dream. "I know we're poor, Ma, but I can do it. Pop says it's all out there in Spain. You just have to reach out and take it. He should know. He's Spanish, just like me."

Alfy saw the fire of the quick temper, the glare that often sent Hernando scurrying over the wall of the Saint Louis Cemetery to hide among the graves. "Yes, you're Spanish just like him, and you're a little black just like him. Now your pipe dreams are just like his!"

Alfonso never doubted what she meant or completely forgave her for saying it. He fled, scaled the wall of the cemetery, and hid in a mausoleum until nightfall. It rained heavily that night. He got soaked trying to seal out the water with a gravestone. He thought he would freeze, but he did not go home for supper. It was only pork and collard greens. That was a little black. When his legs grew numb from crouching in the cold and his bowels had to be emptied, he squatted and shit in the rain beside a tomb, thinking that was a little black. Later he heard his father searching the aisles for him, the great Spanish liar Hernando, and he tried to stop breathing. He wanted to hide in the old grave until he died.

From that day on, Alfonso knew about black. Black was the way they ate, worked, dressed, and talked—the stockings on their heads, the ignorant patois, the respect for any man who was not black. It was boys shuffling their feet and snapping their fingers to the rhythms that came out of the bars on Rampart Street. Black was the endless talk about "poontang." Black was Treme decaying before their eyes. Strewn piled garbage brought rats. Abandoned cars rotted in the streets. Broken windows were never repaired. There was a pool of mud under every tree. People tracked it into the houses until the floors and stairs were caked with it. Not one of them had the spirit to care.

Their refuge had been the cemetery, a place to hide among speechless corpses. At night they went over the walls, taking along any girls bold enough to chance it. Inside they first paid homage to Marie LaVeau, the voodoo queen who was buried there, obeying the command on her tomb, *"Passants priez pour elle."* They prayed a black ritual, marking a cross on the gravestone with a slate, stamping their feet. "Cas' a good spell, Marie. Don't fogit us now." Then they prowled among the graves and talked of everyone dead since Napoleon. The girls clung to them and pretended they were too frightened to feel the fingers probing under their dresses. It was the game of being black. Alfonso learned to masturbate in the cemetery, to drink cheap wine, and to fear the world outside.

He had recently passed it to look over a place in the wall where some bricks had fallen away. He heard the voice of the caretaker, a brown man named Buddy, as he lectured a group of tourists near the gate. Alfonso had heard the speech many times and could picture every gesture. With the tap-tap of his pointer, Buddy said, "In Loo-siana, we bury folks above the ground. "Heah's why." He stomped the ground. "Ground's too soft. It's the water table. Turn a spade o' dirt and you make a well." Tap-tap. He pointed to the sunken burial chambers, rented family vaults, crumbling monuments to once distinguished people. It was a resting place for the rich dead of New Orleans and a playground for the poor children of Treme. Alfonso saw plastic flowers stacked against a tomb. In an aisle beside a rusted mausoleum gate, a condom lay coiled like a transparent eel.

Alfonso gave the seafood bundle to his wife, happy to be rid of it and the solitude of his thoughts. He dropped into a chair, weary of heat and rumination. He needed a time to clean his mind with cool breezes and salt sea air. Since the promising meeting with Vosbien, he had secretly planned a vacation for his family. A Florida beach where he could relax with drinks and cool leafy foods. A time to recharge his mind. "I can set myself on a beach," he said, "lying out under a tree and drinking something with mint leaves."

Corrine looked at him suspiciously. "Al, are you trying to say something?"

He checked his watch. Vosbien's call had not come. It was still early. How long could he sit on the news? Where was his confidence? He made his decision. "Where's Michelle?"

"In her room as always. Al, please tell me. I'll explode."

"Get her. I want her to hear." When she returned with Michelle, Alfonso had spread some old maps on the floor. He spoke with excitement. "This time we could dip down the West Coast of Florida. A million things to see. Remember the little place in Cocoa Beach."

"Al, you got the job!"

"It's practically clinched. I've known since I came back from Cleveland. Vosbien had to take it to his board. Just a formality. He promised he'd call today. I told him I'd need a month to make the break. He wanted me right away, but I insisted. I'm not exactly a pushover, you know."

Corrine had been concentrating on her daughter's coldness. "Michelle, a vacation. A whole month!"

"I don't want a vacation."

Alfonso stood, trampling his maps. "But you do. We all need one after all we've been through."

A look of caution from Corrine stopped him. She needed a moment to consider her daughter. In their zeal to escape the city, they had ignored her condition. They would have her sit on a beach for their pleasure, plumply over-dressed. Somehow Corrine had to win back her confidence. She said, "The vacation isn't all that necessary. It's too cool this time of the year anyway. We can fly directly to Cleveland and have fun looking for a house together."

As Alfonso's dream faded, his enthusiasm stalled. He was willing to make the compromise if it brought Michelle out of her present depression. "Sure. That'd be okay by me. Mr. Vosbien would love me for it."

"I think I'd better make myself clear," Michelle said. "I am not going on a vacation, and I'm not going to Cleveland. It isn't necessary to run anymore."

"But, sweetheart," Alfonso said. "Our plans, the new job. We don't have to stay in this town another minute."

Corrine stopped him a second time, an order to allow her to handle it. Michelle seemed bitter, resolute. She had to be dealt with tenderly. "Michelle, it's what we've been hoping for all along for you and the child."

Michelle could hear the sound of distant drummers. The parade was approaching. This one was devoted to children. There would be floats of elephants, giraffes, lions and tigers. She caught a flash image of her unquickened fetus. She had tried not to look but glimpsed it for the span of a heartbeat. The sight had burned in her mind, the meat-red cells, moist and shimmering. She had staggered away and found a cab, sick and unable to cry. "Mother and Daddy, I have something important to tell you," she said, surprised by the strength in her voice. "I had the child aborted."

Corrine felt as if she had been struck. She had to sit to keep her legs from giving way. But in a moment, shock turned into relief that the deed had been done and Michelle was standing before them, safe and healthful. The mother could only look at her daughter with admiration. Again she had greatly underestimated her. The little girl was a woman with more courage than any of them had suspected. "Michelle . . . how?"

"I went to a woman who did it illegally. I didn't tell you because the decision was mine alone. Mother, I could never run away. Mark can come home now. I hope he can forgive me."

Alfonso was dumbstruck. "You got an *illegal abortion?*"

"Please be quiet," Corrine said. She took her daughter to her room, put her to bed, and sat quietly beside her. It was the only assurance she could offer.

When she returned, the parade was passing. They could hear the cheers as each float went by, and the pleas of the children, "Throw me something, mister!" A passing brass band prohibited talk for a few minutes. Alfonso sat frozen in a chair. He had pulled down all the shades in the house, as if the crowd could see the truth through the windows. "What have we done, Corrine?"

"It's done, Al. I wish it wasn't. I was getting used to the idea of a grandchild. But now that it's gone, we'll live without it. We don't have to be frightened for it now."

As the moment of shock passed, Alfonso was visibly relieved. Even if they failed to go to Cleveland, no new birth certificate would be issued under the signature of the Registrar's successor. Their secret might be safe after all. He felt great admiration for his daughter as he realized he did not know her at all. "To think she went through that all alone," he said.

"Yes, Al. She's a woman."

The parade passed and the crowd quickly dispersed. In the silence, Michelle could hear the streetcar tracks ring when a car was many blocks away. The call from Mr. Vosbien came that evening. She heard her father answer, argue, plead, "But the fall line, the bopper balls, the ionization thing. What do you mean you've decided not to expand? Mr. Vosbien, I'm a good salesman . . . a family man. My family is depending on this move. We made plans. No, I don't know if I'll be available in a year . . . Mr. Vosbien?"

Late that night, Michelle felt the hemorrhage begin. She had to live it all over again, the wretched house, the kind face of Mrs. George and her gravelly voice. Rubber gloves, a bare table, a probe. Then the prick, the jolt of an electric shock. The fetus sliding out, moist and warm between her legs. She looked at it for a moment and would remember it forever. . . .

She screamed with all her strength—"Daddy—I don't want to die!" She passed into unconsciousness as she heard the rush of her father's footsteps on the stairs.

Mark was in a hurry, absurdly so after wasting so much time. Now he was a pedestrian with hundreds of miles ahead of him. Grand Bayou's bus station was a cafe set back from the road. He was told that a bus bound for New Orleans would be passing through at eight o'clock that night, but that the seats would probably all be filled. People were going to the city for the Mardi Gras. Mark said he would stand on the bus and bought a ticket. The telephone lines were also busy. When he finally got a ring from Papa's phone, there was no answer. He called Matt, who said, "Where are you?"

"In a town called Grand Bayou. Matt, Papa isn't answering his telephone. I tried several. . . ."

"Bad news, Mark. Papa died three days ago." Even in an expected death, there was a prick of shock to recover from. There was a long silence, a pause to think of the words left unsaid. "Mark? Are you there?"

"Yes, I heard you."

"He died in his sleep. It was an easy death. Emma found him in the morning."

"Matt, I'm getting a bus. I'll be home by morning."

He ordered food, sat over the plate until it grew cold, and pushed it away, his thoughts dwelling on a time of their lives when they were all together. He remembered two little boys who had rushed to greet their father when he came home from his railroad job. He was strong then and was able to sweep them off their feet and hold them high over his head. "When you get so big that I can't do that, you'll be men," he had said. Papa had done all he could to make them men. He was dead.

With an hour still to wait for the bus, he managed to reach the DeJoie house. A neighbor who identified herself as Charlotte answered, hedged for a moment, but finally told the truth. "They rushed her to the hospital an hour ago hemorrhaging. The poor thing got an illegal abortion. I just came in to lock up the house."

"What hospital?"

"Hotel Dieu."

Mark had to drag the news into the gay atmosphere of a bus full of people headed for a holiday. Dry tastes and aches from the alcohol still lingered. He stood for as long as he could and then sat in an aisle next to a restroom full of sloshing urine. The ride seemed eternal. It was nearly noon when the bus reached the terminal on Tulane Avenue. The street was filled with people heading downtown for the Saturday parade. He walked fast to the hospital.

Alfonso and Corrine were sitting in a waiting room, grimly supporting each other. Alfonso said, "She's going to be all right, thank God. I had no idea she would do such a thing. The doctor wants to talk to you."

Dr. Mort Krasner had finished a busy morning. He had taken calls from the Mayor, an officer of the Civil Service Commission, and several irate City Councilmen. Each call had to do with the final disposition of Pearl LaCroix. Mort explained over and over in detail that he would be prepared to testify at her hearings on all charges listed in his letter of dismissal. He also told them of Michelle DeJoie, the result of Miss LaCroix's strict adherence to the law. By noontime, they were demanding the Registrar's hide. Mort wished he could make the last charge official, the near death of a young girl after an illegal abortion.

The night before, he had saved Michelle's life, removing her appendix in the bargain, a bit of *lagniappe*. Now as he sat alone, he considered the relationship of the two events, LaCroix, the cause, and Michelle, the almost fatal result. If ever he had harbored some sympathy for the Registrar's twenty-five years of service, the girl had tipped the scale. Even as he was putting the sutures in her belly, he was congratulating himself for moving boldly. The attendant publicity would be painful for her and her family, for he knew that Miss LaCroix would drag out everything she could at the hearing. But he felt that his action might save other young girls from the abortionists. These were facts he could not bring up publicly to the Civil Service Commission, but they would always be in his mind.

"Mark Dennick is here," the nurse said, and Mort went out to greet him.

"I fixed the trouble and took out her appendix, Mark. Everything else is there. She's going to be all right in a few days."

"Can I see her?"

"In a minute. I want to talk to you first. Do you know that your father signed a complaint against Miss LaCroix?"

"Yes," Mark said, "Papa's name was in the papers. I was shocked. Why would he want to make the whole mess public?"

Mort checked his watch and thought of his schedule ahead. "Mark, I wrote the complaint. I was surprised at how quickly he signed it. I think he sensed the evil of the Registrar, that she had to be disposed of. At any rate, for the next few weeks the news isn't going to be good for the DeJoie family. If it's any consolation to you, I've heard good repercussions already."

"What good can come of making Michelle a public issue?"

"Plenty. I've been on the phone to several angry Councilmen this morning. They're talking about a city ordinance to reorganize the Bureau of Vital Statistics. When I told them about Michelle, they almost swore they'd get action. Word leaked to Baton Rouge fast. There's talk about legislation. Do you know what that means?"

"To change the Jim Crow laws?"

"Yes." Mort stopped, an attempt to restrain his enthusiasm. "Of course, it's only talk, but who knows? I can tell you one thing. It will happen in time. It's got to happen."

"Doctor, Papa must have known Michelle would be publicly humiliated."

"Yes, I think he did. He also knew that your name would be dragged into it. I guess he thought it necessary. It's what I wanted you to understand."

In signing the simple complaint, Papa had left a legacy of no small proportions, starting state-wide repercussions that might someday lead to the elimination of unfair laws and demagogues like Miss LaCroix. It was a gamble, but one taken deliberately and wisely. Papa, an honest man to his death, had decided that the truth must be told so that his son could no longer hide. From

190

the grave, the old man had taken the situation out of Mark's hands. "I think I understand better than you know, Doctor. Could I see Michelle now?"

She was drugged but awake, her eyes heavy-lidded. She recognized him and held his hand. "I'm glad you're home. I'm sorry I caused you so much trouble."

"Michelle, I want to explain about Papa's complaint. The publicity will be nasty."

She breathed deeply, gratefully. "Not to me it won't. I welcome it. It's like being reborn. My parents are upset because they're afraid. Soon they'll realize they won't have to pretend anymore. I thank your father for his wisdom."

It was as if she and Papa had collaborated in the necessary act. Either of them had the courage to do it. "Michelle, let's get out of here before it happens. The doctor says you'll be all right in a few days. We'll get that train to Washington right away."

She closed her eyes, worn out of patience. "Mark, no! Don't you see I can't run away. I'm going to stay here to see it through. I might even enjoy it."

"But we can never be together here."

"Is that so important now? I know you would have married me if I let you. I also know you tried your best to accept me. You're not completely to blame. No one's completely to blame, not even the Registrar."

It was a measure of the girl that she could forgive even the Registrar. Mark knew that she meant their relationship had been doomed from the moment they walked into that office. It was finished for reasons still not clearly perceptible to him, based on who they were and the time they lived in. The circumstances had set irresistible forces in motion. The futility of fighting them had occurred to her a long time ago.

Outside, the parade had ended. People were dispersing in all directions. Traffic was stalled. Mark had to walk to the house on Esplanade, threading his way through cars and people. *The Oregon Trail* was upside down on the shelf. He first read the note from Papa, handwriting like an electrocardiogram, a transmission from death. When he read Papa's prayer, he said one in return.

There was a check for five thousand dollars, Mark's share of the Tammany property deal, pinned to a note from his brother, which awarded him the family car. Mark then read all of the clippings Matt had left on the dismissal of Miss LaCroix. A great deal had happened in the few days dawdled away in Grand Bayou. The direction of his life had changed, and it was dragging him helplessly along behind.

The telephone immediately took charge. He slammed it down on William, and it rang at once. It was Emma reporting on her novena for Papa at Saint Louis Cathedral. She loved to walk to the old church in the French Quarter opposite Jackson Square. After her method of fairness, she would allot the prayers fifty per cent for Papa, thirty per cent for the child in limbo, and twenty per cent for the DeJoie girl. Mark ripped the telephone out of the wall.

He got stuck in another parade en route to his brother's house. Jefferson Highway was clogged for hours. He waited it out in the toxic smell of his own exhaust, listening to the brass of a faraway band. Matt was enjoying a long weekend, a time to let his beard grow. "I should have warned you about the parade. The Saturday before Mardi Gras is murder out here. But's it's an easy one for us to watch. We just walk out to the highway."

They sat in the yard with beers. Somewhere a backyard fire burned. Boys and dogs prowled past on the levee. Marylene brought dinner, peppers stuffed with shrimp, and they ate under a magnolia tree. Matt brought up his plans. "I thought I'd buy a shack in Grand Isle with my share of the money. Fishing, swimming. It'd be good for the kids. A place for them to run." Saint Tammany had been their own place to run. All the years of their wilderness was now typed out on a piece of paper, validated by an anonymous banker. Matt went on, "Something to leave the kids a long time from now, a little security. . . ."

It was as if the dream had been passed genetically from father to son. Papa had succeeded in implanting his legacy. This family of sons would see that it was carried out.

As if to dispose of the subject, Matt brought up Michelle. "Is she going to be all right?"

"Yes. Doctor Krasner took out her appendix while he was at it. She was drugged but cheerful, not at all upset by this whole mess. She said she didn't want to see me again."

"Well, I can understand that. The whole affair was impossible from the beginning."

Marylene ran into the house, unable to listen.

"I think the publicity is going to be nasty," Mark said. "Michelle doesn't seem to mind. She wants the truth to come out."

"Mark, the best thing you can do is forget about it. Chewing on it won't do a damn bit of good."

That night Mark sat alone in the living room of the house on Esplanade, listening to the marching drummers as the Crewe of Proteus wound its way through the French Quarter. Gloria appeared at the door. Her silk dress was untidy, her face tired from the long drive down from Grand Bayou. She came in cautiously and sat on the floor beside his chair. "I didn't know if you would throw me out, but I had to come. Please let me stay."

"You know we'll have to face Clarey."

"Yes. I can with you."

When the Army psychiatrist was satisfied that Clarey was in control, he pronounced him fit and signed the release. It was Mardi Gras Day, a week after Clarey had been transferred to Veteran's Hospital. "They figured I was ready to be turned loose on the unwary public," he said to his father who came in the car to pick him up. "I still feel a bit rocky, but I'll be okay in a few days."

"Good. You can come home now and live a proper life with your family."

That meant that Clarey was now going to be retired alongside the retired Colonel and the retired Colonel's wife to live happily ever after. He was not prepared for it. "Dad, I'm not exactly ready for a rocking chair. I got a pretty good job offer while I was in the hospital."

The Colonel was startled. Clarey had not sought work since his military retirement. He had shown little interest in any kind of future. The hospital stay had produced some changes. "What sort of a job?"

"Moose Hagen called me. He's a fighter friend of mine, a pretty good middleweight. They need an assistant trainer over at the Poydras Gymnasium. Dad, it's something I can really do. I like being around fighters. They think like me."

The Colonel was delighted by the enthusiasm, but it was difficult for him to place his ailing son in such an occupation. "Are you strong enough for a job like that?"

"It isn't a big deal. Assistant trainer is a nice title for keeping track of equipment and seeing that fighters go through the ropes on time. Moose thought of me when the old guy quit. He said he'd put in a good word for me. I'm meeting with him and the boss tonight."

"On Mardi Gras Day?"

194

"Sure. The gym's closed. Moose said it'd be a good time to show me around. The boss works every night."

The Colonel was fully in favor of any employment Clarey was capable of. Doing a job he liked would be a sure step toward rehabilitation. "Well, you seem to have the job already. I just hope you're not rushing things. You could use some rest at home."

"Dad, please don't worry. I'm ready for a job like this. Something important happened to straighten out my mind."

"I expect your mother will have something to say about it."

As they approached South Claiborne Avenue, traffic stopped dead. A flat-bed truck decorated like the chambers of hell, en route to parade with the Krewe of Orleaneans, had stalled at an intersection. Lady and gentleman devils aboard seemed already drunk. They brandished paper-mâché pitchforks, drank from Dixie cups, and kissed one another with wine-stained tongues. No one cared a damn about the traffic jam.

The Colonel apologized for the delay. It was getting close to lunch time. "I should have gone the back way. Traffic will be murder from here on."

"I don't mind. It's quite a show after being trapped in a hospital." For the week, Clarey had been confined to a bed, a hallway, and a large screened porch that looked out over a baseball diamond. He watched men in wheelchairs play paraplegic softball, but tired of the game and a television set that flickered in a corner of the room. His bedmates were two old soldiers on either side who stared out blankly from their memories of the war against the Kaiser, obediently eating the food chewed into mush by a machine in the kitchen. In the boredom, Clarey had to look at his life. The condition of it—drunk, profligate, humbug lover —was inescapable. The shock of seeing it plainly laid open sobered him.

"By the way," the Colonel said. "Mark Dennick called. I told him you were coming home today."

The truth had come from Matt. Clarey had called him to commiserate over Papa Dennick's death. Matt quickly explained that Gloria and Mark were living in the house on Esplanade. An importance given the word "living" somehow encompassed love as well as life. The implication was clear in the presentiment of his tone. Gloria was spreading her legs for another man, a dear old friend. A brother was put on the spot to report it. Clarey cursed the blank unknowing faces of the old soldiers and slammed his good fist into a wall.

With the two middle knuckles of his hand broken and taped up tight, some of the anger went out of him. The image of Gloria spread-eagled in Mark's bed cooled. Had he expected less from a self-serving woman and a man of wavering resolution? Clarey himself had thrown them together. *Take care of her, Mark.* Had he sensed their mutual need, secretly wished for salvation? The humbug lover had bowed out.

The knuckles untaped and taped again was an interval to ease his resentment. The pains healed in parallel. He loved Mark and Gloria too much to hate them. At last the impossible affair was over. Without Gloria, the future was uncluttered. Because she was gone, there was no longer the worry of holding on to her. He had been freed from the damnable pretense of potency. As he had explained cryptically to his father, something important had happened to straighten out his mind. Unfortunately, Mark now expected a confrontation. It was to be his punishment. Clarey wished he could somehow avoid it.

Sober and alone, he had to face the future squarely. The doctors had diagnosed nutritional cirrhosis, a disease he could live with if he took care. They assured him he could return to a life of physical activity, but they also made it clear that another drink of whiskey could kill him. Clarey was not an old soldier waiting around to die. Nor was he doomed to play softball in a wheelchair. The call from Moose Hagen had come at a good time.

The Colonel maneuvered past the truckload of devils and drove a wide circle to come up Saint Claude Avenue the back way. It was a mistake. Floats pulled by tractors jammed the avenue all the way to Canal Street. Traffic stalled in a livid haze of diesel exhaust. The Colonel looked at his watch and cursed. The drive from the hospital had already consumed an hour. The Mardi Gras had a way of tying everything up.

Clarey was braced for the argument with his mother. She was not as quick as the Colonel to grasp the change that had come over him. True that his behavior had been less than stable since

196

his separation from the service. Also true that his physical condition was far from normal. Clarey listened quietly to the lecture, but he stubbornly insisted on taking the job.

"Must you do it tonight?" she said helplessly. "There must be a million people out on the streets."

"The boss wants to talk to me right away. I'll stick close to the river. That way I'll miss the bodies."

But Decatur Street fronting the *batture* was mobbed with staggering people. It took him an hour to reach the gym. In a doorway nearby, a teenaged boy was ending his Mardi Gras celebration. He was slumped unconscious, a wine bottle clamped in his groin, his face smeared with vomit.

Moose Hagen took the left-handed shake. "Come on in, Clarey. You look good."

Michelle watched the Mardi Gras festivities from her bedroom window. Floats, marching bands, strutting majorettes. Batons and bobbing horns and clarinets. The thick motley crowd was bundled against a cool February sun. Children clamored to be hoisted to their fathers' shoulders. Their faces were eager and happy, their arms outstretched, pleading for a prize. As a child, Michelle had been among them, held high in Alfonso's arms, like them begging for riches. She drew the curtains as her mother brought in lunch, chicken broth with rice, hot tea and lemon.

"Tired of watching the parade?" Corrine said.

"Watching the people made me think of myself. How happy they are to catch a worthless string of beads, I thought. But then I understood. The beads are a treasure to their imaginations. For a silly moment they can have all the wealth they ever dreamed of. Mardi Gras is being what you're not for a day."

Corrine opened the curtains and looked out over the crowd. Rex, their make-believe king, was passing on his float. He stood, arms akimbo, majestic beside his gilded throne, blessing the throngs with a gesture of his jeweled hands. "You sound terribly bitter."

"I didn't mean it to sound that way. I'm really relieved. The way you feel in the morning after a nightmare. How comfortable to look at all your petty troubles."

"Michelle, if we've lived a life of deception, it was because we had to. We knew what Treme was like, the looks of pity, the sly smile. We could think of nothing but to get out of it. I know you can't understand it because you never experienced it, but I wish you wouldn't hate us for it."

"Mother, I could never hate you. And I do understand it better than you know."

Corrine studied her daughter's face. It had gained a serenity, as if she possessed some new wisdom. "Have you truly forgiven us?"

"What is there to forgive?"

"The truths we didn't tell you. Now it will come out. It will be a shock. I'm ready for it."

"Mother, do you expect the neighbors to burn the house down? They're more likely to laugh and say it's better than being Irish. You and Daddy aren't guilty of anything."

"We could have faced what we were years ago."

Michelle grimaced at the persistent need to believe there was something corrupt in the DeJoie blood. She clearly saw her task, to wipe away the self-doubt, to do it decisively even if it meant hurting her mother. "Corrine," she said, feeling it necessary to reverse the roles, "what exactly are you?"

Corrine was shocked. Her daughter was demanding a direct statement of fact. She could not answer.

"Is it such a goddamned horrible curse that you have to make crap of your life with self-pity? You and Daddy trapped yourselves into thinking that way years ago because everyone else was thinking the same. The time of ignorance is over. Do you know why you're now ready to face what you are?"

"I suppose . . . because it seems so easy for you. You make us the cowards."

"Cowards? No. You had good reason to be afraid. In your day there was Treme and the back of the bus." She went to the window, drew the curtains wide apart, and gestured to the crowd. "I can tell you why you're ready to let it out. Because the people are ready to let you."

"I'm not so sure about that."

"Then let me tell you about a theory I've worked out all by

198

myself. Michelle, the social scientist. It has to do with change, the way the human race becomes civilized in stages. A hundred years ago, the good Creole plantation owners kept their brown girls hidden on Goodchildren Street or in a Storyville brothel. It was quite the thing to do, a neat setup for them. A breed of *filles de joie*. Maybe ladies of the evening were scarce then, I don't know. The ladies of Goodchildren Street were told they were second-rate so they believed it and were perfectly willing to remain a concubine to some rich white man. Eventually, they created a whole race of in-between people. That's us. Not long ago it was fashionable still for a boy to keep a questionable girl in a secret place. He could even give her children. It continued the line. But it all had to be hidden away. That was the rule. It hadn't changed much in your time. Is it any wonder you feared what you were? Now I know it's changing. Lo, the age of social conscience. I can feel it. Mark was not as horrified as his father was. My reaction was different from yours. I can be honest and proud of what I am because the people are ready to permit it. Isn't that nice of the people? The ladies of Goodchildren had their lot. You had yours. Mine will be a lot better."

The speech filled Corrine with great joy. She had tears in her eyes, a smile on her lips. Her child had lectured her with deft blunt facts to simplify an enormous complexity, one the mother had feared to examine.

Michelle raised her teacup in a mock toast. "To the bad ladies of Goodchildren Street."

Corrine returned the gesture. "And the frightened ladies of Treme." They sat quietly as Rex drummed by outside.

Mark spent most of Mardi Gras morning alternately pacing the length of the house on Esplanade and rocking nervously on the gallery beside Gloria. She knew the cause of his agitation. He had warned that they would have to face Clarey. She had tried hard to think of a way to talk him out of it, found no satisfactory approach, and left the subject alone, hoping to be left out of the confrontation. When he had walked through the house a dozen times, she said, "Mark, he obviously doesn't want to see you. Why force it?"

"Because I know what he thinks. I've got to explain."

His agitation increased as the day wore on. They watched costumes pass heading for the French Quarter. There were elves, gorillas, jolly green giants, robots, men dressed as beautiful women. After noon, people began to mass at Beauregard Square and the Municipal Auditorium to greet the floats of Rex. Later the floats were abandoned on a side street. They looked awkward and cheap without people to cheer them. As it grew dark, they could hear the music of the marching bands and the noise of the crowd. They could almost smell the popcorn and cotton candy. Mark came out of his chair. "All right. If he won't come here, I'll go to him."

Gloria said nothing. She was grateful she had not been asked to go along.

The Colonel told Mark that Clarey was at the Poydras Gym applying for a job. As Mark threaded his way through the mob on Canal Street, a drunken cowboy was being cheered because he had no seat in his pants and no underwear on either. Mardi Gras was a day to be what you wanted to be.

Moose Hagen let Mark in and explained that Clarey was somewhere back in the dressing rooms doing an inventory of equipment. "It was his idea to start right away," Moose said. "Lucky for us. The place is a goddamned mess."

Mark found him sitting quietly on a training table, a cone of light above him sharpening his features, the tattoo of drums from the street sounding faintly in the bare-walled room. He smiled and began as if he, rather than Mark, owed an explanation. "I meant to come see you right away, but I had to come here first. Mark, I got the job. Assistant trainer. I keep the bums in line, tape their hands, check equipment, things like that. This is a job I can do."

"I'm happy for you, Clarey."

"Being around fighters is almost like being back in the ring. I know what makes them tick."

Even in the harsh light, Clarey looked good. He had gained weight. His face had new color. The claw hand had lost its tautness. "Clarey, I came to talk about Gloria."

He seemed not to hear. He left the table and began opening

and closing lockers, a distraction to delay the conversation. "Will you look at the way gear is stacked in here? I have to straighten it all out tonight. I'll be here until dawn. Fighters are really lousy housekeepers."

"Clarey, will you please listen to me!"

He stopped, slammed a locker closed, but kept his back to his friend. "Mark, I don't give a damn about Gloria. I'm finished with her now. I was killing myself over her, going crazy thinking how it used to be. No love of that kind could ever help me." He walked out of the darkness, examining his taped knuckles. "So you see, you don't have to make excuses. If it hadn't been you, it would have been someone else. It took a while to get over it. Finally I've got her out of my mind. Now I can start over here. The gym is where I belong. You'll see, I'll be in top shape again."

The strength of the old Clarey, the Saint Mary's middle-weight with the will to win, was a disarming surprise. Mark had come for atonement, for condemnation, but Clarey had no wrath left in him. They left the locker room and walked to the ring. It was in a bigger room, surrounded by folding chairs. Clarey climbed through the ropes, pulled them to check the tension, threw his body against them. Mark watched from ringside, listening to Clarey's monotone of criticism.

"Things are going to be in shape with me around here. These ropes are too slack. A fighter could go through them if he lost his balance. The mat's in good shape, though. The footing's firm except in the corners. . . ."

"Clarey, I couldn't stand being alone. I'm sorry."

"For Christssake, Mark—cut it out! You're sorry for me? That's kind. But I pity you. You're a special product of this place. In a fight, you're too willing to join. You're quick to take up the ways of the people you claim to hate so much. Maybe that's why you've been running away all your life, because you knew in the end you would turn out like them. Now you can go on with it, maybe even keep Michelle in a secret place across town if she'll have you. . ." He paused to check his angry tone. He had not meant to be so harsh. "I guess you don't deserve that. I just keep thinking of Michelle. The end of this is a rotten deal for her. She's quite a girl to go through what she did. You lost a lot when you lost her."

In the silence that followed, a roar from the crowd outside seemed a cheer that the speech had at last been made by someone.

"I haven't lost her yet, Clarey. When I have something to offer, I'll go to her."

"What could you offer now?"

"A job. Some kind of future."

It was difficult for Clarey to accept the evidence of Mark's ignorance. He actually did not understand the strength of the girl, that she would never have done what she did had she thought there was the slightest prospect of a future for them. He climbed back through the ropes and dropped to ringside, unable to destroy his friend's last hope. "Sure, well, you come around when I get this place in shape. You'll see the changes. What these bums need is a tough trainer. I'll have no prima donnas. . . ."

"Clarey, I'll clear out of town if you want."

"Oh, crap! Sure, go ahead. But you'd better take Gloria with you. I think you're going to need her. Tell her. . . ." He stopped and reflected, as if to see a long way into the past. "Never mind. It wouldn't make any difference now."

As Mark let himself out, he heard the assistant trainer going through the lockers again, rehearsing orders he would later issue to all those fighters under his reign. "What am I, a housekeeper? Get all this junk out of here. These lockers have to be cleaned out right away. . . ."

Canal Street was littered with beer cans and debris. The people had all gone home. Mark headed for the house on Esplanade. Gloria would be waiting.

Following the Mardi Gras, the New Orleans weather turned raw, as if winter had waited for the end of the holiday. The wind and rain approached the fury of a hurricane for days, and the dark skies underscored Mark's depression. He had little to say each day. The house on Esplanade, with all its shades drawn, was a dark cavern, moldy and damp, much too dreary for Gloria. She thought a move would improve his spirit. He quickly agreed. He was tired of living under Aunt Emma's surveillance.

Gloria inquired to see if her old apartment was available. It was not. It would contain unpleasant memories anyway, she reasoned, and took a place for them on Saint Peter Street in the French Quarter, a furnished apartment above a restaurant named the Gumbo Shop. It was two rooms of peeling wallpaper and a gallery that trembled under the weight of one person. Gloria loved it. Mark settled into it without comment, bringing only his personal articles and some books. Then he padlocked the house, mailed the key to his brother, and took up life in the narrow orbit of the apartment, where he wrote letters to Michelle, and the Gumbo Shop, where he took his meals. He never mailed any of the letters. Gloria found the shreds of them in the wastebasket.

When the weather cleared at last, they took long walks in the French Quarter or drove to Lake Pontchartrain to look at wedges of sail on the water. Gloria seemed happy and quiet, no longer the self-serving girl of Grand Bayou eager for excitement. She had found Mark. She was grateful to be settled, at home with him in a small apartment without frills. Mark was aloof and distant, alone with his thoughts. If he spoke at all, he seemed to be talking to himself. One night they had parked at the lake, and as usual Mark stared out over the black water. Gloria tried to probe his thoughts, an attempt to draw him out. "Most times I feel alone with you, Mark. I wish you'd talk to me. I'd like to help."

He owed her that. She had helped by being patient. "I was

203

just thinking of a place Papa owned across the lake when we were kids. When I look out at the water I can almost see it. We called it, 'Our Wilderness.' It was just an old shack and a vegetable garden. We loved it better than our home. Papa sold it before he died. I'd like to have a place like it someday."

She was pleased to hear of the ambition. It was evidence that he was beginning to think of the future—their future, she hoped. "I'd say that's a good idea. Lots of good property in Saint Tammany. I hear they still have wild turkey in the woods. When the Causeway opens, land will go sky high."

"Papa gave his away for five hundred dollars an acre."

"Mark, why not buy some now? Not a whole lot. Just a little acre by a stream. I could get a job and help out."

It was clear that Gloria was trying hard to include herself in on a dream. From the days at Grand Bayou, he had been aware of her feelings. She had confessed her affair and accepted the punishment, hoping that forgiveness would allow her to remain with Mark. He had permitted it, perhaps unfairly, because of the depression that descended on him when he was alone. Each night she came into his bed and he said nothing, while he thought of Michelle and the letter he had written and destroyed that day. Still, Gloria was a comfort because she cared. He feared he might hurt her. He could not fault her for assuming a role in his future, but he had yet to deal finally with Michelle. Before he could do that, he had to show that there was substance to his life. "I suppose it's time I started looking for work," he said.

"Then it's settled. I'm going to get a job tomorrow. We'll have our wilderness in no time."

The hearings on the Registrar's dismissal began in March. Mark followed the story in the newspapers. The publicity was not as ugly as everyone had expected, except perhaps for Miss LaCroix. Michelle's name was mentioned only once under the byline of Joseph Deschamps. Dr. Krasner was reading Stephen Dennick's complaint into the record when the Registrar snapped, "Michelle DeJoie was of mixed blood. It was my duty to inform the father of his son's intentions." The remark passed without comment from the members of the Civil Service Commission. No one but the reporter seemed even to notice it. The horrible truth everyone had feared was an anticlimax, overshadowed by the real conflict, the dismissal of Pearl LaCroix.

As Dr. Krasner substantiated each charge against her, she replied with outbursts until she was warned by the Commission Chairman. When she was given a chance to defend herself, she accused high officials of meddling with departmental procedures, hypocrisy, duplicity, and lax public morals. Dr. Krasner demanded that she make a specific charge. She could not. "They were subtle about it," she said. "They wanted to be soft on the law." She ended with a long speech which said no more than that she was only trying to do her job. Her remarks, instead of vindicating her, inspired an editorial recommending a complete review of administration policy with regard to vital information on private individuals. Miss LaCroix lost her right to reinstatement. Krasner and Hurley had won half their battle.

The other half was still a dream. They had no test case to execute their *mandamus* plan. There was an implication in the editorial that the state legislature might be willing to take up the issue of the Jim Crow laws. It seemed a weak promise. The white constituency of New Orleans would soon forget it.

"What does it all mean?" Gloria said.

"Not very much, I don't think. A momentary compassion. It comes too late. The laws will stay on the books until someone takes a case to court."

"But surely things are better without that woman."

"I don't know. There's another like her in her place."

"Mark, if I'd known what you were going through, I could have helped somehow."

"No one could have helped, Gloria. No one but me."

With the Registrar disposed of, Mark could think of other things. He took a job in the public relations department of a local brewery. The office was headed by an ex-professional football player, Archie Davis, a huge friendly man of hometown origin. He was a national sports figure, having helped the Green Bay Packers win several championships. But Archie knew very little about anything but football. Mark was hired to write press releases and correspondence.

205

He liked the job. The brewery was within walking distance of the apartment. On clear days, he could share a box lunch with Gloria in Jackson Square. Archie took to Mark immediately, complimenting him on his ability with words and accepting him as a personal friend. In a short time, Gloria saw extraordinary improvements in his disposition. It was a turn up from the long period of depression.

Before long Mark realized that Archie's talents were being wasted. He was an outgoing and clever man, always cracking jokes. The company had him waiting around the plant to shake hands with visitors. Mark hit on an idea. He wrote a long memorandum entitled, "Archie Davis Talks for Charity," addressed to the General Manager. In it he suggested that Archie be lent free, courtesy of the brewery, to civic organizations where he would give talks on his glorious days with the Packers. Archie could put it over with films and jokes. The proceeds would go to charity. The company would gain a public image from any newspaper coverage.

Archie was given the go-ahead immediately. "Mark, you're a genius!" he said. "Football is what I know about, not public relations. I could talk about football all day. I don't have to be trapped in this office."

That night Mark told Gloria of his plan. She listened as she prepared supper, enforcing his enthusiasm wherever she could. But after the meal, she sat bitterly dejected as he drafted a letter to Michelle to tell her of his success. Mark made a special trip to the mailbox, and when he returned, Gloria was gone. There was evidence that she had hastily packed a bag. He had to struggle against an impulse to go after her, but he thought of Michelle and could not bring himself to use Gloria any more.

She returned at dawn, looking weary and pale, and began unpacking her suitcase of cosmetics and underwear. "I've been walking the streets," she said. "I guess I'm not very smart. I wanted to leave to hurt you. I just kept walking around the block. I thought you'd come after me. That makes me the ass."

"Gloria, I've got to see Michelle again. There might be a way to fix things. I owe her that much."

"Yes, I know. I knew it all along. Like I said, I'm not very

smart. But we're alike, us two. I'll be waiting if you need me."
She tossed her empty suitcase into a closet. "Ole Glory has always
been a free-floater, but when I got out there on the street, I realized I didn't have anywhere else to go."

"Archie Davis Talks for Charity," started successfully. The first
talk was to the Ladies Auxiliary of the Knights of Columbus.
Ladies paying to hear football talked about! Mark, who had
helped Archie write the speech, was in the first row. Archie was
brief and funny. A slow-motion film compared the beefy players
to ballet dancers with their moves of strength and grace. The
ladies applauded for five minutes. The speech was covered in the
sports pages. The next day, a memo came down from the General
Manager. "Men who drink beer read the sports pages," it said
succinctly.

The athlete propped his feet triumphantly on his desk. "Mark,
with your brains you'll be running this department soon. Hell—
I think you already are!"

Mark had to take the thought home with him. The maligned
youth of the do-nothing fifties had not often considered the
prospect of success. He had rejected Papa's work ethic. The railroad had seemed the prescribed life. Was his present situation any
different? He was now an aspiring junior executive with success
at hand. His life seemed laid out as patently as Papa had planned
it. The folly was that Mark had fought it so aggressively.

The campaign continued successfully. Archie's talks had a
down-home flavor that charmed the big city audiences. Before
long he was in demand, earning cash for charity and good will
for the company. He seemed to have found an avocation, something he could do as well as football. He was grateful to Mark
and they became good friends. "We'd be an unbeatable team out
on our own," he said one day.

Mark was surprised. "You'd leave the brewery?"

"I've been thinking about it. This town doesn't have a really
good public relations firm. That is if you'd be willing to come
along. I'd have to have you for the creative end, but we'd be equal
partners."

Archie was ambitious. He sensed the limitations in their ar-

207

rangement with the brewery. On their own, the possibilities were boundless. Rather than disloyalty, it was a normal process of growth. "I'd have to think about it," Mark said.

He had decided to join Archie in his bold move when Michelle's letter arrived. It was a long one, written in her precise hand.

Dear Mark,

I was very happy to read about your new job and your success. I always knew it would happen once you gave it a chance. As for me, my life hasn't changed very much. I still have my job at the library. It leaves me time to think, to put things in their proper places. We have both been through heartbreak, and I regret it had to be that way. I certainly do not believe you were to blame although you keep insisting on it. Nor was anyone directly. Now that I can put our relationship so far in the past, I know it would never have worked no matter how hard we tried. We are different kinds of people, Mark. Please try to understand.

My parents are doing as well as can be expected. Their terrible fears were groundless, of course. They expected to be snubbed and pitied. Nothing of that sort happened. When Miss LaCroix took the stand and mentioned my name, I thought they would die. They refused to go out of the house. Charlotte (our neighbor and good friend) came over and laughed, saying she had a crazy aunt who claimed she was a Hottentot. Before long Mother and Daddy were laughing with her. All this mess for a big joke. Not one of my friends at the library have said, "You poor thing." I think I would laugh if they ever did. My parents go out now. They don't look down at the sidewalk. Think of all the time they wasted. All that suffering for nothing.

I wrote to an old friend and schoolmate who is now living in her home country of Bolivia. She is racially mixed like me. I'm plain but she's exotic, brown as a coffee bean. She is working in a hospital in Santa Cruz, teaching handicapped children. I think I might like to try that. But I'm unsettled just yet. From South America I plan to go abroad and look at the Sorbonne. I might like to study there for a while. Suddenly I feel smothered here. I'd come back speaking better French than Mother. Hers is straight out of Lutcher, La. I will give her a challenge to think about.

208

Mark, I do think of you often, and I suppose I will love you always in my way. I am preserving some memories of Pass Christian. Nothing can take that away from me. I will write to you in my travels. Please try to understand why I can't see you. I'm afraid to do that just yet.

Love,

Michelle

Mark read the letter several times and put it away in a drawer. But he could not conceal his bitterness from Gloria, which she saw as evidence that the affair at last had ended. She could not have known that Mark intended to see Michelle against her will. He now had a plan for the future to offer her.

The letter from Michelle, although disappointing, gave Mark a pause for reflection. He saw his future laid out before him. It was set and comfortable, a long way removed from the many conflicts that had delivered it to him. There would be a cash settlement following the sale of the house on Esplanade. There would be the firm of Davis and Dennick, an office in the French Quarter or in a newer building on the other side of Canal Street, a profitable, respectable business. There would be a house in Metairie or Chef Menteur, a life with a woman, children. Surely, he would even own a piece of land in Saint Tammany Parish, a smaller place, perhaps, than Papa's, to serve as a wilderness. The prospects were good for happiness and security, his father's dream for him, but with one omission. Michelle would not be a part of it.

It was why he carefully studied the alternatives he might offer her when he gained the courage to seek a confrontation. Again he could offer marriage—that one-way train to Washington, the unknown. Again she would no doubt refuse to desert family and friends, her familiar life. Indeed, Mark would have to give up his own future, the brewery, Archie's plans. With marriage at last put aside, there was none but the old-fashioned alternative, to live with her secretly. He thought it a dark proposition to offer a woman of Michelle's character, that private arrangement of the Creole gentleman, but he saw no other solution.

On two successive afternoons, Mark left the brewery early, drove to the Loyola University campus, and parked near the library. Each day his confidence faltered and he left before her shift ended, driving his car roughly back to the French Quarter. He understood the nature of his failure. He feared she might refuse him. That would leave him with a sterile, if well-structured, future.

The third day he resolved to be decisive. It was a warm spring afternoon. The university neighborhood was quiet, the air sweet with the scent of newly mown lawns, the sky filled with ragged thunderheads. Students sat about in the shade of great oak trees among piles of textbooks. Mark recalled his years at the university. They had been a comfortable interlude in his life. As he waited, he indulged in the impossible melancholy of returning to a world as uncomplicated.

At five minutes to four, he left the car and waited at the library door, nervously shifting his stand and checking his watch. Michelle appeared promptly at four, not at all surprised to see him, and dug in her purse for a cigarette. She lit it between two brown fingers as he approached her.

"I had to see you, Michelle. I have some things to say."

Her face was unpainted, her hair swept back. In the afternoon sun she seemed older, her manner displaying an unfamiliar maturity. "All right, Mark. If it's so important to you, I'll listen."

"My car is just over there."

"I'd rather walk in the park. You remember our place at the aviaries? I go there often now."

They crossed Saint Charles Avenue, entered Audubon Park, and sat on stone benches near the bird cages. They had used the place on autumn nights when the birds roosted quietly. In the bright spring daylight, the restless pitch of mating birds prohibited conversation. They walked past a house of caged monkeys and sat near a reptile pit filled with alligators and beer cans.

Mark sought a way to begin. "How are your parents?"

"As well as can be expected. Suffering with their new found freedom. Learning, I hope, that the world isn't filled with bigots anymore."

"The publicity wasn't as mean as they thought it would be."

"Good thing, too. Daddy didn't get the job in Cleveland. His mistress saw to that. She called up Mr. Vosbien and told him everything."

"Mistress?"

"Daddy's had her for years, tucked away in a little house on Claiborne Avenue. Josianne Fontanet, a little lady half his age. When he found out what she did, he broke down and confessed it all to Mother. He doesn't need the other woman anymore be-

211

cause he doesn't have anything to prove. I think a lot of her now. I'd like to meet her someday."

"What a mess this has been for everyone."

"Yes, even for Madame LaCroix. Mother and Daddy relished her end. I felt sorry for her."

"Dr. Krasner's bittersweet victory. His dream was to fire her. Father Hurley wanted more. He had a plan to start an action *in mandamus*. It would have made us a test case, knocking around in the courts for years if I'd agreed to it. I didn't have the heart to involve you."

"Someday, someone will have to take the punishment. The laws have to be changed."

"The people have to change first."

"They will. Just as you have. A lot of your bitterness is gone, but you seem sad."

"Quite a few things have come clear to me, Michelle. Looking back, I can understand Papa's great dream for me on the railroad. It was all he could give. I rejected it as the blueprinted life, but I couldn't escape it. It's funny—the way my life is now, I couldn't do a damn thing in the next twenty years to offend either Papa or Uncle William. On my own I've found the same thing Papa wanted for me."

"I respect his memory. Whatever he believed, he knew Miss LaCroix was dangerous. In his place, I wonder if I would have had the courage to sign such a complaint."

"Papa had a way of doing what he thought right, like making Uncle William come across with a railroad job for me in exchange for the Saint Tammany property. He knew William would get it from us eventually anyway. I'm going to have some of that land back someday."

Michelle did not doubt that he would. "I know you'll be a great success."

"And you? What are your plans?"

"Oh, my life hasn't changed much. I'm still at the library. I catch the streetcar every morning at eight. I eat my lunch in the reading room upstairs with Donny. I catch the streetcar home every night."

"But you said you planned to travel."

"That's how I convince myself I should get out in the world. I write down commitments. I don't know. Maybe I'll go. I have enough money in my savings. By the way, how's the job in the brewery? I was thrilled to hear about it."

It was the opening he needed, the future he could offer her. "Michelle, I'm doing well. I'm all but running the office. There's a better opportunity than that. Archie Davis is thinking of taking me in, setting up a public relations firm on our own. We'd fill a need. There isn't a really good firm in all of New Orleans."

"I'm proud of your success, Mark."

"It came as a surprise to me. I didn't do much. Everything fell into place. Matt says I'm a born publicist. Glib without saying anything."

The mention of Matt's name conjured a painful memory for Michelle, one she had tried to discard. It was a picture of her, the accepted outsider, in the yard of the house on Esplanade. The memory was damnably clear: tables laden with spicy foods, a garden of elephant ears, roses on trellises, stunted banana trees, Marylene's healthful pregnancy. Michelle would carry it with her forever. "How are Marylene and the baby?"

"She was more upset than anyone by what's happened. She doesn't have much to say to me these days. I can't blame her. I live a devious life."

"You're living with that girl, Gloria, aren't you?"

Mark was startled, trapped, unable to lie his way out of it.

"Clarey told me, but not to hurt you. He wanted me to understand how much you needed her. He came to see me at the library. We had a long talk."

Damn—of course she would know! She would have heard it from Clarey or Marylene or anyone with eyes to see him blatantly shacking up with a flashy blonde in a cozy French Quarter apartment. Only the ass, Mark Dennick, would not have realized it until told at the moment he was to ask Michelle to do the same. That she had learned it from Clarey was a perfect justice. Heartbroken Clarey, who in spite of everything, wanted Michelle to understand. Mark could find no words for reply.

A class of school children on a field trip marched by in ranks and broke at the monkeyhouse. The animals were conditioned to the sight of little humans. They chattered and begged for food with arms stretched through the bars. With the fact of Gloria out in the open, Mark's plan seemed absurd. Impulsively, he forced it. "Michelle—come with me to Pass Christian. We'll take a week, get a room at that little motel. What was it called?—the Shamrock. . . ." He stopped. The absurdity overruled the impulse.

But Michelle was moved. Only Mark could intrude on her memories of Pass Christian. She well remembered the cabin floating in a puddle of chalk, the gritty showerstall, smells of cabbage and piny mops. Not long ago she would have been helpless to refuse. Willingly, she would have been swept into his car, driven madly to the coast, in bed the moment they were alone in their cottage. Now it seemed unthinkable. "Mark, maybe I'd like to go somewhere for a week and sleep with you. Maybe I need that now to know I'm the same person I always was. But I'm not."

"That's your invention. You are the same."

"Mark, a lot has happened to both of us. We're not the young lovers who ran to Pass Christian. We're different people. Don't you see that?"

"No, I don't. Sure, things have happened, but my feelings haven't changed about you. I still think about you the same way. I still want you."

She wondered if it were possible that he did not grasp the change that had occurred in both of them, or in his desperation, was simply unable to admit to them. "Do you, Mark? Do you really want me?"

Yes, he thought, even in the only way possible, the dark proposition. She could refuse or accept, but the question had to be asked. "Michelle . . . I'm doing well on my job. I'm going to do better in the future. I could afford. . . ." He gagged on the well-rehearsed sentence, unable to say it.

"I'm glad you can't ask that, Mark. I'd be tempted to live with you."

"Is it such a shock? It's the only way left to us."

She was neither surprised nor offended. She had long ago prepared herself for the proposition. This afternoon she had sensed it coming in his tone, in his desperate need to talk to her. She

214

also knew he had arrived at it quite honestly. It was the pattern handed down by the Creole gentlemen and the dark ladies of Goodchildren Street.

Michelle thought of Josianne Fontanet. She and Alfonso had been together secretly for years, although for reasons apart from the ones that were driving Mark to strike the bargain. How had it been for Josianne? How would it be for Michelle, who had a darker secret? A private woman of a successful man, loved, cared for. A house of modest furniture, a garden . . . children? Yes, perhaps those as well. Children spoiled the happy vision. Under the law, they would have their names inscribed in the folios of the Bureau of Vital Statistics.

"I wonder how many girls are living that way today?" she said. "As many as a hundred years ago? A tiny house in a nice neighborhood a discreet mile from a man's proper family. You would have to have a proper family and children to bear your name."

"A family isn't all that important to me."

"Then I feel sorry for you. It's very important to me."

"Michelle, there's no other way we can be together. Is anything more important than that?"

Never had she been so sweetly tempted in her life. She loved Mark still. Of that she was sure. With all his failing resolution, he was good. He would love her and care for her. She could be the woman in his home. She could do private things for him, be in his arms each night, but secretly, with the name M. DeJoie on the doorbell. That last detail ruined it all. "I'm sorry, Mark. That life would be impossible for me."

"Goddamnit—why?"

"Because of what I am. Living with you, being your mistress, I could do that. I'm no squirming virgin who needs a marriage license to come across. But living with you secretly because of what I am—that turns the picture ugly. I couldn't live that way for a day."

"Please . . . will you take time to think it over?"

"I've thought about it more than you know."

"Michelle, you may change your mind. It might be too late."

She glared at him, her jaw fixed, determination in the deep

angles of her mouth. "You sweet fool. Don't you see it's already too late?"

Mark had only a moment to absorb the truth. She turned and ran through the trees to the streetcar stop. He watched the awkward grace of her stride, the whipping lace of white petticoats leaving him behind. She boarded the car. It lurched, rang a warning, and started around a bend, the back of her head a dark speck in a window.

He sat alone until it was feeding time at the monkeyhouse. The school children, their field trip over, were forming into ranks. They balked at leaving. As he watched them, he remembered Clarey's words spoken in the gym. Mark Dennick was a child of this town, quick to accept the ways of the people he distrusted. He had become one of them. Michelle had not; she was a step into the future. They were different kinds of people. How strange and different the young lovers of Pass Christian seemed now.

The voice of the oracle, Clarey, nudged him again, underscored by shrieks from the monkeyhouse: *You lost a lot when you lost her.* Mark could fix the moment he had lost her in his mind. It was on that morning they first learned the truth in the Office of the Registrar.

Near twilight, he walked to his car. The university buildings were lighting up for night classes. A light rain began as he pulled into Saint Charles Avenue. Gloria would be waiting supper.

216